STONE: HER RUTHLESS ENFORCER

---

50 LOVING STATES, NORTH CAROLINA

THEODORA TAYLOR

Book Editing: Author Designs

Cover Design: Najla Qambar

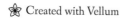 Created with Vellum

PROLOGUE

"Hey, Naima."

I freeze, inside the empty rectangle of my doorless kitchen, a spike of fear replacing my early morning yawn.

There is a man sitting at my kitchen table. A total stranger I've never seen before. And, even scarier than that....

A gun rested on the otherwise empty kitchen table in front of him. Lethal and almost as menacing as the stranger's non-smiling mouth. How did he know my name?

Fear pumps through my body. And to think just a few moments ago, I'd been wondering if even a large cup of coffee would be enough to get me alert and out the door this morning.

I'm wide awake now, no coffee needed.

"Sit down, Naima," the stranger says. He has a thick Jersey accent, but his voice lacks any emotion whatsoever. There was no emotion in his cold black eyes either. The single kitchen light I always leave on reflected off his completely shaven head. But other than that, he's all shadow.

And though he hasn't touched the gun on the table, it feels like he's pointing it straight at me.

I stand there, my body stuck in a rictus of previously unknown terror. What does he want? Why is he here?

The midnight black suit he wears looks like it was specifically tailored to fit over his huge, hulking body. It probably cost more than the entire monthly rent on this townhouse, which I used to share with my blind parents before they moved to the Dominican Republic to retire way more cheaply than they would have been able to here in New York. He's dressed for business, but I'm a social worker, living paycheck to paycheck. I can barely afford rent now that I'm handling it alone, much less a suit anywhere close to the quality of the one he's wearing. If he came here to rob me, he's incredibly stupid.

But this stranger doesn't strike me as stupid.

"Sit down," he says again. "We can do this the easy way or the dead way."

Both my body and mind scream in protest as I fight my primal flight instinct to obey his ruthless command. Like I said, this stranger doesn't strike me as stupid, or flippant either. He said he'd kill me if I don't sit down, and I believe him.

Eyeing him warily, I take a seat in the chair furthest away from him at the table.

The stranger is technically handsome with tanned skin I'm

almost sure isn't due to the summer sun but genetics. He has ebony eyes, and what I'm guessing would be black hair to match, if he hadn't shaven his head bald. His coloring and Jersey accent put me in mind of my best friend Amber's ex-husband, Luca.

The ex-husband who now heads the Ferraro Crime Family.

My heart ices over with a new layer of fear. Is this stranger related to my best friend's crime boss ex-husband? He pronounced my name perfectly, which is unusual for a first meet.

Usually people call me Nay-ma, Nay-ima, Nah-ima, Nancy —pretty much anything but the Nigh-eema, my parents intended when they named me after the social worker who helped them when they decided to start a family after losing their eyesight due to early onset macular degeneration.

The fact that this guy knows how to say my name further convinces me that though Luca Ferraro isn't currently in the room, he's somehow behind this visit.

"What do you want?" I was going for a demanding tone, but the words come out shaky. I'm not nearly as brave as Amber would have been if this happened to her. Unlike me, she doesn't take *ish* from anybody—or use substitute words for shit. She even fought off a gun man last year when he tried to come after one of her clients.

But I can barely talk to the scary dude on the other side of the table, and I'm not at all confident I won't pee my pants if he actually picks up that gun. For the first time, I wish I had actually finished those self-defense classes Amber encouraged me to take. At least then, I wouldn't feel so weak right now, so totally at this man's mercy.

"What do I want?" he repeats with a cold smile. "Just a little bit of conversation."

His words might have reassured me if his smile got anywhere near his eyes. Or if he didn't raise one large, beefy hand and place it on the gun, before adding, "About your bestie, Amber."

"No. No, no way!" I answer immediately. She is my best friend and I will do whatever it takes to protect her. "You might as well kill me, because I'm not telling you anything!"

"Alright then," he answers, just as immediately. "Have it your way."

He raises the gun.

"No, don't..." I cry out, suddenly not feeling so brave.

But he squeezes the trigger anyway and the gun goes off with a loud *BEEP! BEEP! BEEP!*

I LURCH UP IN BED, BREATHING HARD AS THE ALARM clock blares on my nightstand. *Oh God...oh God, I'm dead!*

It takes several seconds before the truth sinks in...that I've just woken up from a dream...a traumatic memory, of something that had happened nearly a year ago. A nightmare... albeit with revisions.

I hadn't been brave that day. With a gun in the room, I'd done exactly as Stone said. Answered all of his questions, and even called Amber, so that she could walk straight into Luca Ferrarro's perfectly laid trap.

I'd been so naïve back then. Kept thinking that the more I

co-operated the more chance Amber and I would have of getting out of the situation alive. But a year later, shame washes over me, remembering how easily I'd rolled over for the granite-face stranger, who turned out to be Stone Ferraro, Luca's cousin and the Ferraro family's most ruthless enforcer.

I'm always encouraging self-compassion to my vision-impaired clients. Be gentle with yourself, I tell them. Don't get too hung up on all your mistakes. Learn from them and let them—blah, blah, blah. As I climb out of bed this morning even more tired than when I went to sleep, I've got to admit, it's hard as heck to practice what I preach.

Climbing into the shower and scrubbing my skin especially hard with Dove Extra Moisturizing body wash isn't nearly enough to make me feel clean, though. I'm even more frustrated with myself by the time I climb out.

When will I stop having that nightmare? I wonder, as I push aside all my usual business casual to get to a black dress at the far end of the rack. When will I get over what's happened since waking up to find Stone at my kitchen table a year ago?

I blame it on the day as I pull on the black dress I bought when my parents' original landlord died. That had been just three months before I inadvertently pushed my best friend straight into the arms of Luca Ferraro, the future don of the Ferraro family. At the time, I'd thought her fellow law student was simply rich, generous, and outrageously handsome to boot.

"You're so lucky," I remember telling Amber, and I'd secretly wished I was beautiful like her. Beautiful enough to land a guy like that. I was a few years older than her. And I'd thought I was the wise one in our friendship back then.

Ha. Stupid—that was all I'd been before Stone showed up at my kitchen table. Stupid and naïve.

Amber and I had made plans before that moment. She was pregnant—I'd thought by some anonymous sperm donor. We'd decided to raise her baby together, create a new family in the townhouse I could barely afford on my own. It was the perfect solution for my own boring and stale life...a dream come true.

Until Stone showed up and it all fell apart.

Memories of Amber and Luca's rekindled romance mix with ones from my unexpected love story with Stone's identical twin, Rock. He was supposed to make up for losing Amber and the baby to the ex-husband who turned out to be its real father. He almost did.

Until that, too, fell apart.

Stone had hated me, and I guess, what they say about twins is true. Eventually Rock decided to dump me on his brother's advice. Then he died the very next day, without telling anyone that we were no longer a thing.

I zip up the dress I haven't worn in several years and look at myself in the mirror on the back of my door. I was born in this house, a house without any full-length mirrors, and I can still remember how guilty I'd felt when I'd gone down to Target when I was fifteen to buy this one with my birthday money. Like it was a betrayal of my parents to add something only a sighted person would need to our domicile. Even now, with both my parents and the prospect of living with Amber long gone, it remains the only item specifically made for sighted people in the house.

However, I don't love what I see in my secretly bought mirror. Thanks to the thirty pounds I've put on, the dress is now too tight, verging on lewd. I'll have to grab a cardigan to button over it, so that people don't think I'm trying to flash them at my dead ex-boyfriend's funeral. My dark curls also aren't playing along with my somber look. I was supposed to get a long-needed trim last week after my annual physical.

But the doctor's news at that appointment had so stunned me that I never made it in. Now, here I am with flyaway curls and a split-ends problem that makes me wish my Haitian mother and Dominican father had never met in that Macular Degeneration support group. My curls are the kind of frizzy, dry mess that would take at least an hour with a flat iron to fix.

But Rock's funeral is in less than that. Sighing, I return to the town house's single bathroom to consult with the patron saint of bad hair days. St. Scünchi No Slip Grip headband goes over my hair, pulling the huge mess into a puff. I rub in a cheap CC cream that evens out my smoky brown complexion, brush on some mascara, grab the cardigan and try again with the mirror.

A little better, I decide, but not putting in much effort feels strange, considering I used to spend hours getting ready for my daily mandated dates with Rock. He was my first and maybe last chance at real romance, and I wouldn't have even dreamed of opening the door to him in anything less than full hair and make-up...all the way up until he dumped me.

But Rock's dead now. My okayest will have to do.

My phone's ding interrupts the second outfit check.

It's a text message from Aunt Mari, with a suggestion for a two-bedroom apartment in Charlotte, along with another admonishment about how, ***"You know you could just stay with Yara and her three kids. She could really use the help, since her husband's been deployed again and all that oldest daughter of hers knows how to do is play on her phone."***

Her admonishment tugs at my heart. It must be so hard for Aunt Mari's daughter, Yara. Aunt Mari and her can't live together because they have one of those oil and water mother-daughter relationships. And raising three kids with a husband away has to be so—

I cut myself off right there. That's Too Nice Naima talking. Always giving too much of herself to others, only to be left behind when the people I build up move on.

Refusing to case work my cousin, I tap on the apartment link—holy macaroni, is that really the price of a one-bedroom? I'm paying twice that for our place in Jackson Heights...

No, not our place. My place, I remind myself. Just my place now.

I've *got* to start remembering that. I type a quick note of thanks to Aunt Mari and hit send.

Then it's time to go.

A wave of grief crashes over me. Rock hadn't been the tough twin. He'd hated to fight and couldn't bring himself to kill.

"I know how it looks on the outside, but I swear I was born into the wrong family. I've been suspecting that from the time I was a kid. Stone took to all the backroom deals and gun stuff real natural, just like our dad, but I taught myself computers because I knew that would never be me. Anyway, that's all I want. To marry a normal woman, so we can settle down and have a normal life. You keep asking why a guy like me would be interested in a girl like you. But you're a sweet social worker. You wouldn't have nothing to do with my family if you weren't trying to help your friend. Believe me, you're exactly what I want. Because on the inside you're just like me."

He told me that as we walked home from yet another amazing dinner date. And that ended up being the night we finally made love.

And now he was dead. Guilt, regret, and resentment swirl around my chest in a confusing grief.

God, I don't want to go to this funeral. But I order a Lyft anyway and even pay the extra so that I don't have to share it.

The funeral is just as I'd expected it to be. Long and super Catholic. As the priest drones on about tragedy and lives cut short, I remember Rock's and my first date. He'd told me stories about all the stuff he used to do to keep from falling asleep during Mass. Shouting Amen after every hymn, writing computer code by hand on the back of the offering card, and even shoplifting some smelling salts from the local Walgreens.

I laughed until tears were coming out of my eyes, and thought, so this is what a spectacular first date feels like.

But at Rock's funeral, my eyes remain bone dry. I don't shed a single tear. There are too many other things to think about, too many worries fretting up my mind.

"You should have sat up front with us," Amber says, later when we're all gathered around the gravesite at a famous Queens' cemetery, known as the final resting place for many of the organized crime world's biggest household names. And now Rock.

Despite being blind and having her four-month-old baby on her hip, Amber managed to find me in the large crowd of her husband's and Rock's Italian family members. I can't say I'm surprised. Amber's always been amazing that way, and as I turn to face her and the baby she named Luca Jr, my chest pangs with what might have been if Stone hadn't shown up at my kitchen table.

"Hi, Amber," I say, glad not for the first time, that she can't see me.

"Why didn't you find me as soon as you got here?" she answers, staying on point like she often does. She's a natural born lawyer. I thought that the first time we met to set up her freshman year dorm room at Hunter's College. And I continue to think it now as we stand beside Rock's grave.

I glance around and end up feeling even more self-conscious. Amber is easily the most beautiful person I know in real life, and the gorgeous blue-eyed baby boy sleeping contentedly on her shoulder hasn't taken away from that sheen. As always, a lot of people are staring at her, which means they're staring at us.

She doesn't know that this happens everywhere she goes. Has been happening ever since I met her. I used to shove the self-conscious feelings down. Used to tell myself it didn't matter. And then act like I really believed that.

Today is different, though. Today I mumble, "I'm not part of the family," and drop my eyes to my feet, so that I don't have to look at her or anyone else.

"You're part of my family," Amber says. "That's true no matter what."

No matter what. I wish that were true. I wish things were really as simple as she decided they were after she accepted Luca's second marriage proposal.

"Nai..." she says with a sigh when I don't answer. "I know how sensitive you are, that you're hurting. I am, too. I mean, I was..."

A sad shadow falls over Amber's face, reminding me that she has traumatic memories of her own. Ones that are way worse than mine. I feel all sorts of petty for not wanting to come here this morning. Not just because Rock's funeral would be sad, but also because I didn't want the pain of seeing Amber with her perfect family and the baby we were supposed to raise together.

"I'm sorry I didn't sit next to you..." I say, meaning it.

I've got to tell her.

"I know this isn't the best place," I take a steadying breath and rip the Band-Aid off. "But I wanted to tell you first that I've gotten a job in North Carolina. So I'm moving there... ah, next week."

Amber didn't use to be so great about showing emotion. She

used to be closed off and a little distant. Even with those she loved.

But today, standing beside Rock's grave with her baby, her mouth drops open and she lets out a woof of air. Like I kicked her. "What? Why are you just now telling me this?"

"I only got the offer three days ago." Not a lie. But not the exact truth either. It's true I only got the offer three days ago, but I applied for the job shortly after that doctor's appointment.

"The fact that they made you the offer means that you must have applied for the job. I'm assuming this offer didn't come out of the blue."

Darn, Amber. Of course, she picks up on that omission. I swear she's like a bloodhound with the real truth and nothing but the truth. Encouraging her to apply to law school has come back to bite me.

I squirm under Amber's interrogation, all the true answers wanting to come out. But I keep them locked behind my clamped lips. I'm not that naïve girl at the table anymore. I know better now. Telling her the truth won't solve anything. Only make it worse.

"One of my dad's sisters lives in Charlotte. All her children are grown and out of the nest, and she's been begging me to move down there ever since my parents left New York. A special position as an advocate for college-age foster youth just came up. And I think...I think it'll be a perfect fit."

Amber's head jerks back. "So you're just leaving?"

I waiver, wanting and wishing like I often do that things had turned out differently. That Stone had never shown up at my kitchen table and that Amber and I had raised her baby together as we planned, without his sperm donor ever finding out.

But that's a stupid, selfish wish, especially now.

Luckily, the priest saves me from having to answer her hurt question. He calls for our attention, and we all turn to face where he's standing behind Rock's now closed casket.

More sermonizing, then it's finally time to lower Rock's body into a ground. A terrible sound rises from the other side of the audience's semi-circle as soon as the gleaming black and gold casket starts its descent.

It's Rock's mother. Her entire body shakes as she weeps into her hands, and I suspect she would fall to her knees if not for Luca holding her up with a strong arm around her shoulders.

On the other side of her stands Stone and a much older version of the man in the mugshot on the Wikipedia page for Stanley Ferraro. Stone and Rock's father, on temporary release from his double lifetime sentence for several counts of pretty much everything a mafioso can be sent to prison for. Stanley had originally been slated to become the Ferraro's Family's next head, but that Don title ended up going to Luca's father when his brother caught a lifetime, and then some, prison sentence.

If things had worked out differently, Stone would be the current head of the Ferraro family. But they didn't and now he's the one standing by as his father does absolutely nothing to console his grieving wife.

That might be because he's in handcuffs chained directly to

his waist. But I don't think so. His expression is a total mirror of his granite-faced son's. He's a craggier Stone with a full head of grey hair. Hard, emotionless, and apparently incapable of providing even a measure of comfort to the woman barely standing beside them.

Looking at the two expressionless men, I try to find a pang of sympathy somewhere in my soul. Try to forgive. Try not to hate Stone, like I've hated him since I found him at my kitchen table. But observing him watch his brother get lowered into the ground with the same cold, uncaring expression he wore when he told me to sit down, I can't. I just can't.

I throw my dirt and go. No stopping to give my condolences to Rock's mother, who I doubt I could look in the eye anyway. No saying good-bye to Amber. I just go and don't look back.

The air is less cold on the other side of the cemetery's entrance. And as I order another Lyft, I breathe heavily, feeling like I've narrowly escaped something. Joe, a Latino-looking guy in a black Prius is my savior and he's on his way. All I have to do is meet him at the curb.

But then...

"Hey, Naima."

I freeze at the sound of Stone's voice. It sends shivers down my back now just as it did back then. And I no longer have to worry about catching my breath. It disappears as he comes to stand in front of me, somehow looming larger than Rock ever did, even though they are—were—identical twins.

He blocks my access to the road. "I don't know how they do

it at your kind of Catholic funerals, but at ours, you usually say something to the mother of the deceased. Especially when the deceased is your dead boyfriend."

A thousand defenses come to mind, none of which I dare to say out loud. Not to this man.

"I'll send a card," I lie. Then, as long as I'm racking up the sins, I add, "I have some place to be. An important appointment."

A beat, as his eyes flicker up and down my body. Not the way Rock's did when we first met, but like a man, who couldn't be more disgusted. "You're lying," he says. "But go, run."

Again, I could defend myself. Again, I don't. Instead I happily take the invitation and start to push past him. But then he grabs hold of my arm, his meaty hand a vice around my shoulder. "Hear you're moving."

My heart pounds with fear at his words. Is he tracing my emails and calls, like Luca used to do Amber? If so, how much does he know about the real reason I'm moving?

"Amber's all upset about it," he says, cutting off my panicked thoughts.

Oh...Amber. A pang of guilt hits me along with another useless wish that things had turned out differently.

"Dick move, Almonte," Stone says, as if giving voice to my thoughts. "Better ways to deal with your bullshit crush."

"I'm not leaving because of Amber," I say, my lips tightening.

Now that's the truth, but Stone shakes his head at me like he's caught me telling another bold-faced lie.

I'm once again gripped by the same anger that made me knee him in the crotch the last time we talked. I hate this, hate the way he makes me feel like someone I'm not. Someone spiteful and fighty. Someone so infuriated, she has to resort to knee punches instead of words.

"Just let me by, okay?" I say. "I don't...I don't want to do this. Not today."

Stone's hand tightens on my shoulder, the direct opposite of what I asked. I'm considering another knee to his crotch, like the last time we talked to each other. But then I see the look on his face and stop.

Mainly because there actually is a look on his face. Not a cold and neutral expression, but a furrowed brow above eyes that are...well, not soft, but not as hard as they were when they lowered his brother into the ground.

And just like that, my baseline compassion boots back up.

"Stone," I say softly. "I'm sorry. I'm sorry about your brother. I can't even fathom how hard this must be for you."

"Yeah," he says, the word falling like a pebble between us.

He looks at me. And I look at him. One thin line of human connection tentatively forming between us.

Then his lips come crashing down on top of mine.

I'm shocked. At least I should be, but I'm not given a chance. His kiss is immediately relentless and all-consuming. There's no chance for my mind to process or wander as it sometimes did when I was making out with Rock. From the moment our mouths touch, Stone plunges and plunders, demanding and then taking every ounce of my attention.

But I can't blame the surprise of the kiss for what happened next. How instead of pushing Stone away, I threw my arms around his neck, pulling myself into his savage kiss even deeper. How instead of feeling repulsed by this unexpected assault, my body thrilled with a hum unlike anything I've ever felt before. Not caring where I was, who this was. Just wanting more and more.

Until suddenly Stone pulls away, as abruptly as he attacked me.

I stumble back a little, not understanding. Not comprehending. How he could so suddenly stop doing something that had felt so good?

But he does. And even worse, his face has gone expressionless again.

"I don't get it," he says, his words as soft as bullets shooting out a silenced gun. "I still don't fucking get what Rock ever saw in you."

The words slice my heart open, just as the phone I'm still holding vibrates in my hand. I look down at it to see that Joe, my Lyft driver, is here.

And by the time I look back up, Stone is gone.

Like he was never even there.

Okay, then...

Sometimes you ask God for a sign that you've made the right decision. Sometimes he just gives you one whether you asked for it or not.

This is my freaking sign, I decide right there and then.

I, Naima Almonte, am a freaking mess. I need to get the heck out of New York City. And this...what happened with Stone...how I responded to his kiss...confirms it.

Bye, New York.

Hello, Charlotte.

CHAPTER ONE

"I just don't understand why you would move down here if you're not going to let me move in with you."

I bite back my frustration and take a steadying breath. "*Tia*..."

"Okay, okay, at least let me set you up. Come to church with me tomorrow, *mija*, there's a man I want you to meet. He is a little skinny but other than that, perfect for you. His name is Luis!"

Eight months later, I'm still certain my decision to move to Charlotte was a good one. But I am regretting answering my aunt Mari's call while rushing around the best I can to get ready for work.

"Thank you, but no thank you," I say in Spanish to her latest invitation to join her for church this Sunday.

"Oh, come on, *mija*, Luis will not bite. And he needs a nice, responsible girl like you to keep him off these streets. Plus, his baby's mother is blonde, and he hates her, so I do not think he will mind your dark skin."

Wow.

I still don't quite know how to respond to the blatant colorism often spewed by the older relatives on the Dominican side of my family tree. On one hand, respect your elders. My father would flip out if he heard I talked back to his older sister for any reason.

On the other hand, if I had to take one more phone call from Aunt Mari about some potential candidate she'd dredged up along with her equally colorist church members, I will scream loud enough for the way less color struck Dominicans in New York to hear it. And don't even get me started on how I have to constantly remind her that I don't just consider myself a dark Latina, but black. You know, thanks to the Haitian mother, she and some of my other older relatives still can't believe my father lowered himself to marry.

"Sorry, Tia Mari," I say instead. Then I switch back to English to tell her, "Hard pass."

"You're right maybe we should wait until you lose all that weight," Aunt Mari says cheerily.

I glare at the phone. "Okay, I've got to go, *Titi.*"

"Wait, we still haven't talked about me moving in with you!"

"So sorry, Titi, I'm going to be late for work. Not hanging up on you," I promise. Then I do just that.

Only to get hit with another pang of guilt. No matter what

kind of new leaf I've decided to turn over here, the old Too Nice Naima, who tries her best to like everyone and wants everyone to like her back is still lurking around.

Too Nice Naima would have gone with her aunt to church to dutifully meet Luis. Then, depending on the level of his sad background story, Too Nice Naima would not only date him, but also spend the majority of her outside work time and energy trying to fix him, all the way up until he left her for somebody better.

Believe me, I'm grateful for my aunt after she not only found me my current job and showed up with several cousins to help me move into my new apartment in a nice neighborhood near the college where I do most of my outreach work. But this move, this new job and this upcoming new phase in my life—it's meant to be a fresh start. It's a chance to break all my old patterns, and her trying to set me up isn't part of the plan.

As I make my way down to the bus stop, I decide I need to nip this in the bud. Tell her I'm not just reluctant to date in my current circumstances, but off the idea of love and relationships altogether.

"I've had enough hurt and disappointment in my life.," I could tell her truthfully. "Too much to be prayed away. Sorry."

Unlike on the New York subway, a man moves out of his seat as soon as I climb on the bus outside my apartment building, which is already stuffed with people headed into downtown Charlotte.

I sigh as soon as I sit down, taking a moment to catch my

breath as I often have to these days after any sort of fast movement.

I didn't have the dream last night.

Again.

That shouldn't make me anxious, but it does. Obviously, having a recurring dream about the most traumatic experience of your life for nearly a year straight wasn't fun. But for some reason, its absence feels even more worrying. Mainly because of what had come before that first dreamless night.

A cemetery kiss that hadn't disgusted or repelled me, but had turned me on, like no other kiss ever had before.

I still don't fucking get what Rock ever saw in you.

Yeah, me either, Stone, I think, staring out the window at Charlotte's charming landscapes as the bus ferries me into work.

What is wrong with me that several months and six hundred miles from New York later, I'm still obsessing over that kiss?

CHAPTER TWO

CHARLOTTE'S SOCIAL WORK DEPARTMENT IS understaffed and underfunded, which I don't like for my clients, but appreciate for myself. My workday passes by just as quickly as every other has since I finished up my training period. It's filled with urgent paperwork, filings, and a ton of delegation for anything that involves next month when I won't be here.

Unfortunately, I have a check-in scheduled with one of my most heartbreaking clients tonight. A homeless college student, living in her car, now that she's been kicked out of the foster care system. I feel tired just thinking about meeting with her.

Not because I don't want to help her, but because I'm not sure I can.

Nonetheless at exactly 5:45, I step into our meeting/conference room where Cami Marino is already waiting for me. Pacing back and forth in front of the conference table, instead of sitting at it, like most of my clients do.

"Cami, why don't you sit down," I say, steeling my heart against the twenty-year old's huge brown eyes.

She reminds me a little of Amber, because she's the secret daughter of an Italian father, and also has light brown skin. But other than that, Cami's nothing like Amber. She's normal twenty-year-old cute as opposed to arrestingly beautiful. And right now, her eyes are crazed and frightened, as opposed to crackling with determination.

But like Amber, she's a hard worker who's overcome enormous obstacles to excel at college. Despite having lost her mother to an overdose and being forced to live out of her car, Cami just made the Chancellor's list after finishing her junior year at University of North Carolina at Charlotte. She's also nearing the same age Amber was when we went from being a social worker and her client to true friends.

I have to remind myself of how well that turned out as I place her case file down on the table. *Don't get too close,* the new Not Nice Naima warns me.

"I'm sorry," she apologizes. "But I can't sit down. I've got to know what's going on with my sister. Did the other social worker get the proof she needs to get her away from our dad?"

I regard her with a sympathetic tilt of my head. "Cami, even if the other social worker found something, I couldn't tell you about it," I remind her. "That's not how this works."

"I just need to know if she's alright. I need to make sure he's not doing to her what he did to me," Cami mumbles into her scuffed tennis shoes. She's dressed in sweatpants and a thin t-shirt over an ill-fitting bra, and she's let her hair grow into a wild, super dry fro, in desperate need of a deep conditioning and a long detangling session.

Observing how bad she looks—even for a college student, makes my heart hurt. I've read that poor grooming is a classic symptom of sexual abuse. On a subconscious level, victims transform themselves to be less appealing, so as not to suffer the so-called attraction they think they might have invited upon themselves.

Looking at her hunched shoulders, I hate that the system has now pitted me against the girl who came into our office six months ago to report her formerly secret father for sexual abuse, in the hopes of adopting her little sister. Cami feared her sister might be in danger, now that the girl's mother had died.

Carlos Marino was a prominent member of the community, the executive director of a top accounting firm. And the head of the agency had seemed more concerned with investigating quietly than Cami's story about having endured a sexual relationship with her father when she was a little girl around Talia's age.

Now here we were in this meeting room with Cami asking me for answers I wasn't allowed to give.

"How are you doing at college?" I ask, trying to steer the conversation back to our check-in. "Are you able to keep up with classes, considering everything."

"I'm fine," she answers, balling her fist. "All that matters is my sister. Can you just maybe nod if she looks okay."

"I've got a box of supplies for you. Razors, maxi pads, stuff like that," I say, instead of answering her question. "Right at my desk. It was a little too heavy for me to lift right now, but if you want to come with me—"

She slams a hand against the table. "Fuck your supplies. I keep on telling you, the only reason I'm here is because of my sister!"

I can't tell her the truth. That the case file on her sister reads more like an indictment of Cami than her father.

I think of one excerpt from the interview with her dad: *Camille is a very bitter and disturbed girl. She threatened to do something like this if I didn't give her money...*

Carlos Marino's condemnations of his estranged daughter's motivations took up more space on the report than the short interview the social worker did with her half-sister, Talia.

But I believe Cami. I believe her story, even if that other social worker doesn't. And that just makes it worse as my purposefully neutral gaze connects with her angry one.

"I'm sorry," I tell her truthfully. "I wish I could tell you more. I wish I could do more."

Compassion can be a soul breaker for some of these kids. And Cami starts sobbing on the other side of the table. I heave myself out of my seat and go to her. Wrap my arms around her and try to take on some of the pain radiating off of her in waves.

NOT SURPRISINGLY, I FEEL TIRED, BORDERING ON weary, when I get out of my Lyft that night. I'd been thinking of making myself dinner and taking a long hot shower when I first left work. But over the course of my Lyft ride, that plan has morphed into a microwave Amy's Dinner and falling face down into my bed without so much as brushing my teeth or washing my face.

I bemoan the alcohol-free state of my apartment, as I climb the stairs to my one-bedroom. What I wouldn't give for a nice, huge glass of—

I stop, my tiredness slipping away when I see the hulking figure standing outside my door.

Every nerve ending surges to life with such speed my head spins. I'm fully awake now, just like I was when I walked into my kitchen on that fateful day last year.

Because Stone is here. Standing in front of my apartment door. His eyes glued to my belly.

Which is about eight months pregnant with his brother's baby.

CHAPTER THREE

"STONE," I SAY, OUT OF BREATH EVEN THOUGH I'M standing still. "What are you doing here?"

His eyes flick from my belly to my face. Back down to my belly. Then... "Is it Rock's?"

Panic lodges in my throat, like a piece of meat, threatening to choke me to death. I've gone through a lot to keep this secret. Abandoned my post, moved across state lines and ghosted my best friend. All so I could cut my baby's ties to the mafia family its father was trying to escape.

It feels wildly unfair to get caught now in my very deliberate sin of omission. Not earlier on in the pregnancy, but at the tail end of my third trimester, when I barely have enough energy to get up the stairs to my apartment, much less fight.

Lie, the new much bitchier Naima I'm trying to be urges. *A lie will solve everything.*

I open my mouth, ready to say whatever it takes to make this cold-eyed killer go away.

But then he says, "And if you're thinking about telling me anything less than the God's honest, remember what happened when Amber lied to Luca about the exact same thing."

Not the exact same thing. This baby isn't Stone's, it's his brother's. His *dead* brother's, which means Stone has absolutely no rights here. But the Ferraro Family's number one enforcer remains disturbingly effective at the art of intimidation. Despite my silent counter argument, I do exactly as he says. I remember what happened when Amber lied to Luca.

Stone at my kitchen table—that's what happened when Amber lied to Luca about who was the father of her baby. Also, this isn't Luca standing between me and my front door right now. Stone is the guy, bad guys like Luca call in for jobs too dirty for them to handle.

Oh God... A sharp pain zips across my pelvis at the thought of what Stone will do if he catches me in a lie, and my over-burdened bladder threatens to release.

"I've got to use the bathroom. Like, right now."

I try to push past him, but he shifts to stand in front of me. "Is it Rock's?" he asks again, without an ounce of sympathy in his expression.

"It doesn't matter either way," I answer.

"The fuck it doesn't matter," Stone answers, his voice vicious and lethal.

I visibly squirm, bouncing from foot to foot. "I really, really have to pee. So unless you want me to have an accident..."

A beat. Then he takes a very deliberate step aside.

Unlocking the door feels like it takes a century with Stone's cold gaze, lasering into me. But finally, I manage to get it open. And though, I wasn't lying about my need to pee, with a burst of speed, I didn't know I was still capable of at this late stage of pregnancy, I dart inside, making a quick decision to slam the door between me and the enforcer who showed up out of the blue.

Then I put myself at further risk of peeing my pants in order to flip both locks and pull the chain before I make a mad dash to the bathroom.

Relief floods through me when my bottom finally hits the toilet seat. But I know it's only temporary. I've escaped the ruthless enforcer. I'm safe...for now. But I already know...

Eventually I'm going to have to deal with Stone.

That eventually hits me hard, and suddenly I can't breathe for the elephant of dread sitting on my chest. I've been found out by the Ferraro family's most ruthless enforcer. And I have no idea how I'm going to get myself or my innocent baby out of this mess?

CHAPTER FOUR

Eventually comes much sooner than expected.

The very next morning I walk into the kitchen to find Stone at the table, just like back in New York. Same sharp dark suit, same shaven head, same Stone-y expression.

But this time there's no gun, sitting in front of him. No, the thing laid out on the kitchen table is even worse. A single sheet form with three horrific words written across the top.

"Is that...?" I start to ask, only to have the rest of the question die in my throat.

Appearing to give zero eff-words about my stricken look, Stone supplies, "Yeah, it's a marriage license. You and me are getting married. Today."

I blink at him, once again not sure if he's for real or a terrible nightmare. "Excuse me?"

"You heard me. Don't act like this is a surprise."

"I'm not acting," I assure him, holding up both hands. "I am truly very surprised. Just like any woman would be if she walked into her kitchen to find the brother of her baby's dead father waiting—with a marriage license application already printed out."

Stone shrugs as if I'm the ridiculous one in this situation, not him. "What'd you think was going to happen after I saw the state of you?"

"I didn't think you'd ever see," I answer truthfully.

Stone narrows his eyes at me. "So you thought, what? You'd just keep this from me forever? Like Amber tried to do Luca?"

"No, not like Amber and Luca," I answer. Then I remind him. "You're not this baby's father."

"Yeah, and that's why we've got to get married," he says, tapping on the documents with one thick finger. "The lawyer I consulted is saying I can't adopt this kid until it's out. But being married to its mother will speed things along. What are you, like, nine months already? If we do this right, I could be in place before the ink on the birth certificate dries."

As my mother often says when my father is getting on her last nerve, "*Ayayay....*" I rub a hand over my face and turn to the Keurig. "I need coffee. Real coffee."

I can tell Stone has plans to be difficult with a generous splash of scary to get what he wants.

"And then we'll go down to the courthouse."

I scowl at him over my shoulder as I fill the reservoir with water. "And *then*, I call the police, because you're not supposed to be in my house."

"This isn't a house. It's an apartment," Stone sneers, looking around my home like he found me living in some kind of hovel, not in a reasonably priced two-bedroom. "And it's way too small to raise a kid in anyways."

I bristle with irritation but I keep my voice carefully composed as I say, "I grew up in a duplex. This is fine. More than adequate."

"I want my kid to grow up in a house," Stone answers behind me, his voice stubborn.

"Cool. By all means, do that when you have a kid," I say, punching a finger into the brew button. "But since this isn't your baby..."

"You should've told me," Stone mutters. "Given me more time to prepare."

Funny I thought, I'd started to lose my accent after so many months in a southern state where many of my clients called me ma'am. But it comes back in full effect as I ask, "Prepare for *what*? Just in case me moving hundreds of miles away hasn't already clued you in, I don't want you or any other Ferraro in this baby's life!"

"Any other Ferraro, including Amber, right?" he asks, standing up from the table.

Especially not Amber, I think to myself, before answering, "No, not Amber either."

With a sigh, I turn around to face him. "I don't need Amber

or anyone else to raise my child in North Carolina without all your crime family drama."

Stone pauses in a way I hope means, he's truly considering my words, and/or realizing I'm not going to go along with his crazy marriage plan.

However, I find out in the next moment it totally doesn't.

"If this is about that lesbo crush you had on Amber, you're going to have to let that shit go. It ain't happening, especially now that she's in two kids deep with Luca. Those two fuck non-stop, you know. It ain't even natural. No way she's leaving him for you."

My coffee's beeping at me to get it, but for several moments on end, all I can do is stare at Stone. So grossly offended, my mind short-circuits trying to figure out how to answer his offensive accusation.

I finally settle on a fierce. "Get out!"

Stone starts walking. But not toward the door. I watch open-mouthed as he strolls over to my Keurig, pulls out my NY SOCIAL WORK department mug, and oh, my God...actually takes a sip of the coffee I just brewed for myself.

He pulls a face. "Whoa, this is strong." Then, without warning, he dumps the entire mug in the sink. "I don't think you're supposed to be drinking real coffee anyways."

Okay, being a social worker is all about keeping your composure, no matter what. Which I always do. I've lost count of how many heartfelt thank yous and apologies I've received, commending me for my patience, no matter what my angry and frustrated clients threw at me. And I've been even better here in North Carolina, where people's voices sound like warm honey instead of cracked concrete.

But Stone...freaking Stone.

"Get out!" I find myself screaming at him. "Get out before I call the police—"

I cut off. Not because I've gotten a hold of myself, but because of the cramp that suddenly seizes across my mid-section, cutting and bright.

"Ow!" I say, doubling over.

"Fuck, what's going on with you?" Stone demands, glaring at me, like I just decided to be in pain on purpose.

"I'm fine," I say, trying to undouble, despite the lingering ache of the cramp. "Or at least I will be when you go. So, please, get—ooooowwww."

I double over again.

"All right, fuck this shit..." The next thing I know, the guy I was just yelling at to get out of my apartment picks me up and cradles me to his chest, like I weigh nothing at all.

"We're going to the hospital," he declares before carrying me out of my own front door.

CHAPTER FIVE

STONE IS TOTALLY WRONG. I TELL HIM THAT OVER AND over again after he deposits me into his large black SUV, then proceeds to race toward the closest hospital like he's a cop with a license to run stop signs and lights wherever he sees fit.

"It's probably just Braxton Hicks," I insist. "I feel fine, and the baby's not due for another three weeks."

"You're an idiot," he answers. Then he ignores me until he screeches to a halt in front of the ER.

I'm pretty sure Stone was never in the army, but he sounds like some kind of drill sergeant, issuing orders from the moment he hauls me out of the huge black car's backseat.

"Get a birthing suite ready. She's about to pop!" he yells to the woman working at the front desk.

"Please stop yelling, and I'm not about to pop," I throw an apologetic look at the woman behind the glass window. "I feel fine now."

But then as if punishing me for daring to disagree with the world's biggest butthole, another cramp doubles me over.

"Her contractions are about ten minutes apart. Birthing Suite. Now." Stone commands. "Whatever you'd set aside for the biggest sports star, I want her in it."

These people don't know Stone from Adam, but somehow, they end up doing exactly as commanded. Less than fifteen minutes after we arrive, I find myself in a birthing suite that looks like a really nice apartment, not the sterile labor and delivery rooms I saw on the tour with my single mother's Lamaze class.

And less than fifteen minutes after that, the head nurse of the maternity ward declares that I'm in the early stages of labor and sends another nurse off to page my obstetrician.

I can't even bring myself to look Stone in the eye after the announcement. Stone, who's still freaking here, standing right by my bedside. Somewhere along the way, he'd assured, or more likely scared the staff into believing he was my husband and should be allowed to stay.

"You sure this is the best you've got?" he asks, glancing around the room, like it's not twice as big as a Manhattan studio apartment.

The head nurse informs him that the babies of five football stars, eleven basketball players, and one major country music singer have all been born in this very room. "Believe me, your wife is in the best of hands," she tells Stone.

"I'm not his—" I start to say.

Only to be cut off by Stone's terse "She better be."

The nurse finds an excuse to leave the room shortly after that.

I open my mouth to tell him he can go, too, but cut off when another cramp tears through me.

"Hurts like a motherfucker, huh?" To my surprise, Stone enfolds my hand in his much larger one. "Just breathe, and it'll be over soon."

Suddenly, remembering all the Lamaze lessons that flew out of my head earlier, I breathe, holding on tight to his hand. And just like Stone promised, the pain soon begins to ebb.

For a moment, I feel grateful. Stone's here, and I know I'm safe with him. A warm sense of security rolls over me, and suddenly I'm glad he's here and I am not alone...

....which is totally crazy! Ugh, hormones. *Get it together, Almonte,* I chide myself. The last thing I should feel with a man as ruthless and uncompromising as Stone is safe.

"Where's my phone?" I ask him. "I need to call my Aunt Mari.

Stone drops my hand like it's a dead subway rat. "Left it in the car," he answers.

"Could you go get it?" I ask between clenched teeth. "She's the one who's supposed to be here with me, not you."

"Well, I ain't leaving your side," he answers. With that, he walks over to the birthing suite's couch and takes a seat. Like the conversation is over and decided. He even pulls a pair of readers out of his jacket pocket and opens the *Architectural Digest,* sitting on the coffee table, really settling in.

I'm thoroughly outraged...and a tiny bit thrilled.

Which is so, so wrong, I remind myself.

"You know, I could ask the nurses to kick you out," I threaten, now totally anxious to swap out the ruthless enforcer with my at least sort of biddable aunt.

"Yeah, you do that." Stone flips a page of his magazine. "Good luck paying for this room on a social worker's salary."

I never curse. It's not kind, and it's not necessary. But I come close to calling this bully a slew of names as I answer, "You're the one who made them put me in this room!"

"Yeah, and you're welcome. Now give me some peace and quiet, while I look at what's popping in Sedona."

Ayayay! I've never met somebody so infuriating in my life. But another contraction interrupts whatever reply I could have come up with.

For the next few hours I writhe around on the bed in intermittent pain, while he flips through magazines, like whatever's in there is way more interesting than what's happening with me as the contractions get longer and closer together. At least I think he's ignoring what's happening with me.

Even though he's several feet away and reading, he somehow senses when I get past my threshold level for pain.

"Time for the epidural," he tells the nurse, just as I'm deciding to abandon my all-natural birth plan after a particularly agonizing contraction. "Get the drug guy in here for her."

There's some relief after the anesthesiologist pays me a visit with his needle kit. Then there's some more grumbling from me about how Stone needs to give me my purse and go, because my Aunt Mari will be here as soon as I let her know I'm in labor. However, this one-sided exchange is directly followed by a whole lot more not going anywhere from Stone.

Soon after that, the obstetrician appears and announces it's time to push.

"If you want to hold your wife's hand, give her some words of encouragement, now would be a good time," the head nurse tells Stone. Probably surprised by his lack of reaction to his supposed baby's big debut.

I shake my head at the nurse. "He's not my..."

I trail off when instead of continuing to flip through his magazine, Stone rises from the couch like a statue suddenly come to life and crosses the room.

The next thing I know, his much larger hand closes around mine again. "C'mon," he grunts.

C'mon. Not exactly the words of encouragement the nurse was hinting at. I toy with the idea of telling the nurses to kick him out. I was the mother after all, and what I said went.

But then I'd lose his hand. And strangely, I'm finding the hand, if not his single word directive to c'mon, comforting.

I've been alone for so long. Alone and on my own. That's the way I wanted it. The way I insisted it would have to be after I decided to move to North Carolina.

But Stone's hand...I need it. I hold on to it and squeeze it as the nurse directs me to use energy I don't have to push and push some more.

"C'mon," he says when I break down crying and tell the nurse, I'm not sure I can do this. "You're doing this. C'mon."

It's been ten hours since I arrived in this unexpectedly nice birthing suite. Whatever strength I had coming in was spent on withstanding all those contractions. But Stone squeezes his hand around mine and somewhere, someplace I find the will to bear down two more times.

Then Stone says, "I can see her. I can see her head!" and my baby girl comes wailing into the world.

I feel a lot of things after I finally push the baby out of my body. Embarrassment that Stone saw everything below my waist as I went through the birthing process. Anger that he took the scissors from the doctor and cut the cord, like he had any right whatsoever to be here. Resentment at the unemotional thumbs up he gives me after the nurses finishes taking the baby through her AGPAR tests.

But as soon as the nurse places the surprisingly pink little girl in my arms, joy immediately wipes out all that embarrassment, anger, and resentment.

"You're here!" I cry, smiling down at her.

She settles in my arms, like she's been waiting for this moment, too. And soon after, all I hear in the room is the beep of the monitoring machines, and the sound of her soft baby snores.

"She all right?" Stone asks above me, his voice quiet. "Fell asleep awfully quick. She just came down the slide."

I let out a chuckle at his observation, probably because I'm still high on just-had-a-baby euphoria. "She's fine. She's just worn out." But then I have to ask, "Why are you still here?"

"Ssh!" he answers. "The kid's trying to sleep."

I quiet, fret my lip, then ask, "Stone?"

"Yeah?"

"Did you already tell Luca?"

A wary beat. Then, "I called him this morning, and told him you were pregnant. But that was before I had all the details."

"So he doesn't know the baby is Rock's."

"Not until I tell him."

"Could you not tell him?" I ask, scrunching up my face hopefully. "If you tell him, then he'll tell Amber. And this is already complicated enough as it is."

I expect questions. Maybe even another accusation of being a lesbian.

But instead Stone goes silent. For a long, long time. Until, finally, he looks down at Garnet, then back up at me and says, "Okay."

CHAPTER SIX

STONE EVENTUALLY LEAVES. NOT THE SEVERAL TIMES I ask him to, but sometime in the night, while I'm fast asleep.

No goodbyes. I wake up in the early morning to the sight of an empty couch.

I don't want to be surprised, but I am.

I'm not leaving your side. The memory of his words floats through my mind as I gingerly get out of bed to pick up the baby. But I guess he'd only meant during the birth.

Good. I'm glad he's gone. At least that's what I tell myself as I put a lot more mental power than I currently have in reserve into trying to coax the baby to latch on to one of my breasts.

It's not until she's drank her small fill and nodded back off that I see the item now resting on my nightstand.

A phone. *My* phone!

Oh my God, yes! I snatch it up, to see a screen full of notifications. From work colleagues, cousins and aunts. They all seemed to know I had a baby girl. And a few of them even mention the pictures being "so cute."

Apparently, Stone contacted my boss and Aunt Mari, who then let everybody else know I had given birth. I shake my head at the phone, not sure how to take that. Normally I'd feel grateful. But this isn't a normal situation. And Stone for sure isn't a neighborhood saint.

I think about the marriage documents on the breakfast table. Who does that? Who breaks into his brother's ex-girl-friend's apartment with a marriage license form to fill out, then makes sure everyone on her phone tree knows she's given birth?

Before I can come anywhere close to answering those questions for myself, the pediatrician comes into the room to check the baby over.

"Looks good," he says after taking several measurements. "Have you decided on a name?"

"Garnet," I answer, a sad pang squeezing my heart.

I'd named my daughter after my favorite character from the animated series, *Steven Universe*. But in that moment, a memory hits me. Hugging my then client Amber after she told me she'd been accepted into Columbia Law.

I'd believed in her and encouraged her to apply, and I couldn't have been prouder of her for getting into New York's world-famous law school.

"If I ever have a little girl, I'm going to name her after you," I'd told her in that moment. "Because I want her to be fierce and bold and brave. Just like you."

But I'd found another gem to name my little girl after. And my friendship with Amber feels done now. For reasons I still can't fully explain—to myself or Amber.

The pediatrician's visit, small as it is, takes a lot out of me. I snooze some more, until my doctor wakes me up. She looks over my charts on a tablet, tells me both the baby and me look great. "Would you like to be discharged tomorrow morning or stay on for a couple more days to recover?"

I frown surprised, since my insurance paperwork clearly stated that, barring any complications, I'd only be allowed to stay for 48 hours in the hospital after giving birth. "I can stay longer? I didn't think my insurance would be good with that."

The nurse and the doctor exchange looks before the nurse says, "You can stay as long as you want, hon."

Wow... But no, I decide. I want to go home the next morning. As homey as they've made this birthing suite look, I'm already dreaming about my own bed and maybe even a bath. In hot, not lukewarm water as all the books I read insisted. Ooh, maybe I'd even order some sushi. It's been so long!

"I'd like to go home tomorrow morning. Thanks though."

The staff actually looks disappointed. I guess they don't get people in the birthing suite as often as they'd like, and they were hoping for a few extra nights.

The next morning, I eat some breakfast, then call Aunt Mari while I'm waiting for the discharge paperwork.

"*Mi amor*, why didn't you call on the Facetime," she demands as soon as she picks up. "I want to see the baby."

It's funny how little I use Facetime after growing up with visually impaired parents and then taking on a former best friend who had also no need of it. "You can see her in person when you come pick me up," I answer with a laugh. "I just got discharged."

"When I pick you up? But I'm already setting up at the *casa*," she says. "That boyfriend of yours said he'd get you home. By the way, *mija*, why didn't you tell me there was a new man in the picture. He's so *guapo*. Quiet and a little scary. But *guapo*. Like my movie boyfriend, Vin Diesel, just without the pointy head."

Usually I'm only slightly chagrinned by Aunt Mari's beauty over everything value system—and her inappropriate obsession with Vin Diesel—but today, I can't even.

"Okay, I'm not sure what Stone told you. But I definitely need a ride home. Do you mind coming to get me?"

"Yes, I mind. I still have cleaning to do before you get here. Why can't you just let your boyfriend bring you? You see, this is why you young girls stay so single. You can't let a man be a man."

"I'm single by choice, Aunt Mari," I remind her.

"I wouldn't be single by anything if I had a man looked like that in my bed."

"He's not in my bed. And he's not my boyfriend..."

"Hey, you ready to go?" a now familiar voice interrupts our argument.

I look up to see Stone at the suite's door, wearing a white linen suit and black everything else.

CHAPTER SEVEN

FOR A MOMENT, I FORGET MY WORDS. SOMETHING HOT and unfamiliar tumbles inside my belly. He's so...and this is weird to say, because I dated his twin...but Stone's arresting in a way his brother just wasn't.

Rock had stayed smiling from the moment we met. He was so animated, I never got a good chance to see his sober face. Not until he dumped me.

But Stone's face is a perfect work of art. Sharp everything and clean classic lines. I can actually see how he and Amber's preternaturally gorgeous husband could be related. *He is*...I realize then. He is *guapo*. Just like my aunt said.

"Is that him?" my aunt demands on the other side of the phone. "*Tu novio muy guapo?* Tell him hola for me!"

I hang up on Aunt Mari. Then tamp down a strong urge to adjust my hair. I can't help but notice how hot he is and how hot I'm not in the moment. Add that to the fact that he's wearing a well-tailored suit, while I'm wearing a weird diaper made of mesh underwear and industrial pads under my hospital gown, and yeah....cue all the self-conscious feelings.

But then I remember the circumstances. That I'm a woman who just gave birth. And that he's a man who intruded on that birth. A man who keeps on intruding on what should have been my magical moment with my baby.

"Why are you here?" I ask, irritation dissipating that silly bout of self-consciousness.

"To take you and the baby home," he answers, like I'm an idiot for asking. "Would have been here sooner, but I was finishing up the crib when I got the call you'd been discharged."

My heart all but gives out in gratitude that I won't have to figure out the crib when I get home. But then it occurs to me to ask, "Wait, why would they call to tell you I was being discharged?"

"Why do you think? Because I slipped the nurse a couple of hundys. Keep up."

I'm trying to keep up. Believe me. But talking to Stone feels like trying to swim in quicksand. The harder I fight, the more stuck I feel.

"They're coming through with the wheelchair soon. You need me to get your shit together?" he asks.

Before I can answer, he's opening the cabinet and grabbing my purse. I guess that was a rhetorical question.

"Stone, wait, I don't want..." I try to sit up straighter, so he'll take my next words seriously, but the action is painful, and makes me feel even weaker. "I don't want you to take me home."

Stone stops, turns to look at me, his eyes two cold, dark pits.

"Naima, pay close attention to my next words. Only one of the three people in this room give a shit what you want. And that person ain't me."

Wow. I'm from freaking New York, but for moments on end, all I can do is sit there. Completely stunned that anybody could be so rude.

"You ready to go?" Stone asks impatiently, like he has a whole list of places he'd rather be than here, helping me do anything.

There are a bunch of excuses I could try to give about why I let him take me out of the hospital after talking to me that way. Especially since I'd made a vow to leave Too Nice Naima behind in New York.

But listen, I just had a baby. My energy was seriously on the flag, and I plain didn't have any fight left in me.

Less than half an hour later, I find myself dozing off in the front seat of Stone's goon car, not waking up until he kills the engine in front of...

Wait, a minute. My eyes pop all the way open when I see the structure now standing in front of me. Not my homey apartment building.

But a house. An actual house with a yard and a picket fence, like I heard about while watching shows set in suburbs on my TV in Queens.

"What the heck?" I demand. "Where are we?"

"At the new crib. It was a bitch to get it all closed up in one day. I'm talkin' bags of cash. But it's ours, and a notary's stopping by tomorrow so that you can sign the rest of the paperwork. We still got a lot of furniture shopping to do, or we can hire somebody if you want. I think they have interior designers down south, too. But I got the baby's room set up right next to the master suite."

I splutter. Then splutter some more, choking on my outrage, before I finally manage to get out. "I'm not going in there with you. I'm not going anywhere with you!"

He stills. Looks at me. "Don't be stupid," he says, his voice filled with lethal menace.

And I shrink back. Remembering the table. Remembering how he held the cocked revolver to my head as he talked to Amber. Then dragged me out of my own house at gunpoint. "Don't be stupid," he warned, when I tried to fight him as he opened the back door of a Suburban. Then he'd shoved me in the backseat. Easily.

But I had been stupid.

Not only had I done nothing to try to escape from the swanky Manhattan condo Luca had imprisoned Amber in, using my life as leverage over her. I'd decided to take Stockholm to the next level by getting involved with Stone's identical twin brother. Then I'd somehow convinced myself everything would work out. Until it hadn't in ways that left Rock dead and Amber and me estranged.

I'd been so, so stupid back then.

But not now. "I will scream. I will call the police," I tell him, all my Queens coming out to shine.

But Stone just gives me a cold Jersey smile and answers, "Yeah, do that. I love these small towns. Everybody's so easy to pay off. Ask for Romano when you call 9-1-1 or don't. He's the captain. He'll come out himself regardless of whoever dispatch tries to send.

"I hate you," I tell him, uncharacteristic rage washing over me in vile, vicious waves. "I hate you more than I've ever hated anyone in my life."

"Aw, that's sweet," Stone says with another cold smile. "But what'd I tell you at the hospital about me and your feelings?"

Before I can answer, he gets out of the car. A moment later, the back door opens, and he grabs the carrier with my sleeping baby in it. Leaving me behind, like I'm little more than an afterthought.

This is a nightmare, I tell myself as I watch him carry the baby into the...okay, I want to hate it, but I have to admit, it the house he bought looks fantastic. It's a large, two-story colonial with a cobblestone walkway, two charming bay windows, and a huge front porch. Everything someone born and raised in a two-bedroom New York duplex could want after moving to the much cheaper and warmer south.

But whatever. I will not let this stand. I need time to get my mind and body right and then I'm figuring a way out of this mess. I refuse to let Stone get the better of me.

CHAPTER EIGHT

THREE MONTHS LATER

I find Stone waiting for me when I get off work. He's leaned up against his car, like a bald-headed Jake from *Sixteen Candles*.

"What are you doing here?" I ask, my heart glowing happy at the sight of him.

"I heard you had a good first day back." He pushes off the car and comes forward to stand right in front of me.

"You heard, but how...?" I start to ask, before breaking off with a knowing, "Slipped somebody a couple of hundys, huh?"

He takes another step forward, staring directly into my eyes. He's close now. As close as you can get without kissing. "Everybody in North Carolina's so easy to bribe. Makes my job real easy."

"And what is your job again?" We're standing so close, my stomach is doing somersaults, and for some reason I can't for the life of me remember what he does for a living.

He bites his lip, and the look in his eyes... it makes me feel like I'm the most beautiful girl in the world. Not some weird Haitian-DR hybrid.

"My job is making you happy, *mija*." he answers, his voice soft and full of emotion.

Then he leans forward to kiss me. But...

"Wait." I place a hand on his chest before our lips can touch. "When did you start calling me *mija*?"

He leans back, and the "you're so beautiful" look disappears. "Don't be stupid."

"I'm not. I'm not being stupid," I answer. A heavy anxiety replaces the fluttering butterflies in my stomach.

His face has gone cruel now. No, not cruel. Emotionless. Back to its usual setting. He's no dreamy rom com hero. I remember that now. He's someone much, much worse.

I take a step back to tell him, "I think there's something honestly wrong with you. Something I'm not seeing. What are you hiding from me?"

"Don't be stupid, *mija*. It's time to wake up."

The *mija*...it bothers me even more than his "don't be stupid" catchphrase for some reason.

"Why are you calling me *mija*?"

"*Mija*, wake up!"

My eyes pop open to find Aunt Mari standing over my bed and shaking me.

"Oh, you're awake!" she says as if she had nothing to do with me being ripped out of dream land. "I'm making *mangu*. Come, come get up, so you have enough time to eat a good breakfast before work."

I glance at my phone charging on the nightstand. It's six in the morning, but my aunt is already dressed in one of those bodycon dresses that cling to everything you want men to notice and hides everything you don't. I have never in my life been able to find a dress that does this for my own body, but my aunt has a closet full of them. And of course, she's also sporting her signature dark red mermaid tresses and full makeup. Aunt Mari is like the "beauty" version of the army. She does more to get pretty before 9am than most people do all day.

"How did you even get in here?" My voice is little more than a sleepy croak as I sit up on one elbow and watch her throw open all the curtains in my room.

I locked the door last night. Just as I had every night since Stone forced me to move into this house.

Not that I think he really wants me like that.

Only in my dreams—which I totally need to stop having. *Seriously, what the heck, Subconscious? Not cool!*

But locking the door before I go to sleep with the baby in her bedside bassinet, makes me feel, if not safe, at least like I have some control over our current living arrangements. Even if it's just one tiny little push button lock.

"*Tu novio* showed me how," Aunt Mari answers, her brown

eyes twinkling as she shatters even that small illusion of control. "It was so easy. He said I could take just any old key and twist it in the lock."

"He's not my boyfriend," I remind her for the millionth time as Aunt Mari decides to do a clean and bustle around my room like she's been invited.

"Go take a shower and make up your face. Men like women who put in some effort," she answers before launching into a noisy all-Spanish sermon about how my generation has forgotten that women need to take care of themselves, and that's why we can never keep a man.

Luckily Garnet sleeps like a rock. Even with light flooding into the room and Aunt Mari's sermonizing, she stays peacefully asleep. Which leaves me free to shower and okay, okay Aunt Mari, rub on some foundation and a little mascara. The bare minimum by Aunt Mari's standards, but I didn't inherit that Beauty all You Can Beauty gene from my Dominican side of the family.

It's not like I need to worry about looking pretty right now anyway, I decide right before I wake up my adorable three-month-old by smoothing a hand over her soft black curls. *This is all the complication I want or need in my life.* I nurse Garnet before putting on my clothes for work.

Too bad the first thing I see when Garnet and I enter the kitchen is the ruthless enforcer who refuses to move out of the house he's been forcing me to live in for the last few months. Stone's seated at the round breakfast table and being fussed over by Aunt Mari.

"Isn't it so nice to have a big, strong man in the house?"

Aunt Mari asks as she sets a *Los Tres Golpes* down in front of the hulking Italian.

No, it isn't, I think, eyeing his plate filled with fried eggs, fried cheese, fried Dominican salami, and last but not least, *mangu,* mashed plantains, with sautéed red onions on top. Stone has no right to be here at my breakfast table. Eating all my favorite Dominican breakfast treats. And ugh... looking better than any man with his severely limited emotional capacity should in a linen suit and open-collar shirt.

"Don't worry, I made you a plate, too, mija," Aunt Mari says. She sets my own *Los Tres Golpes* down in front of me and takes Garnet out of my arms, leaving me free to eat.

My mood lightens as I scarf down her delicious food, and I darn near sing a happy hallelujah song, when she replaces my empty plate with a cup of coffee, all while balancing Garnet in one arm like an old pro.

The original plan had been for Aunt Mari to only stay for a few days, but three months later, I find myself not minding that she's moved herself in with the full blessing of Stone and her six children who brought over all her stuff after church a few Sundays ago.

"Mai's right. This house is too big for just you and your *novio* and your baby," Osner, one of my cousins, called out to me as he and Jhonny, Aunt Mari's other son, carried in a divan.

"He's not my boyfriend," I answered, even as I led them to the downstairs room where Aunt Mari had decided she would be staying permanently after talking it over with Stone.

I'd been annoyed then, but I have to admit it's really working out as I sip my coffee to the soundtrack of Aunt Mari's crooning to Garnet in nonsense Spanish.

The scene would warm my heart—if not for the hulking presence on the other side of the breakfast table, drinking his own cup of coffee, and scrolling through his phone.

I can't believe Stone is still here after three months. He still hasn't found the right threat to make me take his lethal hand in marriage. And he flies back to New York four out of seven days of the week. Yet he's managed to insinuate himself into every other aspect of my life.

This house has both our names on it. And guess what I can see from the kitchen window...the matching His and Hers Cadillac Escalades he leased, sitting in the driveway.

He also forced an interior designer on me a couple of months ago. "Either work with him, or let him decide, I don't give a shit. But my kid ain't growing up in an empty house."

Despite his weekly four-day absence and his not-ever-going-to-happen status as my husband, he seems hell bent on us pretending we're one of those normal suburban families. Why?

I have no frickin' clue. He's barely here, and as for "his kid," he has yet to touch his niece, much less establish any kind of connection that could be described as a father-child relationship. He sleeps in the guestroom the few days he's here, and so far I haven't had to worry about making nice with him. Other than at meal times, I rarely see him.

Aunt Mari loves him, and always fusses over him when he's

down from New York. But to me, it feels like I'm living with a ghost. A huge, scary ghost, who dresses in expensive suits and only haunts the house on Sunday, Mondays, and Tuesdays.

But somehow I'd ended up working with the interior decorator to furnish *our* house with a modern mix of Herman Miller and Bernhardt Design furniture, along with some imported pieces from the Dominican Republic and Haiti to keep it from appearing too much like an interior design magazine spread.

So now I'm eating my breakfast in a house that looks exactly like what it is, a home that belongs to the two of us. And after I'm done doing that, I'll be hopping into the oversized car Stone bought me to drive into the office. Anyone looking at us from the outside would think we were some kind of happy family.

But we're not. We're definitely not. Which was why I spent most of my leave applying for jobs in the Dominican Republic, the one place Stone couldn't easily ramrod his way into my and Garnet's life. All I need is for one job offer to come through. Just one, and this weird living under the same roof with a man I despise nightmare will be over.

I'll be able to raise Garnet exactly as I planned. Just me and her. Far away from the Ferraro family and all their nonsense.

Thinking of that possibility brings me some solace as Stone and I drink our coffees in complete silence.

At least it does until we reach the next part of our now usual morning routine.

Stone sets his cup aside and pulls out a small, velvet box. "Here ya go."

I stoically continue to sip my coffee. Pretending like I can't hear any evil, can't see any evil...

Unfortunately, Stone is totally all right with speaking evil. "Stop playing and put it on already. I don't want you going into the office today without a ring on your finger."

With that, he pops open the box. As usual, it feels like getting shot point blank right through the heart with his gun when he does this, and the ring he's trying to make me wear is the bullet. This ring...it's even more impossible not to look at than Luca Ferraro. French set with a huge princess cut diamond right in the middle. All the carats. It's basically everything I secretly online shopped for when I thought Rock and I might go the distance. Only super-sized.

As always, my heart stops ticking for a few seconds as I helplessly stare at the exquisite ring Stone's trying to make me wear. There was a time I wanted the whole nine yards, a ring, a wedding, a man to love me and call me his own. One who I would adore in return. This ring reminds me of those silly dreams and make emotions drum in my throat.

But then I remember who's doing the offering. No, *offering* is the wrong word. More like, who's ordering me to wear his ring, even though I've already said, "No way, Jose" to marrying him, like, a million times.

I think there's something honestly wrong with you. Something I'm not seeing. What are you hiding from me?

The dream lingers, my subconscious tugging at me to open a case file on the emotionless man, commanding me to wear a ring that looks like it costs way more than two months of my salary. Maybe more than I make in an entire year.

But no, no. I'm not going to do that. He isn't one of my clients. And I refuse to case file him. I mean, how hard did I learn my lesson after doing that with both Rock and Amber? I'm Not Nice Naima now, I remind myself. I'm hard and cold. No more trying to understand anyone the state isn't paying me to help. No more overextending myself for people who don't appreciate or want me in their lives.

With those thoughts placed solidly in my mind, I get up from the table, kiss the baby in Aunt Mari's arms, then head off to my first day of work. Leaving Stone and the gorgeous ring I refuse to accept, much less wear, behind.

But even as I escape the ring gauntlet yet again, it feels like a temporary release. Like I'm the mouse who thinks she has a chance in hell. And Stone's the lion who's just biding his time.

CHAPTER NINE

"Thank you for your interest. After discussing our Facetime interview with my colleagues, we have decided that we would love to have you join our team. Here are the details...."

The message from the director of Organizacion Dominicana de Ciegos appears in my inbox right before my lunch break. And, oh my God, it's exactly the offer I've been waiting for!

The Dominican Republic doesn't have much in the way of government infrastructure, but after applying to several non-profits for the visually impaired, the ODC, a rehab center for the newly blind, had agreed to let me do a Facetime interview. The conversation had been scheduled for one of Stone's out-of-town days, thank goodness, and apparently, it had gone well. Not only were they offering me a job as a training course teacher for their youth program, but they were also willing to give me a whole month to get my affairs in order before I moved permanently to the Dominican Republic. It would be half the pay I'm getting now, but at a much lower cost of living than the States. And I'd be near my parents.

"Isn't that great?" I ask, when I call my mother and father during my lunch break.

However, my parents don't seem nearly as enthused about the prospect of me moving as I am. "Why do you want to come here, so far away from your boyfriend?" my mother asks, her Haitian Creole accent even thicker now that she's moved back to Hispaniola, even though the assisted living facility they currently reside in is on the Dominican Republic side.

"He's not my boyfriend."

"That's not what Mari said," my father replies, his Dominican accent just as thick as my mother's Haitian Creole one. "She said this Stone *tipo* asks to marry you every morning and is offering to raise that fatherless child of yours. I say you should take the deal."

Oh my God, Aunt Mari told them that? I should have known she wouldn't be able to resist spreading that piece of juicy gossip across international lines.

"Marriage is not a business transaction, papa." I rub the side of my head. This conversation isn't going nearly the way I thought it would when I decided to call with my good news. "And besides, I don't want to marry him. I want to move to the DR with Garnet and be closer to you."

"Why would you want to do that now?" my mother asks, like she's talking to a complete stranger, not the mother of her only grandchild. "Your boyfriend is rich and drives a

Cadillac. We're poor and you know, the facility banned papa from driving after that golf cart accident."

"Wait, what accident?" I demand, seriously alarmed, because my severely visually impaired father shouldn't be driving anything with four wheels.

"Oh, your faithless *père* is cheating on me again, you know. Another dumb slut nurse. She let him sweet talk her into allowing him to drive one of the golf carts but then did not properly supervise his foolishness."

"You cannot fault her, *mi amor*," my father chides. "It easy for women to become distracted when gazing upon my fine features. This is something you would know if you were not blind as the bat."

"Naima, say goodbye to your father now for the very last time. As soon as we end this call, I am going to replace his Viagra with cyanide."

"You are a selfish, selfish woman. You should learn to share instead of scaring all of my girlfriends away. If you were nicer, we could have a threesome. Or maybe even a fivesome!"

"Naima, please check for me if his will is in order. The judge will most likely pass everything to you after I am sent to jail for his murder. But I want to make sure you have something left over from his worthless life."

"Mama, you know he doesn't have a will..." I say, rolling my eyes at their antics. My blind mother has been accusing my blind father of cheating on her for as long as I can remember. As for my father, he's utterly devoted to the Haitian woman his family didn't initially approve of him marrying.

And, from what I can tell, has never cheated on her in his life. But for some reason he derives great joy from encouraging her delusions.

Normally I let them play out their little routine, but today I just don't have the patience. "Can we get back to the conversation about me moving to the DR?" I ask.

"*Ayayay*! This again?" my mother answers. "We have already told you to stay right where you are with the rich boyfriend who wants to marry you."

"And why would you even think about abandoning your Aunt Mari after moving her in with you?" my father asks, in the same tone prosecutors use to accuse defendants of heinous crimes.

"I didn't move her in with me," I point out. "And I'm sure she'll be just fine if I leave her here in North Carolina with her six children."

"Six children? Are you sure?" my father asks. "I thought she only had five."

"Yes, I'm really sure, papa," I answer, my tone dry. "I know because all six of them showed up to help her move in, and a few of the older grandkids, too."

"No, that can't be right. There's Jhonny, Heaven, Yara, Osner, Bessy...that's it, right?"

"You're forgetting Alaysha."

"No, that's her oldest gran, isn't it?"

"No, it's her youngest daughter," I answer, rubbing my forehead some more. I can't quite understand how we went off-topic so quickly again.

"Are you sure about that?" my mom asks, her voice totally skeptical. "You know, your *pére* and I were watching one of those telenovelas of his. Turns out the family's youngest daughter was really the daughter of the slutty *oldest* daughter. And you know me. I do not like to talk about anybody. It is not the Lord's way. But naming a daughter Heaven is just asking for the ungodly behavior, *non?*"

Before I can answer a voice appears in the background of the call, announcing the bus for Punta Cana will be leaving on the hour.

"Oh, *cheri*, it was so nice talking to you, but that is the announcement for our two-day Punta Cana excursion. We have to go now, or we won't be able to take seats together, and one of those slutty widows will try to put the moves on your *pére*."

"Love you, *mija*. And say hello to your rich *novio*," my father adds. "Tell him he has my blessing, just send over one of those Cadillacs!"

"Papa, Mama, wait—"

"What will you do with a Cadillac, you blind fool?" my mother demands, before I can finish.

Then they hang up without letting me get in another word.

I look at the phone for a long time after the call ends. I should be amused. I know I should. According to Amber, my mom and dad are cute and completely lovable.

And back when they lived in New York with me, I totally agreed. We felt like an inseparable unit, and I loved my parents. So much, it was easy to let my twenties slip away while I took care of them at night and my clients by the day.

But one day they decided out of the seeming blue to move back to the island. And now I'm a single mom in my late thirties over here, while they seem to be living it up with excursions to Punta Cana.

I should be happy that they're having so much fun in their sunset years. And I am. At least I'm trying to be. I just can't help but feel a little bit dejected that my parent's only response to my announcement was a bunch of jokes about my rich boyfriend and their usual banter.

Like Aunt Mari, they fail to see why Stone's presence in my and Garnet's life is hugely problematic. I can just hear my Aunt Mari complaining to them this morning about how I couldn't appreciate a good, rich, and *guapo* man. And how I was what was wrong with my entire generation of women these days.

She probably said the same thing to Stone after he presented me with that ring command.

Yeah, I need to get away from here, I decide as I return to my desk after making that disappointing phone call outside. For both my sake and Garnet's. Even if my parents were less than encouraging about me moving to Santo Domingo.

I type back an enthusiastic reply to the organization's director. Then I use the rest of my lunch hour to start making plans.

Thank goodness, Stone didn't get himself listed on Garnet's birth certificate. As soon as he leaves tomorrow, I'll buy tickets and order an expedited passport for the baby. Then a month from now when he's out of town, I'll fly out without a word to anyone. We'll finally be free.

The ding of my calendar brings me out of my planning reverie, and my spirit plummets as soon as I see the reminder.

Back to school meeting with Cami (update her on her sister's case if possible).

Crossing my fingers that I'll have something positive for her, I close the reminder and navigate through the system to find the case file on Talia Marino, Cami's little sister.

However, that hope dies as I go over the social worker's final conclusions. I read over passages like "pillar of the community", "reported his oldest daughter threatened to blackmail him if he didn't give her money", "believes she has undiagnosed mental problems", "youngest daughter did not corroborate story." It's a complete exoneration, followed up by a personal testimonial from the social worker herself, who happens to attend the same church as Cami's and Talia's father.

Oh, man. I was looking forward to helping Cami get whatever supplies she needed to begin her senior year at UNCC. Though Cami is a bright, young college student who's overcome sexual abuse and the foster care system to excel as a Computer Science major, the last time we spoke she seemed to barely be holding on due to this case. But now...

With a sigh, I close out the file, wondering how much farther she'll spiral when I tell her that there's nothing she can do to help her sister.

CHAPTER TEN

CAMI'S ONCE AGAIN PACING WHEN I ENTER THE conference room. It feels like a continuation from the conversation we had before I left on maternity leave.

A very sad and disappointing continuation. The box I'm carrying, filled with new school year supplies and a care kit I scored from Homeless Services, suddenly feels too heavy to carry.

I set it down on the conference table, and ask, "Hey, how are you doing, Cami?"

I keep my voice bright and cheery, but I can already see the answer to my question in her appearance. *Not well.*

Her skin is completely broken out, and she has dark circles under her eyes like she hasn't slept in days. She's wearing an oversized UNC Charlotte hoodie, but I can tell she's gotten even skinnier since we talked last. Her legs look like sticks, even though, according to her last check-in with the social worker who stood in for me over the summer, she'd found a part-time job at a local fast food chain.

"I'm dropping out," she announces, barely glancing at the box of supplies I brought in for her. "I saved every penny I could from my summer gig, but it just isn't enough. I've got to drop out and get a second job. That's the only way I'm going to be able to save up enough money to get an apartment for Talia and me."

My stomach sinks. "Cami, that's not a good idea."

"I knew you would say that!" Cami abruptly stops pacing and holds up her hands, as if trying to ward off my reasonable argument. "You think I should finish my degree. Just let my sister go into foster care. But you don't know how it feels."

She hugs herself, her shoulders hunching. "You don't know how it feels to have somebody do things to you like that. I can't let the system have her. I just can't!"

My heart clenches with sadness for both her and her sister. Cami obviously cares so much about her half-sister even though they've never met. And considering her homeless circumstances, her advocacy has been nothing short of heroic. I admire her so, so much. But...

"Talia isn't going into the system," I tell her, ripping the Band-Aid as fast as I can.

Cami drops her arms, her whole body sagging with shock. "What?"

"I'm sorry." I cross the room so that I can be within hugging distance as I tell her the heavily redacted version of the case worker's story. "The social worker interviewed both your father and Talia, but she didn't find any signs of abuse."

"That's because he coached her," Cami insists. "He

coached me the same way. Told me he'd kill my mom if I told anybody about our special time."

Cami's face contorts with pain and disgust. "That's what he called what he did to me. Our special time. And when I talked to Talia, she said that's what he called it too. I told her..." Cami shakes her head, her expression becoming mournful. "I told her she had to report him when the social worker came around, but I guess she was just too scared."

I hold up a hand, a sour taste suddenly springing to my mouth. "What do you mean you talked to Talia? I thought you two had never met."

"I mean, not before her mother died, but after that...yeah. I'm planning on raising her after they put our dad in jail. I didn't want to be a complete stranger." Cami folds her arms again. This time defensively. "Plus, her babysitter doesn't keep that close of an eye on her when she takes her to the playground after school."

"Oh, Cami..." I rub my forehead. "Please tell me none of these conversations took place after you asked me to have a social worker open a case file on Talia."

Cami folds her arms even tighter and looks at the ground. "I had to let her know she wasn't alone in this," she mumbles. "That's what I hated most when he would come over. The feeling that no one else cared about me. I mean, my mom was there, but she was always willing to look the other way if he gave her enough money for drugs."

She looks back up at me. "That's why I had to keep visiting her every day after school. Please believe me."

I study her sharply for a few moments, looking for any sign

of duplicity. But her logic makes sense from a victim's stand-point, if not from a social worker's. And though her father claims she's only in this for the money, here she is after having saved up an entire summer, threatening to drop out because it wasn't enough for a down payment on an apartment.

"I believe you," I conclude in the end. "And I'm sure you only had the best intentions when you talked to your sister. But no one else is going to see it like that. If you talked to her, coached her in any way to make these claims against your father..."

"*They're not claims.*" Cami's eyes beg me to believe her. "He's hurting her. I know he is. Not during the investigation probably. But definitely before and for sure now that they've cleared him."

She unfolds her arms and points an accusing finger at me. "When did that happen, by the way? Where were you even?"

No, I'm not Too Nice Naima anymore. But it's easy not to take offense at her accusing tone when I can see the kind of raw pain she's in. "Out on maternity leave," I answer gently. "But the case worker only informed him this morning of her findings, according to the notes."

"This is bullshit. This is such bullshit. I have to go over there."

Cami tries to push past me to the door, but I grab onto her arm. "Talking to your sister at the park is one thing. If you go over to her house, you're going to give your father grounds to file a restraining order against you."

"I don't care!" Cami answers, trying to tug her thin arm out of my grip. "I can't just leave her with him when I know what he's going to do to her."

"Okay, maybe you don't care, but your next employer most definitely will if you have to explain why there's an arrest on your record when they do a background check," I answer, holding on to her arm as tight as I can. "You've worked so hard, Cami. You've withstood your own mother dying and given up all comforts to get this degree. But all your hard work and sacrifice won't mean anything if you can't get a job. And if you're in jail, how are you going to support your little sister?"

Cami kicks at a chair and yanks her arm away. But I stay calm, setting the temperature, as I wait for my words to sink in through all that helpless rage.

I can tell I've reached her when her expression crumples from angry to despondent. "What can I do?" she asks me. "I've got to do something."

I let out a sad breath and tell her the truth. "Unfortunately, there's not much you can do now. Tomorrow morning, I'll go to the head of the agency, and request for the case to be reopened, this time with another social worker assigned to it. I can cite a conflict of interest. Since the social worker who was put on the case attends the same church as your father. I might be able to argue bias."

This is more than I should be telling any client about a case file totally outside of my department. But I'm rewarded for my lack of discretion, when Cami quickly nods. "Okay, okay. That sounds like a plan. He'll leave her alone if he knows somebody is watching."

"Great. So we've got a plan, but Cami..." I tilt my head to look her in the eye. "You can't go anywhere near your sister. The best thing you can do is return to UNCC next month, keep getting good grades and set yourself up to land a full-time job that will provide you with enough money to take care of you and your sister after you graduate."

I spend an hour going over the new plan with Cami and receive her promise that she'll stay away from her sister this time. We even discuss putting in an Amazon order for her books after she applies for her second to last semester of classes.

But I'm conflicted as I walk her out to the car with the box of supplies. I've given her enough hope to return to school for her senior year, but the chances of my request for a second inquiry being granted is slim at best.

Even if my boss, who was so concerned about Carlos Marino's reputation that he assigned a sympathetic church friend to Talia's case, does grant my request for a review... it's not like I'll be here to see it through. By this time a month from now I'll be in the Dominican Republic. And I'll just have to hope that whoever I'm replaced with takes Cami's case as seriously as I do.

I know I'm totally right to get myself and my baby out of this situation with Stone, but as Cami drives away in her nineties' era Acura, I can't shake the feeling that I'm doing her a huge disservice. Not to mention Talia.

I've finally figured out a way to get out from under Stone's thumb, but I couldn't feel worse.

Which is why I answer my phone, that night when Cami calls, even though I've just gotten Garnet down to bed.

"Hello?" I say. "Are you alright?"

"No, I'm not alright. I'm not alright at all!" Cami's voice comes back watery and broken, like she's stopped sobbing just to answer my question. "I did something. Something so, so bad."

Alarm bells don't just go off—they blare inside my mind. But I force myself to stay on my Calm Social Worker setting as I ask, "Cami, are you safe? Are you in need of medical attention?"

"No, but...but..." she starts sobbing so hard I can barely understand the words coming out of her mouth. Something about her father...and Talia...and seeing something he was about to do on her computer.

CHAPTER ELEVEN

Twenty minutes after rushing out the front door, with an order to Aunt Mari not to take her nightly Lunesta pill yet, I'm standing in the front entrance of a mansion in Myers Park.

Trying not to vomit, as I look down at the completely naked man laid out in front of me.

"Is he dead? I think he's dead," Cami says beside me.

I respectfully have to disagree. Unlike Cami, I don't think her father's dead, I know he is.

There's a kitchen knife with a worn wooden handle lodged where his heart would be. Perfect strike. And exactly zero signs of life. He lies completely still, and his skin has taken on a blue corpse pallor. There's no doubt in my mind that his living spirit has left the building, even before I bend down to take his pulse.

And yep, he's dead all right. Dead as a completely naked doornail.

"Please, tell me he's not dead," Cami pleads above me.

I gather my composure. Both of us completely losing it will only make the situation that much worse. "What happened?" I ask Cami, standing back up.

Her face crumples and her lips tremble. "I wasn't trying to kill him. I just wanted him to stop him from hurting her."

"But why were you even here?" I ask, cupping her shoulder. "After we agreed you'd stay clear?"

Cami looks away, lets out a huff of air.

"Cami, what aren't you telling me?" I ask, alarm bells going off inside my head.

"I hacked his computer, okay?" she answers defiantly. "I've been watching him that way all summer. And he wasn't doing anything suspicious. But when I went to check his feed after I got off my shift, I saw he'd accessed this forum on the dark web. He'd basically spent the whole day watching all these gross videos of father's taking baths with their daughters, and I knew what he had planned, because that's what he used to do to me. Bring me presents and show me videos of stuff he wanted to do during our *special time.*"

She lets out a shuddering breath. "I know I was supposed to wait, but I had such a bad feeling. So I came over here, used the key he keeps underneath the plant to let myself in and I went upstairs to hide in one of the guest rooms. I was just planning to...I don't know, watch the hallway from, like, a crack in the door. But after hiding, I heard the sound of running water, and then he came out of the upstairs bathroom, dressed in nothing but a towel. I watched him...I watched him start walking toward Talia's door. He had, like, this gross hard on because he was so excited."

Cami visibly swallows and more tears pool in her eyes as she tells me, "He used to do that to me, too. Come visit me, when I was too sleepy to fight him off. So I pulled the knife and chased him down the stairs and cornered him at the door. I told him I was going to call the police. And you know what he said?"

Cami shakes her head, more tears streaming. "'Go right ahead. Nobody's going to believe you. My social worker friend gave me the all clear, so everybody knows you're a liar.' That's what he said. But I'm not a liar. I'm not, and I couldn't let him hurt Talia again—oh my God, is he dead? Like, really dead?"

Yes, he's dead. So, so dead. I should tell Cami that, then call the police to take a report. I know all the exact protocols to follow in this situation. But...I can't bring myself to reach for my work phone.

God, I believe her. But her father was right. There's no way the police will. And unfortunately, the fact that she hacked into his computer makes it even worse. I don't have a law degree, but I can easily put together an argument that Cami, the computer science major, planted whatever the police found on his laptop.

I think of the sister who told the social worker that her father had never touched her inappropriately. "Is there any way your sister will corroborate the sexual abuse?"

Cami shakes her head. "I don't know. It took me years to get up the courage to say anything. Even after he stopped messing with me."

Ayayay...my mind works for something, anything that could solve this s-wordy situation. Maybe Talia would support her sister's story. But it wasn't guaranteed. She might even feel like everything that happened was her own fault.

And even if she did testify on her sister's behalf, there was still no telling if a court would believe a homeless black girl over the man, the other social worker had called an "upstanding pillar of the community" in her report. Especially after he went on record, claiming that Cami had a history of mental problems and had attempted to blackmail him for money. Both claims were unsubstantiated, but I could easily see a jury deciding that Cami was the villain in this story.

No...the best-case scenario for this situation was Cami spending months to maybe the rest of her life in jail instead of completing her senior year at UNCC, while her traumatized sister got cycled through the foster system.

I look at the body. Look at Camille...then call my Aunt Mari.

"*Mija*, where you at? I'm not going to be able to take care of the baby tomorrow if I don't get a full night of beauty sleep."

"Do you have Stone's number? I need it."

"Why don't you have Stone's number?" Aunt Mari asks. "He's your boyfriend!"

"He's not—" I start to argue, but then I stop myself and say, "I just don't, *Tia*. Could you please give it to me? It's an emergency."

"What kind of emergency—oh wait, here he is. Just came in

the door. Stone, *mijo*, Naima's trying to get ahold of you. Says it's some kind of emergency."

A voice rumbles in the call's background. Then Stone's on the other end of the line, demanding, "Where are you? Tell me right fucking now."

His imperious demand would have annoyed me just a few minutes ago. But now my heart floods with relief, hearing his voice. "I need your help," I tell him. And I give the address without any argument.

It takes him even less time to get here than it did me.

I open the door and stand back with one arm wrapped around Cami's shoulders. I expect him to come in hot like I did, throwing panicked questions before they all die in his throat.

But Stone's eyes barely flicker when he steps inside the front entrance and sees the dead body lying on the floor.

He simply looks at it, looks at me, then asks, "You okay?"

"We're fine," I say, squeezing Cami's shoulders. "But he isn't."

"Yeah, I can see that. Looks like a story."

"Yes, it's a story for real," I answer, before giving him the short version of what happened.

His eyes light on Cami when I'm done. "So you decided to just go ahead and knife your old man?"

"Stone, don't..." I plead. Cami is no kind of emotional state to handle him right now.

"I didn't mean to," Cami whispers, her voice broken and sad. "I just wanted to stop him from hurting my sister."

"Nah, you need to own that shit," Stone answers coldly. "He came after your little sis, and you did what needed doing. Respect."

Both Cami and I blink at him, probably both shocked that he not only believed her story without any follow up questions, but also gave her kudos for killing a man.

"Um, Cami, maybe you should go upstairs and check on Talia," I say. "Stone and I need to talk about how best to handle this."

"No, don't go back upstairs. This scene's already a DNA nightmare." He points to the grand staircase, leading to the second level of the house. "Sit right there. And don't touch any fucking thing else while the grown-ups figure this shit out."

Cami doesn't have to be told twice. She retreats exactly as instructed, taking a seat on the bottom stair, with her hands carefully placed on her knees.

As soon as she's safely out of earshot, I lower my voice to say, "Thank you for coming. I didn't know what else to do."

"Yeah, if you call the police with that thin story, Lil Miss UNCC is looking at ten-to life, no parole, for being a crazy brat. Even if she had her reasons."

I would have put it, like, any other way. But I have to admit that Stone's assessment of the situation is chillingly spot on.

"Is there anything you can do to help her?"

"I can do more than help her," Stone assures me. "I know

guys that can have all this cleaned up before midnight. As long as Cami doesn't rat anybody out, she can be back in How to Be Too Edumucated 101 tomorrow, like none of this shit ever happened."

"Oh thank God," I say, laying a hand over my still rapidly beating heart. "But how about Talia?"

Stone shrugs. "We'll have to leave her alone overnight. But I'll send in a couple of guys to watch the house."

"Wait, *guys*?" I ask. "You have guys down here? Like other criminals?"

Stone continues on like he didn't hear any of my questions. "As long as you're there when Talia gets put into the system because her dad's nowhere to be found, we're golden."

I nod, his plan crystalizing in my head. "Yes, that could definitely work. I just have to figure out a foster situation. Talia's and Cami's grandparents are dead, and both their parents were only children. There's no one else to take care of them. But I can figure something out."

Stone tilts his head down. "Cami killed for her little sister, you don't think she'd be willing to raise her?"

"On the contrary, I know she wants to do just that," I answer. "And she's old enough, but she's currently living out of her car, which means she wouldn't be eligible as far as the state's concerned."

Stone gives this last obstacle a few seconds of thought, before saying, "I got a place she can stay."

My eyes widen, my whole heart going soft with gratitude. And I find myself smiling up at him as I say, "Oh, Stone..."

"What?" he asks, as if my smile irritates his skin way worse than my usual resentful glare.

"I'm just not used to so much save the day from you," I answer. "I wouldn't have thought you had it in you to be Cami's superhero."

"That's cuz I don't have it in me," he answers bluntly. "I'm no hero, and I don't fuck with capes. My help comes at a cost. Would've thought you'd assume that."

All those warm feelings fade right out of my heart. *Of course, it came at a price.*

"How much?" I ask as bitter disappointment settles in my chest.

"More like *who* much," he answers.

A warning zaps through me and I swallow my instinctive cry of alarm. "What do you mean," I ask softly, my heart beating too hard and too fast.

Those cold, unemotional eyes skip over my face and lingers. But he does not speak. Instead, he pulls out the velvet ring box I left on the table this morning.

CHAPTER TWELVE

"Naima, will you have this man to be your husband? Will you love him, comfort him, honor and keep him, in sickness and in health for as long as you both shall live?" the judge asks me.

I fret my hands in front of me, wishing I'd taken Aunt Mari's suggestion to carry a bridal bouquet. Flowers were totally unnecessary, as was her impulse decision to invite every Almonte within state lines to this sham of a wedding ceremony. But I've got to admit, I could really use something to hold onto as I brace myself to tell the biggest lie of my life.

Stone has already answered his version of the judge's question with a quick "Yeah, sure."

I should do that, too. Just get it over with. But I look around. I have no idea why. Maybe I'm hoping for some kind of lifeline to drop down from the sky and save me.

But no lifelines here in the courthouse chapel.

Only people. There's Aunt Mari, standing behind me. She's wearing a lacy below-the-knee bridesmaid dress, even though I told her she didn't need to put on anything fancy for a simple courthouse wedding. A ridiculously handsome guy named Keane stands directly across from her behind Stone. Apparently, he also didn't get the difference between a witness and an official best man memo. Like Stone, he's wearing an expensive-looking tailored suit.

I hadn't bothered with hair or makeup beyond foundation and mascara this morning. I'd just put on my St. Scünchi headband, then went through my closet and picked the lightest colored thing that fit on my post-pregnancy body. I'd figured the green jersey fit and flare dress would allow me easy access when it came time to feed Garnet after the ceremony was done, but now I'm wishing I'd put a little more thought into my wedding ensemble.

So here I am, the most underdressed member of my own party, squirming in the expectant silence of all the relatives sitting behind the courthouse chapel's wooden rail.

Quite a few of my older female relatives are crying like this five-minute ceremony is just as beautiful as anything they'd seen in a Roman Catholic church. Or maybe they're just relieved that someone agreed to marry their darkest family member. Who knows?

I find Cami in the front row of teary *tias*. Garnet's sleeping peacefully in her arms, and her little sister, Talia is tucked into her side. It's only been a few days since her father "disappeared," but Cami already looks ten times better than she did on that horrible night.

Better and happier. Not just because I'm getting married to

the man she considers her hero, but also because the social worker assigned to her case agreed to let Cami pick her sister up from school yesterday and bring her back to the apartment Stone had arranged for them.

My old apartment, actually. I hadn't known how to feel about that when I stopped by to drop off a move-in basket last night. On one hand, Stone had found an interesting way not to break the lease on the rental I was no longer using. On the other hand, I felt more trapped than ever as I made my way up the stairs to the two-bedroom that used to be mine.

However, my irritation had evaporated when Cami introduced the little white girl clinging to her side to me.

"This is Naima," she'd said, pushing her half-sister forward. "Don't worry. She's nice. She's the one who helped arrange for you to live with me instead of Dad."

I'd expected a conflicted response from the girl. Maybe even some questions about the father who had mysteriously disappeared.

But instead, she raised her brown eyes to mine and whispered, "Thank you."

That was when I knew for sure, what I had only believed in my gut before. Cami hadn't been lying. Everything she'd accused her father of was true.

And now, the sight of Cami sitting with her sister in my wedding audience makes my indecision disappear. Yes, I swore not to be Too Nice Naima anymore. And yes, I know I let myself get too close to a case, just like I swore I wouldn't do again after Amber. But something inside me won't let Too Nice Naima die. Or abandon Cami when I know my agreement to this marriage is the only thing standing between her and a jail sentence.

Believe me, I thought about it when Stone pulled out that ultimatum disguised as a wedding ring. But only for a second. As hard as I'm trying to be these days, the truth is there's no version of me that would have been able to live with herself if I let Cami go to jail for the crime of protecting her sister.

So instead of grabbing my baby and running straight to the nearest passport office, I turn back to the judge, and spit out the word, "Yes," as quick as I can.

Then I concentrate on trying not to faint over the fact that I've just agreed to marry a man I first met over a gun at my kitchen table. A ruthless enforcer, who despite having no real feelings or emotions other than general disdain toward me that I can see, was willing to do anything to force me into this marriage of inconvenience—up to and including blackmailing me over a dead body.

The rest of the civil ceremony happens pretty fast after that. There's a blur of repeated words, then the gorgeous wedding ring I refused on Monday morning gets shoved onto my left ring finger on Saturday afternoon. Then Stone hands me an ultra-modern signet platinum wedding band to push over the thick knuckle of his ring finger.

"Should we just hug or something," I ask quietly when the judge announces that Stone may kiss his bride.

"Don't be stupid," he answers, his eyes flashing.

Then he gathers me up in his arms and hits me with one whammy of a kiss.

You'd think I'd feel nothing after being blackmailed into this moment, but oh my God, it's the graveyard all over again. Stone's lips zap me with the same electric current of instant lust, completely erasing my memory of everything that came before it. And my previously mournful thoughts are soon replaced with an aching desire for this kiss to go on forever and ever. Amen.

But Stone abruptly pulls away with a smirk, then turns to everyone who came to the wedding to say, "Well, that's in the bag."

My family jumps to their feet and claps for us, calling out all sorts of congratulations and good wishes. But I'm left feeling stupid—stupid and so, so messed up. Just like I did outside that graveyard.

Stone might have kissed me, and for a few mind-melting moments I might have liked it. But nothing whatsoever has changed between us, even with this marriage.

Two signatures and a checkmark next to the Married box on one thin form.

That's all we are.

All we'll ever be.

I know that in my sensible mind. So why can't I stop the sudden wish that things were different between us? Why can't I keep myself from imagining what it would be like if Stone wanted me, even just a little bit?

But that's not how the real world works. At least not for me.

"You coming?" he asks me.

Another rhetorical question. He takes me by the elbow and leads me into the fray of my huge Dominican family.

As I'm enveloped in a sea of hugs and kisses, I peep over at Stone whose accepting all the warm congratulations with stoic handshakes.

He seems so aloof and untouchable, even after that kiss. And his expression is as unreadable as his soul.

Plans, you ask? I don't have any. I have no idea whatsoever how I'm going to extricate myself from this marriage mess. Or what this decision means for me and Garnet going forward. What will it be like married to a man like Stone? *Ayayay*.

This is supposed to be the happiest day of my life. But my stomach knots with dread, wondering what comes next.

CHAPTER THIRTEEN

Two hours later, I'm hiding in the walk-in pantry, still in shock and dumbly staring down at my ring.

"There you are. I've been looking all over for you."

A voice with a heavy Boston accent interrupts my "I can't believe I'm now married to Stone Frickin' Ferraro" trance.

I look up to see the guy who greeted Stone with a "Hey, bro, you really doing this? I thought maybe it was a joke when I got your text." That was before he turned to me and introduced himself as "Keane, just Keane."

He's standing in the pantry's open door with a tumbler in his hand. "Guallando" by Fulanito spills in behind him, letting me know that the "itty bitty reception" Aunt Mari insisted on throwing at the house has become a party in full tilt.

"How did you know I was in here?" I ask Keane.

"Oh, I wasn't talking to you, I was talking to Jack." He grabs a bottle of Jack Daniels from a nearby shelf. "There's only so much rum us Boston guys can drink. And Stone's fucked off somewhere, so I had to go whiskey questing by myself. Though I wouldn't have pegged him as a Jack guy."

"I'm sorry he abandoned you," I say quietly, trying not to ogle the man, who used to be a former hockey player, according to one of my male cousins. He's so handsome and clean-cut but talks like a movie about Boston mafia gangs.

My curiosity nudges at me to ask him how he knows Stone exactly, to try to gain insights on the impenetrable man I married.

Don't case file him! Not Nice Naima cuts those thoughts off before they can begin.

"That Jack belongs to my aunt Mari," I say instead. "Stone keeps his stuff on the higher shelf."

Keane looks up and a grin spreads across his handsome face. "Midleton, Score!"

He puts the Jack Daniel's back and brings down a bottle with an old-fashioned label on it. "You want some? I can get another glass."

"No, I'm alright," I answer, pasting on a smile.

It must not have been too convincing. Keane closes the pantry door behind him and asks, "You sure about that? I've become more—I guess you'd call it *perceptive* over the years since marrying a therapist. Plus, hiding in a closet during your own wedding reception ain't exactly screaming all right."

I shake my head. Not sure how to answer that. No, I'm not alright. I just signed up for marriage with a guy who by his own admission doesn't give a single s-word about my feelings or even understand what his brother ever saw in me. I'm definitely not alright.

But it's not like talking about any of this with Stone's best man will help.

As if sensing my dilemma Keane asks, "Stone mentioned you moved down here from New York. You got anybody you can talk to in North Carolina?"

"My family, I guess."

He raises an eyebrow. "You guess or you know?"

I sigh. Real talk, Stone's rich, commanding, and looks like the lead in a Martin Scorsese film, so I'm pretty sure my family likes him way more than their half-Haitian black sheep. I suddenly find myself missing the best friend I left behind with a deep, hollow ache.

When I don't answer his question, Keane comes closer and leans one shoulder against the shelf with the industrial-sized cans of diced tomatoes. "Stone mentioned he invited me down here to be his best man instead of his cousin Luca because for some reason you want to keep this marriage a secret."

"He told you that?" Telling the guy who came all the way down from Boston that he was second on the list to be your best man seems beyond rude, even for Stone.

Keane wags his hand back and forth. "Kinda, I had to do a lot of reading between the lines. You know Stone."

"No, I don't know Stone. That's the problem." The next words escape from my mouth before I can stop them. "I barely know anything about him. He's just this big, mostly silent wall. He hates me. I know he does. But for reasons I still don't fully get, he's hell bent on ruining both of our lives with this marriage."

I clamp my lips, before I can say anything else. I'm not sure why I said that much, and to his best man of all people?

But Keane just opens the bottle of whiskey, pours the tumbler halfway full and offers it to me.

"No, thank you," I say, my voice much more subdued now.

"I insist. It's fucking good whiskey and you need it more than I do."

Giving in, I take the tumbler and tip the golden liquid into my mouth. Keane's right. It is good whiskey. A warm, soothing burn down my throat.

I take one more sip, then hand it back to Keane. "Thank you. Thank you for being nice to me."

"Yeah, I'm good at being nice these days," Keane answers with a wink and a grin. "But you know, it's not something that comes natural. My wife had to teach me, and by teach me, I mean she had to give me an ultimatum before I started acting right."

He crooks his head in the general vicinity of the door. "Stone's probably got it in him to be nice, too."

I snort. "Stone?"

Keane tries to keep a straight face but breaks off with a snicker. "Okay, yeah, that's a long shot. You got me there. You know, I don't think I've ever heard that guy say 'thank you' without it being totally sarcastic?"

"Now *that* I believe," I answer.

We share a chuckle, but then Keane sobers to say, "Let me point out though that my bro, Stone is pulling one hell of a commute to do this co-habitation thing with you. Also, he's crazy loyal to his family, but you told him you didn't want them to know about your wedding, and boom, they're off the guest list. And sorry, but that big-ass ring don't exactly shout, 'my husband fucking hates me.' Know what I mean?"

"Okay, maybe he doesn't full on hate me..." My stupid heart doesn't just skip a beat, it throbs painfully as I look at my perfect, over-the-top, dream ring in a new light. However, then I remind myself and Keane, "But he definitely doesn't like me. I don't think he's even capable of liking anyone like that."

"Not thinking isn't knowing for sure," Keane points out, taking a big sip of whiskey. "All I'm saying is keep your mind open when it comes to Stone. He just might surprise you."

CHAPTER FOURTEEN

"*POR DIOS!* DON'T BE CRUEL. I DON'T HAVE ANY grandchildren yet. I miss the babies so much. I should be allowed to cuddle this little one as long as I wish."

About an hour after my pantry talk with Keane, I find myself in a tug of war over Garnet with one of my middle-age cousins.

"It's time for her to go to bed," I answer as gently as possible...while wrestling my baby away.

"You come to my Stephanie's *quinceañera* next month!" she calls after me when I finally manage to pry Garnet from her.

I make a non-committal sound as I back away. The last thing I need is to get in another one-sided complaint session with one of my relatives about how I never come to any of the family events that seem to take place every single weekend. Aunt Mari's already been fussing at me all day about how I need to do better, since everyone came out to my

STONE: HER RUTHLESS ENFORCER   95

wedding. Even though it wasn't my idea to invite them in the first place.

I rush up the stairs with my drowsy baby before anyone else can invite me to another family event that I won't be attending.

However, I stop cold in the door of my bedroom when I find a pair of polished wingtips where Garnet's crib used to be.

And Stone, lounging on a settee that wasn't there this morning...flipping through a car magazine.

"If you're looking for a place to put her, kid's been relocated next door," he says without looking up from his literally racy reading material.

A place to put her, I grumble to myself. Like she's some object to be stored.

But I take her next door anyway, preferring anywhere that's not in the same vicinity as my now...ugh...husband.

But I suppose this is as good a time as any to switch Garnet to a proper crib, I decide after I lay her down in the yellow-walled room Stone designated as the nursery. She's been sleeping through the night for a couple of weeks now, and it feels like a natural transition.

Garnet falls asleep disturbingly fast. Her little baby snores fill the air before I can even begin to parse through all the understandable dislike and completely baffling lust stirring around my nether regions.

I return to the room just as confused as I left it. What does Stone moving in mean? More playacting like we're a real couple? Or maybe he wants something else. Maybe he wants me, despite what he said at the graveyard.

Dread and Curiosity tug-of-war inside my chest as I open the door to the master suite.

Stone's still on the settee when I enter, showing more interest in his car magazine than he's ever shown in me. And he doesn't look up when I come in.

I decide to use his silence as an opportunity to slip a checkered sleep shirt out of what's now one of two dresser drawers. Matching dresser drawers.

Ayayay...why do I get the eerie feeling that he had all this new furniture bought and put in storage behind my back? All those "no way"s I'd given him, they didn't matter. He'd simply been biding his time during my entire three months of recovery.

With that creepy thought lodged in my head, I take my time in the shower, delaying the inevitable...what? I have no idea. My past discussions with Stone weren't exactly conversations. More like a high-stakes game of chess, disguised as talking. A high-stake game I'd definitely lost.

He's texting on the phone when I come out of the bathroom. But he looks up to eye my flannel sleepshirt with a cold smile. "Nice outfit. Real bride like."

I ignore his sarcastic comment and ask, "Who are you texting?"

"Not Luca, if that's what you're worried about. I told you I wouldn't tell him."

"I wasn't worried," I answer. Stone's callous. And maybe a sociopath. But for whatever reason, it never occurred to me for even a moment that he wouldn't keep his promise. *I trust him,* I realize with a surprised inner jolt.

Pushing that thought aside, I tell him, "I was just wondering who you were texting this late."

"It's not late where he is."

I wait, but when Stone doesn't continue, I'm forced to ask, "Where does he live? And why couldn't he make the wedding?"

A smidge of sympathy tugs at my chest, thinking about how Stone had only one guest compared to every Almonte living in North Carolina.

"Hawaii," Stone answers. He goes back to his texting. "And I didn't expect him to come. He lost his wife and kid in a real fucked up accident a couple of years ago. Hasn't answered a call or text since."

"But you keep on texting anyway..." My heart jerks, not knowing how to reconcile the dead-eye killer I married to the man reaching out to his friend again and again, despite getting no response. "How do you know him? Is he... in your line of work."

"Nah, he's an old college buddy. Same guy who introduced me to Keane." Stone answers.

"You went to college?" I have to ask, because no offense, I never would have guessed. It's even more surprising than the revelation that Stone apparently has a whole two friends outside his New York crime family.

"Yeah, for a couple of years," he answers. "Luca's dad, tried to make us all go when he was the head of the Ferraro family. But I hated that shit. And Rock partied out. So when the dean at Manhattan U. told him he didn't have the grades to come back, I ditched college, too."

"Oh wow, I didn't know that."

Of course, I'd known about Rock failing out of Manhattan University. It was one of his biggest regrets. And he'd been making plans to go back to school when we were together. But he never mentioned that Stone had gone, too.

"You and Rock really used to do everything together," I realize out loud. "I can't imagine how much you miss him."

My sympathetic words hang in the air, Rock's memory hanging over us like a ghost. And Stone's gaze drops to the floor, like he's overcome.

No, he's not nice, I realize in that moment. But he is human. A twin who lost his brother less than a year ago. Today was hard on me. But it was hard on him, too.

Without warning, Too Nice Naima takes over my mouth. "Stone, I'm sorry. I'm so sorry that..."

"So, you want me to eat you out or what?"

I nearly choke on my own spit at the unexpected question. "Um, what?"

"I can't fuck you, but if you want me to get you off, I'm down for that."

More spit choking, as my brain scrambles to come up with a response. I mean, Stone's a Ferraro. I've watched enough mafia movies to know...

"You can't..." I swallow. "You can't have sex with me?"

"Yeah, my penis ain't up for that, but if you want to come, I got you."

I blink several times, my mind trying and failing to fully process all of his words. "But why?" I end up asking him. "Why would you want to ah...service me without getting anything in return?"

Stone shrugs. "Husbandly duties and all that. You were there for the vows, too."

"Yes, but that still doesn't explain why you wouldn't want me to keep up my side of the bargain." *Am I really that repulsive to you?*

I don't get any reassurances from Stone about my unspoken fear. He just shrugs again. "You squeezed out a kid already. Give it a couple of years or three and we'll talk about a little brother."

I widen my eyes. "Wait, you want another kid?"

"Yeah, at least two more. Wasn't planning on any before, but you're a good mom, so why not go to one of them docs that shake our shit up in a petri dish and plug the baby right into ya?"

"That's not how it works. Plus, I'm getting awfully close to forty to be making any big family plans. And did you just say I'm a good mom?" I ask, not sure I really heard that compliment in his confusing plans for our future.

"What? You don't' think you're a good mom?"

"That's not the point," I say.

"Then what is the point?" he asks, unbuttoning his shirt, to reveal an old-fashioned wife beater underneath. "I got an early flight tomorrow and all this conversation feels unnecessary. Do you want me to eat you out or what? Just answer the question already."

"Okay..." I say, raising a hand. I vowed not to case file this guy like I did Rock, but I have to ask, "Should I be worried about your mental health?"

Stone snorts and snatches the wife beater off over his head. "You just like to make shit complicated and I don't."

I thrust my chin defensively. "Stone, look, I'm just trying to understand why you're willing to service me, apparently grow a family with me, but don't want to have penetrative sex with me."

"Yeah well..."

Stone rises to his feet and one step consumes the distance between us. He leans down to speak directly in my ear. "I don't do that poetry and flowers shit, but my tongue is a motherfucker. I can make you feel good if you want. Real good. Or..."

He takes a deliberate step back. "We can turn off the lights, and I'll get up for my flight, first thing tomorrow. Either way, I'm done with questions. So what are we doing here?"

What are we doing here...

I stare up at him, and he stares back down at me at a total conversational impasse.

Until I find myself confessing, "I don't...I don't want a

sexless marriage. But I'm not sure how I should feel about a man who apparently has no desire for me."

It's not a question. But I look to Stone for an answer.

He rolls his neck, that irritated look, flashing across his face, like it's the only other expression in his entire toolbox. Then he growls, "Lay back. Spread your legs. Let me eat you out. If you don't like it, you can tell me to fuck off."

Let me...

Why do I have the feeling that this was as close to a please or even a simple request as I was ever going to get from Stone?

I should pick option number two. Tell him to turn off the light and let him catch his flight. Good temporary riddance.

But I don't.

He looks, so much like Rock, but somehow not the same at all. After three chaste months in separate rooms, I hadn't expected this relationship to involve sex. Even after we said I do.

But now he's doing *all* the offering and giving me another ultimatum. One I find myself powerless to resist. Am I curious or sex-starved. I have no idea.

Either way I take a hold of the hem of my flannel nightshirt with my heart, beating in my throat. I squeeze my fingers around it a couple of times, then pull it off in a quick rush before pushing down my panties in the same manner.

Then...oh God...My heart thunders in my chest as I carefully, lay myself across the bed.

Like a platter offering itself up.

CHAPTER FIFTEEN

I LIE THERE, WAITING. WAITING TO GET SERVICED BY the man, now standing above the bed. The one who told me just a few months ago that he didn't give an s-word about what I want.

Maybe he still doesn't.

His expression doesn't change, but his eyes scan my body as he climbs onto bed. One knee, two, and then his arms.

He's so hulky up top. He installed a workout room in the basement, and I have to wonder just how much time he spends in there. Surely, it's even more than the hour he does right after dinner. Everything on his bare upper body bulges as he crawls over to what I guess is now my side of the bed and places himself between my spread legs.

My thighs tremble when he touches them, even though he hasn't really done anything yet.

"You afraid?" he asks. There's a gleam in his eyes. But I

don't know how to describe it—wicked, sinister, amused. All three words apply.

"It's been...awhile," I answer.

And by awhile, I mean never. No one's ever gone down on me. Not the boys I sort of fumbled around with in college while feeling vaguely guilty about the two blind parents I'd left behind at home. Not Rock...no one has ever kissed me down there.

"You're already wet," Stone observes, his voice flat as a scientist.

"My body's response to knowing something sexual is about to happen," I answer, trying to keep my voice just as clinical and unquavering as his. "It doesn't mean anything, purely biological."

That's true, I know, yet it's also not true. Yes, getting wet when you know sex is coming is a biological response, without any proven link to increased desire. But this feels like more than that. My entire body is pulsing. Dying to find out what will happen next.

He dips his head down between my legs.

He has a large tattoo on his back, I notice. Dark angel wings.

Devils also have wings, I'm suddenly reminded. Right before his tongue enters me with a single plunge.

I gasp out in surprise, a very, very nice surprise. His tongue is warm and sure, working inside of me with more confidence than any dick ever has.

"Stone..." I breathe out, his name little more than a moan as he efficiently stokes the long dormant embers inside of me, licking up and down my slit, before adding two fingers.

Oh wow... oh *wow*. My hips squirm beneath his mouth and on instinct I reach down to cup the sides of his head. He must shave every morning, his skin is bristled with new growth, and the five o'clock shadow on his head scratches beneath my palms as his tongue and fingers work between my legs.

It usually takes so long for me to come with someone else. First I have to calm down and convince myself not to be self-conscious. Assure myself that I don't have to look like Amber or a supermodel to have a guy be into sex with me.

Stone doesn't want to have sex with me. He's made that plain and clear. But for some reason, despite his disdain, and his general zero f-words attitude, I find myself rising embarrassingly fast.

My core greedily clenches, and my hips lift to receive more of his mouth and fingers as my hands tug, trying to bury his tongue even deeper inside of me. I know it's wrong. I know it's dirty. But, I can't help myself. Just a few minutes of Stone, and I've lost all control.

"Oh God... Oh God...Stone." His name comes out a broken plea, right before I crest. Screaming mutely into the fully lit room, as I cream all over his face.

Stars bursts in front of my eyes, as a universe takes over my vision and an ocean fills my ears. Pleasure, unlike anything I've ever known from a toy, my hand, or a real life dick, washes over me. The heat of it completely suffuses my body as I squirm, both enjoying the orgasm and trying to get away from it, because it is just so, very intense.

Somewhere during that, Stone rises up on both knees. Then, with the same cold, almost bored expression, he observes how my body trembles and shakes, long after he's done.

It's so embarrassing. I wait for the orgasm to let go and hate him at the same time. For inserting himself into my life, for blackmailing me into marriage, for eating me out just as good—no, girl, if we're talking for real—even better than he promised.

At least I want to hate him.

But as I come down from my almost painful first oral orgasm, I find myself more curious than annoyed.

I think there's something honestly wrong with you. Something I'm not seeing. What are you hiding from me?

Despite my many promises to myself, I start to open a mental case file on him...

But then, as if shoving me back toward my vow not to case work him, Stone asks, "You good? I want to brush my teeth."

I sit up on bent arms, feeling the opposite of desired. "Yes, of course. Go brush your teeth. And, um, thank you, I guess."

Stone just shrugs as if of all the no big deals in his life, making me come like a frickin' tornado is the least big deal of them all. Then he disappears into the bathroom.

What...the...*heck?*

Do not case file him....do not case file him... I practically chant to myself as I put back on my sleep shirt, then hop under the covers, before he comes back out in a pair of boxer shorts and nothing else.

No awkward post-coital small talk for my husband. Stone deposits his watch and a couple of rings onto a little jewelry tray on top of his dresser. Only their clinks break up the total silence, before he crawls into bed.

Man, he moves quietly for such a big guy. I can only imagine how lethal he must be when he's working.

His work as the Ferraro family's most ruthless enforcer... that's what I should concentrate on instead of going all Nancy Drew on his mental state.

As the orgasm fades away, I try to remember him at my kitchen table, threatening me with his gun. Treating me like a speck of dust he'd gladly wipe out.

I think about that.

Then I reach across the bed and squeeze his junk.

He catches my hand almost immediately and pushes it away. But not so fast that I can't feel he's totally soft.

"Is it me or is it ED?" I ask in the dark.

No answer.

"I'm talking about erectile dysfunction," I say just in case he doesn't understand.

More silence. Not even an irritated grunt of acknowledgement.

"Because if it's ED, there are things we can try."

I keep my tone light and helpful, judgement free. But still no answer.

"If it's me..." I start to say.

"Let me know the next time you need wifeing. Until then, shut up." Stone's voice slices through the dark. Slices through me.

Then he turns over and gives me his back. Leaving me and my mind spinning.

Well, Keane was right about one thing. Stone definitely surprised me tonight.

CHAPTER SIXTEEN

LET ME KNOW THE NEXT TIME YOU NEED WIFEING.

Like his offer to collect my things from the hospital, this, too, turns out to be a rhetorical invitation.

I never ask, but Stone wifes me several more times over the next few months. Pretty much every night he's in Charlotte instead of New York. He seems to have added eating me out to his evening routine. You know, after his expensive whiskey nightcap and right before he brushes his teeth and washes his face.

I wish I could say I hated it as much as I hate him. But I can't.

I still don't like Stone. Like, at all. But I really, really like his mouth. To the point that instead of feeling relieved when he leaves town, I miss him—I mean his mouth. I miss his mouth. Yep, just his mouth.

"Hello...hello...Naima...you there?"

I snap out of my daze to find Shirley, one of my co-workers

at my cubicle entrance. She's an old-timer, close to retirement, and hanging on by a thread if her jowly semi-permanent scowl is any indication. "There's somebody here to see you. A man interested in fostering an older kid."

"All my kids are over 18," I remind her.

Shirley sucks her teeth. "Well, he's asking for you specifically."

"Really me? But none of my kids are eligible for adoption."

"You can tell him that just as easy as me. He's waiting in the conference room."

Shirley doesn't give me a chance to answer before walking away.

Did I say everyone in North Carolina was so nice earlier? Okay, edit that. But luckily my skin is a lot thicker than it used to be, thanks to Stone. Before he invaded my life, I used to take Shirley's snappish tone personally.

Now, her bad attitude seems understated in comparison to my husband. It still sends a shiver down my back to think of him with that term attached...down my back and up another place.

God, what is wrong with me? I wonder as I enter the conference room to direct the potential foster father to another social worker.

However, I slow when I see the man waiting for me.

He stands up when I enter, but that's the only polite thing about him.

Men who walk into our agency wanting to foster usually

hail from the khaki and button up crowd. But this potential father is wearing jeans, paired with a leather jacket, and he's got a military crew cut with a hole in the middle.

I try not to judge on sight alone, but this guy does not in any way look like a man, hoping to enrich his life by fostering a child.

"Hello, Mr..."

"Lunetti," he answers. "And your Nayma, right?"

He doesn't give me a chance to answer. "Before you pull out all the brochures and what not, I should tell you, I'm not looking to adopt just any orphan. There's a specific one. Talia Marino. Her father was a dear friend, and I hear you're the social worker on her case."

I crook my head, alarm bells going off. While I advised and helped smooth over many of the technical details for the main social worker in charge of overseeing Talia's transfer of custody to Cami, my name isn't listed anywhere on the little girl's case file.

"Where did you hear that?" I ask him, keeping my voice neutral.

Mr. Lunetti considers me for a hard second, before answering, "Around."

I love these small towns. Everybody's so easy to pay off.

I slice my eyes toward the agency beyond the room's still open door, wondering which of the workers this guy had gotten to, to know the specifics of Talia's case—my boss? The social worker attached to Talia's file? Really it could be anybody since we all have access to the case system.

"Are you related?" I ask, trying to act like this is business as usual.

"No, but I got a nice farmhouse outside of Durham. A couple of acres. Plus, two boys and a wife who's dying to spoil a little girl. Better than that apartment they're living in anyway."

The alarm bells aren't just ringing now. They're blaring loud as fire trucks inside my head, because this guy knows where Cami and Talia live? "Forgive me, Mr. Lunetti, but I'm fairly sure Talia has already been claimed by a living relative."

"Living..." He leans forwards, his expression avid. "So you're thinking Talia's father ain't living no more? Maybe he more than just disappeared?"

"I'm not here to make any hypotheticals. I'm just telling you that Talia has been taken in by a relative and therefore is not available to adopt...or foster."

Silence greets my announcement, tense and creepy.

Then Lunetti says, "Congrats on your marriage. Tell your husband he needs to pay me a visit."

My skin prickles. Is that a threat? Secret code for something? My brain buffers, trying to figure out how to respond.

I don't have to say anything though. With that weird invitation, Lunetti gets up and walks out of the room. Without so much as a word of goodbye.

I go to the conference room entrance and watch him leave. Staying right where I'm at until he's all the way out the agency door.

Then I burst into action, rushing to my desk and grabbing my purse.

"Need Stone's number!" I text Aunt Mari as I fly out the agency's door, mumbling excuses about not feeling well and cutting out early.

Aunt Mari doesn't answer, even when I call. But I know she has a bad habit of putting her phone on silent, when she's teaching Garnet Spanish (aka watching telenovelas with her baby niece in her lap).

Why oh why was I too stubborn to just ask for Stone's digits after the last time I really needed to get in contact with him? Cursing myself, I jump in my car and head straight to my old apartment.

Cami opens the door on the first knock and her face lights up when she sees me. "Oh, good, you're here, too."

"Too?" I ask.

She opens the door wider and I'm once again greeted with the sight of Stone in my kitchen. But this time instead of sitting at the table, he's at the kitchen counter with Talia putting together an El Paso taco kit.

What the heck?

I stare at Stone and he stares right back at me, like I'm the thing that doesn't belong in this homey scene. Not him.

"Yay! You came for Taco Tuesday!" Talia cheers beside him.

So many questions. But remembering why I came, instead of asking Stone why he's here making tacos, with one of my old aprons covering his grey suit, I say, "Talia, can you go play in your room for a little bit? The adults need to talk."

"Is everything alright?" Talia asks, her eyes becoming worried.

She directs her question not at me or Cami, but at Stone.

"If it ain't, it's gonna be," he answers, voice grim, as he shifts his gaze from their tacos to me. "Now go give those dollies of yours some attention while the grown-ups talk."

"What's wrong?" Cami asks, as soon as her sister is out of earshot. She looks even better than she did at our wedding. There are no more dark circles under her eyes, and her hair lies in two neat French braids. She's gained some much-needed weight, and her skin has cleared up after several months of steady access to hot water.

I hate that I'm about to pop the happy, comfortable bubble she's managed to make here with her sister...and ah, apparently Stone, too. At least on Taco Tuesdays.

"Somebody came by the agency to see me. He said he was interested in foster-to-adopting Talia. But the thing is, he already knew everything about her, including where she lived."

"What? How?" Cami asks, her eyes going wide at my news.

"I'm not sure," I answer her. Then I turn to Stone to tell him, "He congratulated me on our wedding and said you should pay him a visit."

Stone's lips thin. "Did you get a last name? Where he lives?" Stone demands, before I can answer her.

"Um...Lunetti. And he said something about having a farm in Durham."

"Shit. That's the Lunetti Crime Family." He frowns at Cami. "Looks like your father was accounting for some off-paper clients, too. Should've known he didn't get that mansion, pushing tax cuts like H&R Block."

"Are you saying, you think he... worked for the mob?" Cami asks Stone, her voice dropping to a whisper.

"There's a Lunetti asking a bunch of questions about his disappearance, so I ain't just thinking it," Stone answers. He yanks off his apron. "Alright, it's a wrap on Taco Tuesday. Tell your sister to pack her shit up. You're moving in with us."

Then either not aware, or just not caring about Cami's completely devastated look, he says to me, "Get them home. I'll take care of this."

"But how?"

Stone doesn't answer. Just pushes pasts me and leaves out the door, without a word of goodbye.

Exactly like Lunetti.

CHAPTER SEVENTEEN

I TRUST STONE TO KEEP US SAFE. MAYBE I SHOULDN'T but I do. Probably because Stone is the guy Luca, the head of the Ferraro crime family, calls when he needed something protected...or killed.

In any case, it doesn't feel like a lie when I tell Cami and Talia not to worry as I tuck them into the second downstairs bedroom that night. "Everything will be all right. No one's going to hurt you."

"I didn't know Dad was a criminal." Cami tells me when I pull up the covers on her side of the bed. "If I had known..."

That sentence trails off, and I sense, she doesn't know how it should end.

"I'm glad you didn't know," I tell her. "I'm glad Stone is here to help. Please don't worry, everything's going to be alright."

I think they believe me, but I can hear the sisters whispering worriedly as I leave their room.

God, It's so unfair. I wish there was some magic wand I

could wave over this whole messed up situation. One that would not only undo everything that's happened to them, but also ward off any further dangers.

But life isn't fair, and I don't have that kind of wand, I remind myself, as I go next door to check on my widowed aunt. The excitement of moving in and cooking for two new people is no match for her Lunesta. She's already asleep and snoring delicately, just like Garnet, who I find still fast asleep upstairs.

Everyone's accounted for...except for the one man who's the walking definition of taking care of himself. Which is why I shouldn't worry about him. Or over analyze what happened when I went to tell Cami about the man who's stopped by the agency.

It's just, how did Stone go from Taco Tuesday to Liam Neeson a la *Taken* at the drop of a dime?

Because he's the mob version of Liam Neeson, that's how, Not Nice Naima reminds me sternly. *And he does not need your help.*

No, obviously he doesn't. In fact, I have a whole case load folder at work, filled with clients like Cami who truly do need my help. But...

As soon as I walk into the master suite, my eyes fall on Stone's overnight bag.

The overnight bag sitting unzipped on the kind of suitcase stand I only thought they had in hotels before Stone moved in. The wide-open overnight bag I've never been alone with before when Stone is in town. The wide-open overnight bag I might never have another chance to investigate...

To snoop, Not Nice Naima reminds me. *You're not trying to investigate; you're planning to snoop. Through a possible sociopath's things.*

Okay, Not Nice Naima has a point. He didn't even cry at his twin brother's funeral.

No tears, but tacos, that's a different story. I remember how normal he looked in the kitchen of my old apartment. Like a father. A real father, making something easy with his girls. And then there was the way Talia had looked to him when she got scared. Like she trusted him completely.

I think there's something honestly wrong with you. Something I'm not seeing. What are you hiding from me?

*Don't...*Not Nice Naima warns me. *Don't case file him.*

Her warning makes me recall the argument I had with Amber when she thought things were moving too fast between me and Rock.

"You're turning him into a case file. Getting all caught up in his sad backstory. Throwing yourself body and soul into making sure he's rehabilitated, just like you did with me."

I'd been so offended, but she'd been one-hundred percent right. I should have listened to her. Then and now...

Do not case file him. Do not case file him, both Amber and Not Nice Naima warn inside my head, as I force myself to turn my back on Stone's bag and head toward the bathroom to begin my nightly routine.

Thatta girl, they congratulate me—

Right before I break and make a beeline to the overnight bag.

With a wildly beating heart and the voices in my head screaming at me about what an idiot I am for case filing a frickin' enforcer, I unzip it...and take a peek.

"Holy macaroni!" I whisper.

The voices and everything else in the world go quiet when I see what's inside his bag.

CHAPTER EIGHTEEN

STONE COMES IN MUCH LATER THAT NIGHT. QUIETLY.

Not because he doesn't want to wake me. I'm pretty sure that's just his natural setting. Lethal—it's the only way he knows how to move.

He pauses in the doorway when he sees me, though. Probably because I'm sitting on his settee...with his overnight bag in my lap.

If I was hoping to see him actually looked surprised for once, I'm disappointed. His face stays completely expressionless, like always. But at least now I know why.

His emotionless eyes flicker down to the bag. Back up to me. Then he says, "Hey, Naima."

"Hey," I answer.

Casual, like he didn't just come back from probably killing somebody, and I'm not sitting here with his secret in my lap.

Tension pounds thick as a rap bassline between us.

So much silence passes. Suddenly, I miss Queens. Miss the city and all its noise.

"How did things go with Lunetti?" I ask.

"A little more difficult than expected. But I'm taking care of it."

"By taking care of it, you mean what exactly?"

"All a sudden after months and months you want to hear about my day-to-day?"

No, I didn't. The few stories Rock had told me often left me with a sick feeling in my stomach. But for Talia's and Cami's sake I have to ask, "Are the girls in danger?"

"Not on my watch. I let the Lunetti family know they were under my protection."

"And they just accepted that?"

Stone rolls his neck to one side, then the other. Like this scene is giving him a crimp in his neck. "You need wifeing?" he asks.

"No," I answer quietly. Meaning it. I have never been less turned on in my life.

"Alright. Well, then, I'm hittin' the shower—"

He stops talking when I take the bag and turn it over, sending all the pill bottles inside of it spilling out.

"I'm okay with you being, like, the worst communicator in the history of the entire world," I tell him. "But I'm not okay with this."

He stares at me for a hard, lethal second. "You shouldn't be going through my things."

"And you shouldn't be taking meds that weren't prescribed to you. I mean, there's like six different kinds of anti-depressants in here." I pick up one with a dark blue label. "And I'm pretty sure this one is an anti-psychotic..."

He yanks the bag and the pill bottle out of my hands. "You shouldn't be looking through my stuff."

"I should have guessed," I say as I watch him pick up the bottles and start throwing them back into the leather bag. "Not crying at your brother's funeral. The way your frustration tolerance dips at night. That cold fog that surrounds you like a wall. All the pieces are falling into place."

"Not another fucking word, Naima," he growls, snatching up the last three bottles in one beefy hand.

"Of course you don't want me to say anything else. The meds that were totally not prescribed to you are wearing off. If I keep on talking, something dangerous might happen. Like you starting to actually feel something."

His face hardens, and his whole body goes stiff, as if he's trying to hold himself back from doing just that. *"You shouldn't be looking through my shit."*

"And *you* shouldn't be taking unprescribed anti-depressants. I mean, have you ever actually seen a therapist? Even once in your entire life?"

"I don't need to," he answers. "These pills are enough to keep me right."

"Right? That's what you call how you act?" I shoot back, jumping to my feet. "As my North Carolina co-workers would say, 'You is a lie.' How you act, how you treat people. It isn't right. It isn't normal. I mean you refuse to communicate with me. You're totally shut down."

"You know what, I'm tired from spending all night solving *your* fucking problems. I'm done with this conversation."

"Do you think I wouldn't like to be done with this conversation, too? Be done with you? The answer to both those questions is yes! But I can't be done with you, because as it turns out, you're on something—like, a whole lot of somethings—that makes you think it's okay to barge into my life and completely take it over."

"*Our* life," he growls. "The moment you got pregnant with my brother's baby it became our life."

"No, no it didn't," I yell right back. "And if you weren't on a boat load of drugs, you'd see that. You say you're doing this for Rock, but you've never even bothered to touch the daughter you claim to want to adopt so badly. I mean, what would he say if he knew you were doing all these drugs?"

"Who do you think gave them to me!" Stone suddenly roars. "He was the fucking nerd. Who do you think doctored all those prescriptions for me when we were in junior high? Because I couldn't control my temper and nearly killed a kid after he fouled me in a game of basketball? My fucking brother. That was his way of trying to make me halfway normal."

I gasp, covering my hand with my mouth.

I never would have guessed, but when I think about it, I can't say I'm surprised. Rock valued normal. I remember how he assured me I ticked all his boxes. Not because I was funny or cute, but because I was a normal person with a normal job. And wasn't that why he dumped me? Because I couldn't just be perfectly standard, without a shade of gray?

"I'm..." I clamp my lips, then let them go to say, "I'm sorry, Stone. Rock shouldn't have done that. Maybe he was trying to help, but self-diagnosis is dangerous. If you really think you need something to help you handle your emotions, you should see a psychiatrist for an appropriate prescription and seek out therapy. There are several people who take adult clients at the place we're sending Talia. Maybe they could help you, too..."

I break off when Stone angrily zips up his bag. "I'll sleep in the empty bedroom. Don't ever go through my shit again."

He raises a finger, puts it right in my face.

Old Naima would've back down. Would've cowered.

But new Naima stands her ground. Holds the monster's gaze and asks, "Do you need husbanding? Would you like me to suck your dick?"

He doesn't answer. And did I complain about him being an emotionless cypher before? My bad, he's vibrating with rage now. I can practically feel it rolling off of him in waves.

But that still doesn't stop me from pointing out, "You think these drugs are keeping you stable, but they're ruining your life. You're overdosing. That's most likely why you can't get it up. Can't hold normal conversations. You need to see a real doctor before you kill yourself. Before Garnet loses both of her dads. And deny it all you want, but you and I both know she deserves so much better than that."

He lowers his finger from my face. Balls his hand into a fist...then turns and leaves.

Slamming the door so hard behind him, I wonder if they heard it downstairs.

CHAPTER NINETEEN

I WAKE UP THE NEXT MORNING FEELING HUNGOVER, even though I haven't had a thing to drink. Oh my God, is this what a real domestic argument feels like? Thank God, my parents only had completely ridiculous, totally unnecessary ones. I can't imagine growing up like that.

The reason for my yelling hangover comes back loud and clear. Stone, the pills, the overnight bag he took to bed last night instead of me.

God, what a mess...

It's a workday but all I want to do is pull the covers back over my head and pretend that real life doesn't exist for a little while longer.

But then Garnet's voice suddenly crackles from the baby monitor I keep beside my bed. Not exactly a cry, but something else. More like a noise of surprise.

I sit up to look at the video feed on one elbow, just in time to see a figure entering her room. It's Stone, and Stone has a bottle fisted in one of his meaty hands. Motherly instinct wars with confused curiosity as I watch him go over to the crib.

"Hey, Garnet...I'm uh...Stone. Pop, I guess. Whatever you want to call me. I got a bottle. You want it or you only about the tit in the morning?"

He waits, as if he's expecting her to answer. Then when she doesn't, he tries to hand it to her. "Here, take it. I brought it for you."

Okay, wow, mercy replaces curiosity, as I climb out of bed to save both the baby and Stone.

By the time I make it into her room, she's crying, because she can't figure out how to pick up the bottle of breastmilk by herself and Stone's resorted to bribing her. "What do you want? Apple juice? Candy?" He pulls out his billfold. "I got money. How much you want to stop crying?"

Apparently, Garnet isn't nearly as easy to bribe as someone working for the state. She cries even harder when Stone waves a Franklin in her face.

"Thank fuck you're here," Stone says when he sees me in the doorway.

Ayayay, language. But I'm laughing too hard to chastise him as I pick up poor Garnet.

"Yeah, you need to give her a tit," he tells me. "I was trying to feed her. But it went sideways real quick. Now she's mad."

"She's not mad, she's just hungry," I tell him.

But instead of latching her on, like I usually do in the mornings, I make a sudden decision. "Here, hold out your arms."

"Like this?"

Stone holds his arms straight out in front of him. Like he's at a blood draw.

"More like this..." I correct. Settling Garnet on one hip, I crook one his arms, and then the other. Like he's a Ken doll. You know, that one bald Ken doll, who's capable of killing a man twelve different ways, but doesn't know how to hold a baby.

"I don't think this is such a good idea," Stone says as I settle Garnet into his arms.

"No, it's a *great* idea," I answer.

Panic flashes across Stone's face, when Garnet starts to bawl, like I've handed her off to a bear. "Look she's already crying. She wants you."

"She wants her bottle," I correct, fishing it out of the crib.

As if trying to prove my point for me, Garnet calms down as soon as I plug the bottle into her mouth. And, she continues to suckle even after I replace my hand with Stone's.

"See?" I tell him after a few moments of peaceful milk guzzling. "Babies are easy. They just want to be held and fed."

Stone nods. "Yeah, this ain't so hard," he admits. "No wonder Luca doesn't mind doing this shit."

I wince. "We're going to have to have a conversation about the insane amount of language you use around children.

Especially now that Talia's here. But yeah, you've got it. Congratulations."

A few beats, as if he's trying to figure out what a real human should say, then he answers, "Yeah, thanks for showing me."

We both watch Garnet suckle the bottle for a few more moments, then he adds, "And...uh...sorry about last night."

He's not looking at me, but I'm full on staring at him. With my mouth wide open. Did the word "sorry" really just come out of Stone Ferraro's mouth?

Should I say it's alright, so that maybe he'll develop a positive association with saying that word in the future? Or use this unexpected apology as a natural segue into a gentler conversation about his prescription drug abuse? Which is still a huge problem, no matter how many cute babies suckling bottles you insert into it.

"You don't have to worry about those drugs anymore," he tells me, as if reading my mind. "I flushed all of them down the toilet this morning. You were right."

"All of them?" I ask, shaking my head, mind fully blown by the "you were right" cherry on top of the unexpected "sorry" sundae he served up this morning.

But unfortunately, I have to point out. "That might not necessarily be a good thing. If you've been taking them since your teens, it's probably better to see somebody. A psychiatrist, like I said last night."

He goes quiet again. So quiet that for minutes on end, there's no sound in the room, except the sound of Garnet cooing around her bottle.

Which means she's done. I should take it from her, but I remain frozen in front of Stone as I wait for his answer.

"Okay," he says, his voice gruff, but lacking its usual menace. "If that's what you think it takes for me to be a good father, tell me where to go to get my head shrinked. For Garnet. For Rock."

Okay, well, I wouldn't have put it like that. But Stone putting it like anything, quite frankly feels like a win, a huge one.

"I'm just worried is all," he says. "I've done things. Easily. If I'm some kind of monster on the drugs. How will I be off of them? I mean, I've been popping pills ever since I was twelve."

"I don't know how you'll be," I admit. But then I think of what Keane said a few months ago. "Maybe you'll surprise yourself."

Just like he's surprised me. For the first time since I met him at my kitchen table, I reach out to touch Stone on purpose, tentatively laying a hand on his arm.

He tenses. But doesn't push me away. And, it feels....

Wow, I can't believe I'm thinking this. Especially after the way we met, the way we got married, and the way we ugly fought last night.

But this morning....

This morning feels like a fresh start.

CHAPTER TWENTY

"It's not a matter of if I'll get hit by a car, but when."

One of my visually impaired clients told me that back in New York, grumbling about the rise in popularity of hybrid and electric cars.

The morning that began with what has now become Stone's new routine of feeding Garnet her morning bottle was definitely a fresh start. But waiting to see how he responds to coming off his unprescribed pill habit feels like waiting for a car to strike.

I brace for impact, expecting his new drug-free status to disrupt our relationship in some meaningful way.

Maybe he'll wake up next to me one morning and say, "Wait, this is stupid. I don't even like you. Why the hell did I insist we get married? Thank God, I'm off those drugs."

Or maybe he'll turn to me one morning, and decide to touch me for real, to cover me with his body and...

I always cut myself off right there. It's a fresh start for Stone, but not for us. And if Rock and Amber taught me anything, it's that hoping for any kind of happily ever after is a fool's game. At least for me.

But the truth is, not much changes in the weeks following his pill flush.

He's still Stone. He still doesn't talk much. Still looks irritated when I ask him too many questions. Still...ahem... wifes me on the regular, without asking for anything in return.

If Stone has resumed having sexual needs, he either truly doesn't want me that way, or is getting them met from someone else during the four days he's in New York.

I try not to indulge myself in the ego-crushing game of "which of these options would hurt you the worst?"

Instead I track Stone's encouraging progress in other areas.

For instance, he's become a smidge more tactful. "I think you and your sis should stay on with us," he told Cami a few days after he flushed the pills. "This is a better neighborhood. Gated. Plus, you'd be saving me some dough on rent."

I'd been pleasantly surprised when Stone had actually pitched this solution over the dinner table as opposed to commanding Cami and her sister to stay put, like he did with me.

Cami pushed one of her now properly moisturized curls behind her ear, before answering. "I don't know, we've already put you guys out so much. I mean, *Tia* Mari's been having to cook extra for us. And Talia can't walk home from school if we're living here." She finished her counter argument with an apologetic look directed toward Stone. "I'll figure out how to pay you back for rent, I promise."

"Or you can transfer the kid here," Stone answered. "This neighborhood's got great schools."

"But—" Cami started to protest.

"And cooking for six is easy for me," Aunt Mari interrupted with a *pfft* and a wave of her perfectly manicured hand. "At least the two of you have manners. Those boys of mine used to attack my *sancocho* like wolves, without a thank you or a please."

"Yeah, I want to go to school here. Please, Cami," Talia pleads. "I want to stay here, with Tia Mari and all this good food. And I like learning Spanish with her by TV."

With that testimonial, she held her empty bowl and says, "*Por favor*, Tia. Can I have so more."

"You see, she said *por favor!*" Aunt Mari declared, picking up a ladle and waving it in the little girl's direction, as if that one phrase of Spanish was a perfect illustration of her dubious teaching methods.

"You've got to stay here," Aunt Mari insisted, scooping two more spoonfuls of the tasty beef *sancocho* stew she'd made for dinner into Talia's already empty bowl. "At least until we see what will happen when Alejandro discovers the woman he married is actually his fiancée's evil twin sister."

"He's going to be so mad!" Talia exclaimed, practically begging her sister to let them stay with her eyes.

"I don't know," Cami said, still looking unsure.

As silly as I found Aunt Mari and Talia, I also jumped on

their reassurance bandwagon. "Cami, please say yes. It would give me so much more peace of mind to have you stay here."

"And there's always free babysitting, if you're looking to make yourself useful," Stone added, around a jaw full of beef.

I could tell our arguments were getting through her pride wall when Cami nodded and said, "Yes, I want to make myself useful. I want to pay the both of you back for everything you've done."

"Well, free babysitting and not worrying Naima to death is good start," Stone answered. "So you staying or what?"

Obviously Cami agreed after we all ganged up on her. Stone has a somewhat familiar, but technically new way of continuing to get what he wants. Even if he no longer issues blunt commands or shoved women in the back of cars to get them to comply.

Same old Stone. Just a tad, tad bit nicer.

He's also become slightly more expressive since ditching the pills. He smiled when Talia brought home a first trimester report card full of As and Bs. "Better than I ever did," he told her, grabbing a magnet to stick the report up on the fridge.

And he even laughed once when Garnet fell on her butt during an ill-fated attempt to stand on her own.

But other than a super occasional smile and a new routine of feeding Garnet her morning bottle whenever he was in town, not much changed.

I wouldn't say I was surprised. I wasn't expecting miracles, especially since he was still in the process of finding a good therapist with availability when he was in town.

But a slight disappointment begins to set in as the weeks click by and nothing changes for good or for bad. Halloween passes, then Thanksgiving, and then suddenly it's December.

And I have to consider weird questions, like, should I get the husband who will probably be dumping me as soon as he finds a good therapist and comes to his senses a gift?

I discover that Stone has my digits when my phone lights up with a New Jersey number in mid-December, while I'm wrapping donation presents for our agency's annual holiday drive.

"I'm at a toy store. What do you think the kid wants for Christmas?" he asks in answer to my tentative "Hello?"

"Garnet?" I ask, scrambling to catch up.

"Yeah, Garnet. I already got Talia a BB gun."

"Okay, we'll talk about that," I answer. "But I'm assuming since Garnet's not old enough to really know that it's Christmas yet, she'll want whatever age appropriate gift you find in the *toy* aisle. Maybe ask an associate to make sure it's age appropriate. You know, like not a BB gun."

He chuffs. "I like how you always say 'we'll talk about it' when you really mean hell no."

He's being sarcastic, I know. But a weird part of me wants to ask, *"Do you really like it? Like me? Even a little bit?"*

Instead I clear my throat and ask, "So are you coming down

for Christmas? I wasn't sure, since you spent Thanksgiving in New York."

"Yeah, Luca's flying the whole family out to the Tourmaline in Mexico, and I'm not about that resort shit, so I'll stay down there with you."

I can't tell if he's disappointed or resigned to having to pass the holidays with us.

"I'm sorry you won't be able to spend Christmas with your family."

"Don't be stupid," Stone answers. "You're my family. I would've been down there for Thanksgiving, too, if you wasn't insisting on keeping all of this secret."

God, the hope...it's like a stalker, always lurking around the shadows of my heart. Waiting to pounce on any positive thing Stones says. Yes, our marriage is mostly pretend, but I like the idea of Stone wanting to be here with us more than he wants to be with his huge Italian family in New York.

At least he does for now.

I swallow, unable to say, "*Sure let's shout from the New York rooftops that we're married, right before you decide to dump me.*"

So instead I decide to let him know, "Next Christmas I'll probably need to take Garnet to Santo Domingo. Let her meet her grandparents."

"Okay," he says after a long beat of silence.

I wait for him to say something else about me not wanting his family to know. Maybe bring up his mom, Peg, who I'm fairly sure still doesn't know Garnet exists.

Only to be surprised when he says, "I found a head shrink. But she can only meet on Wednesdays. So starting in January, I'll be down there four days instead of three."

My brow lifts with surprise at his announcement. "All to meet with a therapist?"

"Nah, I got business, too. Few things I'm starting up on behalf of the Ferraros. And like I said before, all of you. I like you guys. Like what we have."

His voice sounds softer than usual. Sincere as opposed to its baseline of sarcastic.

And, I know how this will all end, I do. But my stupid heart...it warms at his words, and the thought of him not just deciding to stay on an extra day in North Carolina, but also wanting to stay. Because of us.

"See you in a few days," he says when I find myself too caught up in my battling emotions to answer.

Then, in still typical Stone fashion, he doesn't wait for me to answer before hanging up.

CHAPTER TWENTY-ONE

I wake on Christmas morning in Stone's arms.

I must have rolled sometime in the night. Our bodies now lie so near to each other's, we're sharing the same pillow, and our lips are almost close enough to touch.

Stone's dark eyes are already open, and staring back at me.

"You alright?" I ask him, worried for no reason I can explain.

"I'm fine," he answers. "Trying to decide how a normal person would react to you rolling over on to my side of the bed."

I should be offended. He's acting like I purposefully chose to invade his space while I was sleeping. But before I can stop her, Too Nice Naima wonders out loud, "Is that something you struggle with? Figuring out ways to respond to situations in a way that quote-unquote normal people would?"

He raises his eyebrows. "Well, right now I'm trying to figure out how a normal person would answer that question, so I guess so."

My lips quirk, fighting to contain a smile, as I say, "Sorry for rolling over here in the middle of the night. My body sometimes has trouble making the switch between when you're here and when you're gone."

"Oh. Okay."

We trail off into silence. Then he says, "Got something for you."

He turns and pulls a small package wrapped in gold foil out of his nightstand drawer. "If you don't like it, just let me know what kind of jewelry you prefer, and I'll do better next time."

The same doubts and reservations swirl around my head at his "next time." But they all cut off when I open the box and find the latest Fitbit Smartwatch.

I happily gasp. "This is exactly what I wanted!" My first generation Alta stopped working a few weeks ago. But how did he know...

"Yeah, I was hoping Aunt Mari had at least this one right," he says with a wry half-smile. "She also suggested a gift certificate for a year's worth of blowouts and a diamond tennis bracelet. But neither of those sounded like you."

"No, blowouts and tennis bracelets aren't me at all," I agree, my heart fluttering. "I can't believe you talked to Aunt Mari."

He shakes his head at me. "Why can't you believe that. You're my wife."

I look back at him helplessly. An unspoken "for now" ringing in my head.

"Um, I also got you a gift. Just a small one." I tell him, changing the subject. "But it's downstairs."

He doesn't answer. His eyes just bore into me, like he's trying to read my soul.

No problem whatsoever with sustained eye contact, I note in the case file I'm still trying not to build on him. But I can't tell if it's due to his long conditioned aggression or his even longer conditioned disassociation.

Either way, it feels intimate. No matter the cause, in this moment with his eyes gazing into mine, it feels like something more.

We haven't kissed. Not once since right after the judge, whose name I can no longer remember declared us husband and wife. But right now a kiss, feels like the natural conclusion—the only conclusion—to this Christmas morning conversation.

"Merry Christmas, Stone," I whisper, leaning forward just a couple of more inches on the pillow.

Like a lot of women who grew up way too Catholic, I don't have a lot of experience in bed. But man, am I good at making out.

"You're a helluva kisser," Rock told me after our third date.

As I press into Stone's lips, a small, silly hope that he'll also like the way I kiss unfurls inside of me. I cup my hand around his bristled head, moving my mouth over his as I push in my tongue.

He lets me, opens his mouth slightly, but other than that, nothing. I realize after a few seconds of one-sided kissing. Nothing at all. Except for a slight shift of his body as he moves everything below his neck away from me.

*Wow...*I break off the kiss, cheeks hot with the hit to my pride. I'd obviously read more into his response than there actually was.

"You need wifeing?" he asks when I pull back.

"No," I answer quickly, trying to mask how stupid I feel right now.

This marriage is only about Stone's notion of personal duty, I remind myself. Passion and affection definitely not included. Just like the batteries in the light-up cube I bought for Garnet.

Speaking of which...

"I should get up. It's Christmas morning, and I want to be there when Talia and Cami open their gifts."

Stone doesn't answer, and I take that as my cue to awkwardly roll back to my side of the bed and climb out.

I can feel his dark eyes on my back as I escape to the bathroom. But this time I don't case file. This time I don't misinterpret. Just turn the shower knob on a colder setting and remind my overheated body how he hasn't shown even an ounce of desire for me. Like, ever.

CHAPTER TWENTY-TWO

LUCKILY, HE'S NOT THERE WHEN I COME OUT OF THE shower. He probably decided to get in a gym session before breakfast. He does that sometimes. Not just sometimes, usually, I note. He's usually long gone by the time I wake up. Today was a fluke.

Stop hoping, Almonte, I chide myself. The pills change nothing. It will always, always be the same.

He eventually appears about an hour later, just as I'm feeding Garnet mashed plantains in her high chair and explaining to Cami and Talia that some of the many more presents that appeared under the Christmas tree after they went to bed last night are actually from Santa. Ho, ho, ho!

"I don't believe in Santa. He doesn't really make sense," Talia tells me, eight going on eighty.

At the same time Cami asks, "Why would you do that? You shouldn't have gotten us gifts."

"Cami," I answer, laughing. "Seriously, it's no big deal."

"Yes, it is a big deal," Cami says her eyes flaring with conflicted pride. "You've already done too much for us. And there's no way for us to ever pay you back."

"Well, she likes doing too much for you, me and everybody else," a voice says before I can respond. Stone enters the kitchen, dressed in the New York Knicks Christmas sweater, I put under the tree for him.

"You might as well get to opening all her gifts." He drops two rectangular packages I didn't wrap on the table in front of them, "Mine, too."

The presents are beautifully wrapped in the kind of heavy gold paper, I only ever see in department stores and in the suggestion column on Etsy.

But Talia suspiciously eyes the gift, as if Stone's set a radioactive bomb in front of her. "What do I have to do to open this?" she asks.

Dead silence.

And Aunt Mari shakes her head confused. "What do you mean what do you have to do, *mija*?" she asks her partner in watching telenovela crimes. "It's a present. Haven't you ever gotten a present before?"

Yes, she had. That was the problem. I curse myself in that moment for not anticipating this.

Presents must have been part of Talia's grooming. A transactional exchange designed to get the little girl to do things she didn't want to with her father.

Disgust fills my stomach as I realize how she must be interpreting Stone's gift. One day I might feel some regret for helping Cami cover up that creep's death after she killed him, but it isn't today.

"Talia..." I start to say.

But Stone rolls right on over my carefully crafted response to tell her, "If you like it, say thank you. But other than that, you don't owe me shit."

I cringe at his still way-too-foul for children language.

But Talia begins to tentatively open the present, like she doesn't quite believe Stone's words. And her expression doesn't change much when she sees the top-of-the-line tablet inside.

"I don't want it," she says, shoving it away.

"Talia!" Aunt Mari gasp. Then she lets loose with a stream of Spanish about ungrateful children.

"*Titi*, don't," I say, standing up.

But Garnet, whose been going through a clingy stage, begins to cry.

"It's okay," Cami switches from prideful to desperate to please as she picks up her own gift. "Thank you, Stone! I appreciate it. We both do!"

Cami tears open her own package to reveal another tablet inside. "See Tally, we match! I can use this for school, and you can, too. Stone was only trying to be nice."

Talia doesn't answer. And her face has gone bright red, like she's trying not to explode. Or cry like Garnet.

"If you don't want it, I can give it to any of my grandkids,"

STONE: HER RUTHLESS ENFORCER   145

Aunt Mari offers, glaring at the little girl. "They love i-Anything, and they know how to be grateful. Even the two-year-old knows how to say gracias when somebody gives you a nice gift."

Talia erupts from the chair and runs from the room.

"Talia!" Cami calls.

"I'm sorry. I'm so sorry," she says to Stone. "She's just not ready for...that."

She throws us all another apologetic look before running after her traumatized sister.

CHAPTER TWENTY-THREE

A NORMAN ROCKWELL CHRISTMAS IT IS NOT. IT TAKES over an hour of both Cami and me talking to her, before Talia agrees to come out of the room and open the rest of the presents.

Too soon after that, relatives begin to arrive for the Christmas dinner, which Aunt Mari insisted could only be hosted here, since no one else's house was big enough.

"Wait, what did you do last Christmas?" I asked when our family members start rolling in by the tens.

Aunt Mari sucked her teeth and answered, "Why you no make yourself useful instead of asking me all these questions?"

Soon after that she put Cami, Talia, and me to work, serving up platters of yucca patties as appetizers to tide everyone over until dinner was served around three or four.

"Is she still mad at me?" Talia asks as we bring the empty trays back to the kitchen.

"She wasn't necessarily mad," I answer gently. "She just didn't understand your response."

"I don't want to tell her why," Talia says, her voice low. "But I don't want her to be mad at me."

"You don't have to tell anyone anything you're not comfortable with sharing," I answer. "And Tia Mari's probably already forgotten about it anyway. Do you see how many people she has to cook for?"

Talia laughs, but the shadows don't completely clear from her eyes. She looks over to where Stone's drinking a beer in his favorite chair, watching but not cheering for the basketball game he turned on in the living room. "How about him? I don't want him to be mad either."

"I'll talk to him," I answer. Then I promise. "Everything will be okay."

But that promise feels like a lie as soon as it comes out of my mouth.

Everyone else gets more and more relaxed as bottles of rum disappear and plates of food are consumed. However, Stone stays in his seat, barely talking or responding to what's going on around him, even when my cousins move the couch out of the way and turn the living room into a spontaneous dance floor.

I laughingly hand Garnet off to Aunt Mari and pull Cami and Talia onto the dance floor. With Christmas joy in my heart, I teach them the same moves my blind parents taught me, so that they'll know what to do the next time one of my Dominican family's instant dance parties pops off.

I'm having fun, so much fun. But then the music slows and

couples take over the dance floor. Cousins both younger and older than me, aunts and uncles who've been together for decades—they all dance, not with their children but with each other, holding each other tight. Even Heaven and her second husband, who Aunt Mari told me last Thanksgiving were on the brink of divorce, have found each other again on the dance floor, eyes closed as they sway rhythmically to the music.

"You should ask Stone to dance," Talia says, dropping her hands from our dance circle.

Maybe it's the rum. Maybe it's all the Christmas spirit. I don't know.

I cross the room to go to him, and bend to place a hand on his arm as I ask, "Everybody's dancing. Do you want to dance?"

"Nanh," he answers. His eyes stayed glued to the basketball game.

I'm deeply aware of all the people side-eyeing our conversation. Relatives who will both happily accept invitations to my house and gossip about how my man refused to dance with me after church this coming Sunday.

"One. Just one dance," I say, some unnameable emotion clawing like a desperate animal at my chest. "C'mon, Stone, it's Christmas. Do me this favor, okay?"

"No, you do me a favor." He unglues his eyes from the game. Looks at my hand on his arm, then up at me. "Stop touching me."

I withdraw my hand so fast. It's like I reached out to touch what I thought was a human, and found my palm burned by nitrogen ice.

I can't bring myself to meet anyone's eyes as I rush over to Aunt Mari, who's dancing with Garnet asleep on her chest.

"I need to put the baby down and go to sleep," I tell her. "Tell everyone it's time to go home. I don't want any complaints."

"But, *mija...*"

Aunt Mari stops when she see the tears brimming in my eyes. "Okay, you don't worry about anything. I'll kick everybody out," she says, transferring Garnet to my arms without any further protests.

She probably thinks I need the comfort of a sleeping baby more than she does.

And she's totally right.

CHAPTER TWENTY-FOUR

"HEY, NAIMA, I NEED TO HAVE A TALK WITH YOU."

I turn from putting down Garnet, to find Stone standing in the nursery's door. He's changed out of the sweater I gave him into a pair of jogging pants and a white t-shirt. And his face is grim.

But my heart is grim, so I guess we kind of match. I follow him back to the bedroom, wishing I had enough pride not to notice how his white t-shirt clings to his bulky muscles.

After we enter the master suite, he sits down on the settee. I remember how I chose to sit there, too, the night I confronted him about his pill usage.

And I know he's gearing up for a hard conversation when another expression falls over his face. This one tired, bordering on weary. "We've gotta talk about this morning."

I nod, shame washing over me. "I know. I shouldn't have kissed you. I crossed a line, which is really ironic, since I'm always trying to get you to respect my boundaries."

Another aggrieved sigh, and he says, "Naima..."

"I think I should move into the fifth bedroom," I burst out. "I mean, I know Cami's in there now, but I'm willing to share. And after what happened this morning and downstairs when I asked you to dance, I think...no actually, I know that's what I need to do."

"Da Fuck?" Stone says, his brow lowering into an angry scowl. "That's not how it's supposed to work with husbands and wives. I'm trying to be normal."

I was trying to stay calm, but the word "normal" sets me off. "Then you should divorce me, already, because nothing about this marriage is normal. C'mon, Stone..."

I suddenly feel as tired as he looks. "Our unorthodox sexual dynamic was one thing when you were completely disassociated from our relationship. But it's been months now, and obviously you don't want to do more than the bare minimum with me. And you're right, you are exceedingly excellent with your mouth. But...it's not enough."

Stone frowns again. "Is this because of Amber? You wish it was her tonguing you down instead of me?"

"What?" I ask, momentarily flummoxed by his mention of the best friend I left behind. "No, this has nothing to do with Amber. In fact, I am so sick and tired of being a pillow princess. My natural setting is give, and only receiving was nice at first, but it's beginning to make me feel sick inside. I'd rather have nothing at all than continue on like this with you."

"I make you feel sick inside?" he asks, as if those were the only words he heard in my entire diatribe.

"No, just the opposite!" I answer, wishing it weren't true. "You blackmailed me into this marriage. And up until Rock's funeral, I was still having nightmares about you dragging me out of my home. You used to be the monster that haunted my dreams. Now you're the monster I want to..."

I trail off. Not knowing how to say it. Not knowing how to tell Stone what I've secretly been hoping for since he went off the pills. No matter how much my head tells me not to wish.

But Stone doesn't let me off the hook. "What?" My normally recalcitrant husband finds and holds my gaze as he asks, "I'm the monster you want to *what*, Naima?"

I shake my head. Not out loud. Not to him. The shame of our mismatched desires rolls over me, clogging the words in my throat.

And eventually, Stone stands back up. "Look, Naima..." he says with an aggrieved sigh.

"I'm... I'm going to pack now," I decide before he can finish that sentence. Then I turn to go to my dresser drawer.

But he grabs my arm, and keeps me right where I am with his vice like grip. Easily. "This..." he says, his voice low and angry. "This is what I needed to talk with you about."

Without warning, he plunges his hand down the front of his sweatpants and pulls out...Holy macaroni...is this really what I think it is? *Yes, yes, it is.*

I answer my own questions as I stare at Stone's long, thick, and incredibly hard dick.

CHAPTER TWENTY-FIVE

I DOUBLE-TAKE. EVERY DROP OF WATER EVAPORATING from my throat. "Is that..."

"Yeah," he answers, his voice tight. "Been dealing with it since this morning. I tried jacking off in the shower. Then again right after dinner. But it keeps on coming back."

My eyes probably shouldn't be as big as saucers now. I'm a professional, with a degree, and years of on-the-job training. But I can't keep my face or voice neutral as I stare at the unexpected hard piece of flesh in Stone's hand. "Did you take something? If so, was it prescribed? This looks painful."

"It is painful," he assures me. "And no, I didn't take shit."

"So then why...?" I start to ask

"Don't be stupid," he answers, his eyes blazing hot as he looks down at me.

The realizations hit me like a bird slamming into glass. "Wait, is this..." I shake my head, barely able to believe the supposition that's about to come out of my mouth. "Is this for me?"

"Who else would it be for?"

"But I thought you didn't like me like that. I thought you couldn't even see what Rock saw in me."

"Yeah, and I thought you knew I was literally on drugs when I said that. Lots of them. It took me four of the blue-label bottle pills to get through that shit."

The memory of his face that morning, so cold and blank, comes back to me. "Oh..."

Stone looks away, his uncharacteristic embarrassment obvious. "I wasn't trying to bother you with this, but..."

He trails off. And I try valiantly not to look, but c'mon...

My eyes drift down to the thing in his hand. God, he's huge. Rock was big, too. But Stone is something else. His heavily veined cock strains against his skin, as if it's trying to break out, and I can actually see it pulsing, as it pushes a drop of pre-cum out of its tip.

Suddenly something on me is pulsing, too. Hot and needy between my legs. Without thinking, I place a hand on his chest, bracing myself as I lower myself to my knees.

Stone inhales sharp when my mouth closes around the head of his leaking dick.

"Nai..." he breathes. "Fuck, you don't have to do that..."

But he snakes a large hand around the curve of my neck, guiding my head as I bob my mouth up and down on his dick.

"Stop," he says after a little while, stepping back and forcibly pulling me up to my feet.

"I want to make you come," I tell him, not bothering to hide my disappointment over him cutting me short. "I want to make you come like you did me."

"Yeah, and I want to nut inside of you," he answers, roughly pulling me into him. "Who do you think's gonna win this argument?"

Before I can answer, his lips come crashing down on mine.

You, I reply mentally, sighing into his kiss. *You're going to win this argument. You win.*

This kiss isn't like the one outside the cemetery. Not exploratory or mean. It's dominating and full of intent. And it doesn't stop, even when Stone drops back down on the settee, and pulls me into his lap.

"Fuck I need this. I need you."

He finally lets go of the kiss to deal with my clothing. Bye-bye frilly green Christmas dress. He rips it down the middle, pushes my panties aside, then lifts me up and plunges me down on his dick.

I gasp, then whimper at the sensation of him filling me up.

I think Stone might feel similarly. He has a look on his face that's hard to explain. Like suffering and ecstasy at the same time.

"Aw, fuck, you feel good," he says, his hands finding my butt cheeks and cupping them.

Almost experimentally, he begins to work my hips in short

quick movements, basically using me to fellate his dick. Then, he leans back on the settee to watch the slide of my extremely wet core up and down his length. "Fuck you're wet and tight. Your pussy was made for this fucking right here."

It's lewd and crude. Not anything like the romantic wedding night sex I imagined when I was online shopping for rings.

And I don't care. His cock feels so good inside of me. I don't want poetry. I don't want flowers. All I want is this. This rough fucking. My back arches as I let him take whatever he wants from me.

Stone and I are, I think it's been established, the absolute worst, when it comes to communication. But that night...

That miracle of a Christmas night, we correspond better than we ever have before with only a few words exchange.

"Wanna feel you," he grunts, his hands fall away from by butt.

It's just three words, but I know exactly what he means. He rises and I fall. Colliding in the middle, he takes my mouth again and I gladly surrender, pressing my large soft breasts into his wide hard chest as we begin to move together. Holding me close, his strokes deepen inside of me, his grunts become more and more guttural. A bitten back moan, as I meet him stroke for stroke. I never want this to end, but not sure how much longer I can hold on.

We explode together. Two bodies, two people, two *souls* in total agreement.

Stone falls out of the kiss again with his climax. His back

caves and he shudders as he empties inside of me. His cumload is...I'm not going to lie. A lot. Like enough to make me wonder if his ED wasn't something he'd been dealing with for years, not months as I'd previously assumed.

"You're back," I say when he's finally done.

Breathing hard, he lets his entire body fall back against the settee. Then he looks up at me.

The smile on his face is in no way cold this time. No, it's large. Large, wide, and totally sincere.

CHAPTER TWENTY-SIX

LAST NIGHT, I'D HAD SOME THOUGHT OF MAKING A BIG deal of Boxing Day, too. Anything to distract me from the husband who'd rejected me that morning.

But on December 26th, I wake up to the ding of a text from Aunt Mari: ***"Are you ever going to get up? I made monkey bread."***

I'm picking up the phone to shoot her a quick sorry and ETA when a new text comes through. ***"That's okay. Your husband's bringing your plate upstairs."***

That's all the warning I get before Stone comes through the door with a tray. It's kitted out with coffee, monkey bread and a scramble of eggs and a bunch of vegetables and meats from last night's party. There's also a vase with a flower in it.

"Wow, breakfast in bed," I say, completely unable to hide my surprise.

This is...well, pretty darn romantic. Too romantic. Looking

at the tray gives me a warm and shaky feeling. Like I'm skating on ice underneath a blazing hot sun.

"I just brought it up. Tia Mari made it," he tells me, as if sensing my conflicted response to his thoughtful gesture. "And Talia's the one who decided you just had to have a flower in a vase. Said she saw it on TV, and I was like, what the hell you watching?"

"You're concerned about her watching inappropriate TV, but not about cursing?" I ask, taking the tray from him. "I'm introducing a swear jar tomorrow. You are going to end up paying for that little girl's college."

Stone pulls a bill out of his wallet and tosses it on the tray. "Here's a hundy to start it off. That should hold me through lunch."

I laugh, not just because of the joke, but because Stone actually made it.

However, the amusement fades from his eyes when I laugh.

"What?" I ask, not sure what happened to our moment.

"Nothing," he answers. "I'm just definitely seeing why Rock liked you."

A compliment. I do believe Stone Ferraro just gave me, Naima Almonte an actual compliment. My heart thrills, only to roller coaster drop when I remember the secret I kept from him. The secret I kept from everybody.

"Um, Stone...there's something you should know," I say, setting the tray aside. "I think maybe you should know ... Rock dumped me."

Stone blinks. Then blinks again. "What? No, he didn't."

"Um, actually, yeah, yeah, he did."

Stone stills, sways, then sits down on the bed's edge like he's trying not to fall. "When?" he asks, his expression unreadable.

"A few days before he died," I answer. "But he was a little weird for months before that. After I moved out of Luca's penthouse, he started calling less and less. We went from going out every day, to once a week, then barely once a month, because he was so busy."

I lower my eyes, remembering how confused I'd been. Confused but not surprised. Amber had warned me that she didn't think our relationship was much more than Stockholm Syndrome in disguise. And she'd been right.

"I think he probably would have ghosted me if the circumstances had been different. But since I was his boss's wife's best friend, he had to do me at least the courtesy of breaking up. He...said...um....it was because of you. Because you said I was a lesbian...and that I was probably thinking of Amber when I was fooling around with him. It was super offensive. Our first argument. First and last."

Stone, the man I've already had so many fights with, I've lost count, looks over his shoulder at me. I'm not expecting an apology for his part in our breakup, and I don't get one. He just sits there, visibly stunned that Rock and I weren't the love story he thought we were.

I clear my throat into the new super tense silence, "I understand if this changes your feelings about..." I shake my head, not sure what to call what happened yesterday. It was too passionate and intense to merely be called a meeting of needs. So I settle for, "what happened last night."

When Stone still doesn't answer, I continue on with, "Rock told me he wasn't looking for anything complicated when he broke up with me. After the way he grew up, he wanted a normal life. A normal wife, without any shades of gray. He probably wouldn't have married me, even if he knew I was pregnant."

"No, he wouldn't have," Stone agrees with a somber nod of his head. "Rock never double-dipped. Once a girl was gone, she was gone. You lasted a little longer than most of the other ones, though."

Stone's words hit me like a bowling ball to the chest. "I'm sorry I didn't tell you sooner. But I'm telling you now."

"Yeah...now..." he says, before going quiet again. After a few moments he looks over his shoulder to ask me, "So is it true?"

"Did Rock dump me?" I nod. "Yeah, yeah he did. I wouldn't lie about that."

"No, the part about Amber. Luca doesn't see shit but Amber when she's in the room, but I noticed the way you used to look at her. Like she hung the moon. Plus, there's nice, then there's what you did. Offering to help her take care of her baby, then letting yourself get kidnapped right along with her when Luca came a calling."

"I didn't let myself get kidnapped," I remind him, my voice going from soft to snappish in an instant. "That was all you. And your gun."

"Yeah, maybe at first that was an excuse you could use."

Stone answers. His words are confrontational, but his voice is not. His tone stays a matter-of-fact, Maury reading DNA results to the jerk who refuses to claim his kid, as he says, "Rock told me what happened when Amber convinced Luca to let you go. He said you cried when he told you the good news. And then there's all this stuff with you refusing to tell Amber you've had a baby and married me..."

My chest constricts at the unspoken, but he continues to look me in the eye as he asks "So what's going on with you? You still hung up on Amber or what?"

I squirm under his questions, and I think about the day our friendship fell apart again. How hurt I felt that Amber was basically kicking me out of her life, how betrayed, even though I couldn't quite explain why.

Stone forced me into this marriage. I don't owe him anything. For a moment that feels like a good enough excuse to say nothing. To clamp my lips and fold my arms, like I used to when my mom accused me of filching her *bonbon amidon* starch cookies at Christmas time.

But I guess in the end, Too Nice Naima, just can't stand to be that much of a hypocrite. How many times had I accused Stone of not properly communicating with me?

No, I don't owe him anything, but I find myself confessing. "I don't know what my relationship with Amber was. Friendship. Just friendship. I never expected it to be more. At least at first. I didn't think I had feelings for Amber or any other girl. When my parents were still living with me in New York, I barely had time to go out to dinner, much less any kind of relationship. But then they moved away, and I was all alone, except for Amber, who never seemed to need to spend more than a few days a week with her then boyfriend. So when she got pregnant after breaking up with him, it all felt so logical. Like, yeah, of course we would be a family. We could always be there for each other. I loved that idea. Loved Amber and her unborn child. But then Luca happened, and all those plans went, *poof!* I guess it really is a spectrum like they teach us. Normally, I like guys, but for Amber...I would've changed my mind. I can't say if I was in love with her. But I also can't say I wasn't. That's the truth. The whole truth, as much as I can tell of it."

"Yeah, well..." More quiet. Then Stone says, "You triggered Rock."

I crook my head, surprised by his three-word conclusion. "What do you mean, I..."

"Triggering—isn't that what they call it when you make people relive shit they don't want to relive?"

Once again Stone's definition of a textbook word is crude but not entirely inaccurate. "I'm not talking about your word usage. I'm saying I didn't know Rock had a girlfriend who left him for another woman."

"It wasn't a girlfriend; it was our mom."

"Your mom had a girlfriend?"

"Yeah, and she still does," Stone says. "Her and Luca's mom are both still married. Technically. But when it comes to boning, that's what's up."

I blink, my entire mind shifting to accommodate the idea of the two women, I'd only ever seen in pictures having a torrid affair. "How do you know? Are you sure?"

"Rock and me walked in on them when we came home from college after deciding we didn't need to be there. They'd pretty much set up house. Rock's no fan of our dad, but he loved Luca's dad. And you know how loyal both of us used to be to Luca..."

Used to be. I wonder if he's putting that fealty in the past tense because of what he discovered about his mother, or the wedding I'd asked him to keep secret. "Did you ever tell Luca?" I ask. "Luca or his dad?"

"We thought about it, but why rock the boat? Luca's dad has got a mistress, too. He just doesn't know so does his wife. So in the end we stayed quiet about it. But Rock never forgave her. Barely managed a card and flowers for Mother's Day after that. And you know how he liked to keep his shit black and white. If he thought there was even a chance of you fucking around with Amber behind his back, yeah, I'm not surprised he took that relationship of yours behind the barn to shoot it."

I can't believe it, so many puzzle pieces were finally falling into place about the last doomed month of Rock's and my relationship. But I have to ask , "And how about you? How did you take finding out about your mom and your aunt...by marriage at least."

Stone shrugs. "Popped a couple of blue-labels and kept it moving."

A logical answer, at least for Stone. And it feels like a natural conclusion to our conversation.

But instead of leaving it there, I ask, "And how about now? With me, now that you're off the drugs?"

This time he doesn't just look at me over his shoulder, he full on turns around to face me and sets the tray on the floor.

"Fuck Amber," he answers, his dark eyes blazing inside a face as hard as New York concrete. "Don't matter what or who you were feeling before, I'm your husband now."

Then he captures my lips and covers my body with his.

It's an answer to my question, but not really. Our past...his psychology... Amber, who still doesn't know—all those factors feel like shadows surrounding our relationship. Blocking the light.

Anxiety pings like an engine light in the back of my head, even as Stone creates just enough space between our bodies to raise my sleep shirt and rid me of my panties. His workout pants get shoved down after that, and then he's in. "My fucking wife," he growls low in my ear, right before he begins to slowly stroke inside of me, his movements deep, deliberate, and demanding.

With a needy groan, I twine my legs around his waist, my nails scraping down the back of his workout shirt. God, he makes me ache. Not just for sex, either. And that emotional fact sends another wave of anxiety through me.

He abruptly stops moving on top of me and grabs me by the chin. "Where you at?"

"I'm right here," I answer, telling him what feels like both the obvious truth and a terrible lie.

The hard glint in his eyes lets me know he doesn't believe my truth lie. "Whose wife are you?"

"Yours," I answer, my heart quickening with the word.

"Where you at?" he asks again.

"Here. With *you*."

And this time it doesn't feel like a lie.

The anxiety, Amber, all the secrets we've revealed in less than twelve hours, they all fade away as I look into his dark eyes.

"Stone, I'm right here with you. Please. Please don't stop—"

My plea breaks off, when he drops down on one arm and starts driving into me, his hips thrusting powerfully to the beat of my desperate cries. Desperate and grateful.

Stone heard my truth, and he still wants me. Even more than his brother did.

It feels too good to be true.

I can't believe it. But I can enjoy it, I decide as he pounds into me. I can enjoy it until the wheels come off this relationship, too.

CHAPTER TWENTY-SEVEN

I WAIT AND WAIT. BUT THINGS JUST KEEP GOING OKAY. Stone gets a therapist as promised. Also, a new psychiatrist, who refuses to prescribe anything, since his behemoth patient might look like a monster, but doesn't in fact have any documented psychiatric history. At least not on paper.

"I can't talk about the killing and shit," he tells me after his third therapy appointment.

We're at a toy store during my lunch hour. We're having a special dinner for Talia's birthday tonight, and Stone demanded that I come with him to pick out her present this time. "So I don't fuck it up again."

I didn't really think he fucked it up the first time, but Too Nice Naima stays humming in my background, no matter how hard I try to switch her off. So here we are in a downtown store full of twee toys, trying to find a present for the girl who really doesn't want any presents from men, and something for Stone to talk with his new therapist about.

"Maybe you can talk to her about losing your brother, and some of your childhood stuff. You know, with your Dad."

Stone snorts. "How I'm looking, still whining about my dad hitting me a few times when I was a kid?"

"It's not about how you appear," I point out. "It's more about processing the emotions."

Stone just grunts. And I continue to scan the shelves, wondering how far to push him. It had been a lot more than a few times, according to Rock. I remember the stories he told me, about how Stone was the first to get in front of their father, whenever he tried to come after Rock or their mother.

Rock had said, "My dad would have to knock him unconscious if he wanted to lay a hand on either of us. He was our hero."

I had sensed back then that Rock was only telling me this story to get me to like the twin brother I despised back then. It was important to him to have us get along, and he wanted me to be impressed. But at the time, all I'd been able to think was, "So that's how that monster was created."

But now I'm standing next to the monster. Trying to help him find an appropriate toy, while listening to his play-by-play of what sounds like another mostly silent therapy appointment. "She can't help you if you don't let her in."

Stone grunts again, and then picks up a baseball mitt, hanging out on an end cap.

"Mmm, I don't know if Talia's going to be into baseball," I tell him.

"I wasn't going to get it for Talia, I was going to get it for us," he says. "You know, for the next kid, since it's going to be a boy."

My heart freezes in my chest. "Another kid?"

He rolls his eyes at me. "C'mon don't act like we ain't talked about this before."

Technically, he'd done most of the talking during that ridiculous conversation. Also... "That was before."

"Before what?" He turns to face me. "You mean before we started fucking for real?"

I swallow. "Yes, before... that." How did I go from waiting for the inevitable shoe to drop on our relationship to talking about kids?

He lowers the mitt. "Yeah, I'd think us fucking every night without protection would make another kid in our future obvious."

I'm not sure what to say, and when I finally do answer it feels like I'm carefully picking each word before it comes out of my mouth. "We've only been having sex for a few months. Maybe we should put conversations like this on hold until we're both surer about the next steps."

He looks down at me for a long, tense moment. Then he says, "I'm buying the fucking glove."

I watch him walk away, feeling helpless. And making wishes in my chest that I know better than to utter out loud.

WE NEVER DO FIND A PRESENT FOR TALIA. AND

instead of walking in the door with a beautifully wrapped gift that evening, Stone sticks his head into the kitchen where Aunt Mari, Talia, and me are frosting the cupcakes we'll be having after dinner tonight.

"Hey, Tal, come out here, I need your help with something," he says, not even a hint of happy birthday in his tone, even though the kitchen smells of freshly baked cupcakes and all of Talia's favorite Dominican dishes, bubbling on the stove.

Then he leaves without waiting for her answer.

After exchanging a look with Aunt Mari, we end up following Talia out to the living room and we both gasp when we see Cami waiting there, with what looks like a black and white bulldog puppy in her arms.

"I been complaining about there not being enough testosterone in this house, so I went out and got some," Stone tells Talia. "His name's Stallone. But the thing is, I don't know who's going to walk him and take care of him when I'm out of town. Think you can help me with that?"

"Yes! Yes! Oh my god, yes!" Talia cries. She runs over to her sister and spends the rest of the night cooing over the puppy she somehow knows is her birthday present, even if she is just supposed to be helping Stone out.

I'm trying. God, I'm trying to keep a level head. Our marriage is just a matter of duty. The sex we're having now, a meeting of basic needs. I remind myself and remind myself, but Stone's thoughtful gift, it unnerves me. And even though I haven't been to church in a minute, I send up a prayer. *Please…please, God. Don't let me fall. Don't let me get hurt again.*

"That's a good man you got there," Aunt Mari says as we watch him go over Stallone's crate training with Talia while sipping rum and eating cake. "You are very, very lucky. My Miguel? Bless his heart, but he could not pick out gifts. You know, he gave me a candle for my first birthday after we were wed? For my birthday! I ask him, what kind of gift is this for your wife? And from then on, I made sure to tell him exactly what jewelry and finer things to get me at least a week before my big day, because I knew I could not trust him to pick out the jewelry I deserved himself. I hope you know how lucky you are to have a man like that."

I fret my lip. Not because I disagree. Actually, just the opposite. The house, the ring, the patchwork family, and now the amazing sex...

I know this will eventually run its course, and I know I shouldn't get too attached but...I wanted it. Deep inside where all the old hungers lurked, I feel the need for this thing between me and Stone swells, like a great big wave about to crest. The sensations are so intense my fingers tremble as I pick up Garnet from the living room floor and hold her tight.

Together we watch Stone be exactly the kind of father figure Talia needs in her life. And I try, I try not to make it mean anything.

CHAPTER TWENTY-EIGHT

OVER THE NEXT FEW MONTHS, I DON'T FALL FOR Stone, but I do get used to him. I also discover the daily life changing magic of having someone who truly doesn't give an eff-word in your corner.

My store returns all go into the back of Stone's Cadillac for him to take care of while he's doing whatever he does all day in his tailored suits. And guess who the phone gets passed to when a pushy telemarketer dials me up. I've also learned the hard way, not to complain to Stone about any of my cases.

He still doesn't mess with capes, but one missing college student from my foster roster suddenly reappeared, complaining about how none of the local drug dealers would sell to him. It was almost as if he'd gotten blacklisted.

"More like Stonelisted," I accuse Stone that night when we're walking Stallone around the block. "Tell me the truth, it was you wasn't it."

He just half-smiled and said, "Got some ideas about how

you could interrogate me. It involves a whole lot of you bouncing up and down on my dick."

I ended up interrogating him all night. But I never do get a clear answer.

That's okay, I guess. I enjoy the way we connect in bed. Over our crowded dinner table. During the nightly TV we watch on the couch. And during our daily dog walks with Stallone. After a lot of thought and contemplation, I allow myself this. Allow myself to enjoy him—the crazy, mishmash life I've mosaicked together with him, Garnet, Aunt Mari, Cami, and Talia.

Stone leaves the majority of the parenting to me, but I'm not going to lie, he is fantastic backup. He uses his unusually strong menacing power like a space heater. Often standing in Talia's doorway behind me, when I tell her to clean up her room.

I refuse to put any expectations on him, but if he did stick around, I bet his version of, "You heard your mother," would totally be on point.

He's great with the discipline and occasionally with the feelings stuff, too. I find that out one Sunday morning, a few months into Cami's last semester of college.

Aunt Mari always takes this day "off" and insists on bringing Garnet and Talia with her to church, since there's "one generation in this house the Lord can still save."

So Cami and I are rinsing the dishes after making our own breakfast, while Stone sits at the table. Fresh off his New York morning flight, he's eating the plate of bacon and eggin-a-hole toast I made for him, shortly after he came through the door.

Her phone vibrates right as she's about to put the last plate into the dishwasher, and in typical college girl fashion she pulls it out to check it instead of completing her task.

Only to repocket it as soon as she reads the message. A little too quickly, if you ask me. "Everything okay?" I ask.

"No, it's nothing."

"It sounded like something," I press, my social worker spidey sense totally going off when I see the way she's looking everywhere but at me.

"Well, it isn't," she snaps back at me. "It isn't anything."

"Hey, watch that tone, Marino," Stone says from the table. "She was only asking you a question."

"If you don't want to tell me, you don't have to," I say, reaching out to rub her shoulder. Good cop, to Stone's bad.

"But you gotta be respectful," he reminds her with a squint.

"I'm not trying to be disrespectful. I just don't... don't want to tell you," she answers.

But then she starts fretting her hands, leading me to ask. "Are you safe? Do you feel threatened in any way by whatever was in that text?"

"Threatened?" Stone stands up from the table and demands, "Somebody fucking threatening you?"

"No, I guess not," Cami says. "It's more like I'm confused."

"Maybe we could help with that confusion?" I suggest.

Cami, hesitates, her eyes darting between Stone and me. "I don't know..."

"Just fucking tell her," Stone says, pulling out a hundred from his billfold.

"You know she's only going to gentle voice you til you do," he says, dropping the Benjamin Franklin into the cuss jar I set up on the kitchen counter. "Remember how she broke Talia when she had pinworms?"

Stone clasps his hands and raises his voice about a thousand octaves, as he trills, "You sure you don't want me to take a look? You seem really uncomfortable. And we all want to make sure you're comfortable."

Cami cracks up, but I glare at him, wondering if all the great sex is worth putting up with a man who makes me sound like the pushy version of Snow White.

"Anyway," I say over her laughter. "I'm here for you. Whatever you need."

"I don't need anything," Cami says, shaking her head. "It's just a stupid boy...but kind of not a boy. He's a teacher's assistant from one of my classes last semester. And he was, like, hey, since you're not in my class anymore, want to go see *Weird Science* on Friday night?"

"What's *Weird Science*?" I ask.

"Some stupid shit only geeks like," Stone answers, pulling out his wallet again. "Rock and his geeky Manhattan U friends made me watch it once."

"So he's asking you out on a date?" I say to Cami.

Cami pulls one arm into her side, grasping it nervously. "To hang, yeah. Whatever."

"Do you want to hang out with this guy?" I ask her.

"I don't know. I mean he's cool. He stayed way past his office hours once to help me figure out an assignment problem. He's nice. I think he is. I'm almost sure of it. But I'm..."

She trails off. And though, I'd never press on such a sensitive subject, I can't help but wonder about all the ways she's finishing that sentence inside her head. Not accurately, I sense. She's doing the work with her university therapist. But it's going to be a long time before she learns to see herself outside the lens of what her father did to her.

So, I finish the sentence for her, "Wonderful. You're wonderful. Also, funny and easy-to-talk-to...and so, so bright."

"Double down on that," Stone agrees. "And hey, yo, Cam, all guys ain't like your old man. If they're liking you right, it ain't got conditions on it. You can go to the movies with this dude or whatever, but you don't have to do anything else. Remember, you put that bastard father of yours in the ground. So, from now on, how far you go stays up to you."

Not exactly how I would have put it, but Cami releases a breath I didn't know she was holding until it audibly comes out. "Okay, okay, you're right," she says her voice going a little higher with excitement. "I think I'm going to say yes."

"That's what I'm talking about," Stone says, grabbing a bag of almonds from the cabinet above the cuss jar. "And hey, if this guy tries anything you don't want, let him know you

STONE: HER RUTHLESS ENFORCER   177

have somebody in your life who can make bodies disappear, real easy like."

"Or...have a clear communication about boundaries before engaging in any mutually agreed upon acts of intimacy," I suggest.

Stone pops an almond into his mouth. "If you want, I can show you how to snap a guy's neck, using mostly your own body weight."

"God, you are ridiculous," I say, shaking my head at him.

But Cami's face goes soft as she looks between us. "Seriously, thanks you two. For helping me figure this out, for everything. I don't know how to really say this but living with you guys is like having a mom and dad. You make me feel safe and like I can do anything. I kind of wish I could stay here forever."

My heart melts at her words. "You can stay here. As long as you like. I'm not ever kicking you out."

"Thank you," Cami whispers. Then she closes the distance between us and hugs me tight. Like I really am the mother she's always needed.

"Why did you say 'I'm'?" Stone asks, later when we're walking Stallone after breakfast. "Why did you say 'I'm never going to kick you out,' with Cami earlier?"

I startle. Over the last few months, I've gotten used to talking with Stone over our daily walks. Mostly about light things, like the kids, the latest episode of whatever contest show we're watching with Talia and Cami after dinner, and the Knicks' chances of making the playoffs this year. We never talk about his work, but he likes hearing about the older kids I'm helping. And sometimes we find ourselves in deeper conversations. About my childhood growing up with severely visually-impaired parents, and his childhood growing up as the next don of the Ferraro family.

"Do you ever wonder what if you were the head of the family instead of Luca?" I'd asked him on last night's walk, remembering how often Rock had brought it up.

He'd shrugged. "Rock did, but I was all good. Enforcing seemed a more natural fit for my skillset anyway."

I'd shivered and asked, "And how about now that you're off the pills?"

He'd gone quiet, so long I'd wondered if he was going to answer. Then he quietly says, "I like how you do that."

"Do what?"

"Dig deeper. You're the only who's ever done that with me. Assumed there was something underneath. Sometimes it feels like....I don't know. Like I was living inside a huge piece of cotton. Then one day you came in and got me. Just got me and dragged me out."

Last night, he'd looked down at me over Stallone with something akin to admiration in his eyes.

But today, he's walking almost too fast for me to keep up, asking me questions, I don't quite understand.

"Are you upset that I made Cami promises about never kicking her out, even though the house is in both our names?" I ask him.

"No, I'm upset because you made promises to Cami, like you weren't married to me."

I scrunch my forehead, so confused. "So what? You want me to kick her out at the end of the school year? Even if she doesn't have a job?"

Stone shakes his head at me. "How do you fucking do that?"

"Do what?" I ask, my voice pitching high, because it feels like we're speaking two different languages right now.

"Assume the best and the worst of me at the same damn time? It's like I can't figure out what you want from me."

I stop dead in my tracks. "You're trying to figure out what I want from you?"

"Yeah," answers Stone, stopping as well. "Why is that a surprise?"

The answer to that question is too sad to say out loud. The thing is, sometimes it feels like I've been trying to figure out what other people want since the day I was born. But no one, not Rock, not Amber, not even my parents, has ever tried to figure out what I want from them.

Don't fall, don't fall, don't fall, I pray as I tell Stone the truth. "I don't expect anything from you. Is there something you want from me? Something I'm not giving you?"

He looks at me for a long, tense moment. Then he starts walking again. No more intimate and/or pleasant conversation. Instead we're back to silence, with me not understanding what's got Stone so agitated.

CHAPTER TWENTY-NINE

STONE DISAPPEARS AFTER WE RETURN WITH STALLONE and doesn't reappear, even when Aunt Mari gets home from church with the girls.

"Where's Stone?" Talia demands, used to finding him here when she gets home.

"I'm not sure," I answer.

I pull out my phone and type out a quick, "Where are you?"

But no answer, until later in the day, when Stone comes through the front door still wearing his dark mafia suit, even though he usually changes into something a little bit more comfortable for the Sunday dinner, Aunt Mari claims she has to host here every other week, because no one else's house is big enough.

"Again, what did you do before we moved here?" I asked when it became clear to me that the Sunday dinners were going to be a bi-monthly thing, back in January.

STONE: HER RUTHLESS ENFORCER   181

"Oh, we were so sad and cramped," Aunt Mari answered. "Thank God for Stone."

But thank God isn't what I'm thinking as I watch him half-listen to Talia tell him about how she tried to speak Spanish at Sunday School but nobody really understood her. He seems...off.

Despite the funny details of Talia's story, his face remains a mask.

And by the time Yara rolls in with her three-kid crew, he's nowhere to be found.

"I think I saw him go into the basement," Aunt Mari tells me when I ask.

She's right. I hear the treadmill whirring away as soon as I open the door. Is he working out? But he never works out on Sundays.

A bad feeling comes over me, as I make my way down the metal stairs, to find him running on the treadmill...in his dress shirt and tailored pants. Stone's completely drenched, and his handwoven dress shirt clings to his skin, with huge sweat patches everywhere.

Brow scrunching, I come the rest of the way down the stairs to ask, "Stone? What are you doing?"

No answer.

"Getting a few miles in?" I ask. "In your wingtips?"

Stone still doesn't answer. And I move closer to read the machine's display. It says he's been running for over an hour and a half.

This can't be comfortable. Or sane. His entire face is red. It's like he's torturing himself, and I can't watch.

So I make it stop, punching a finger into the big red button in the middle of the display.

"Hey, what are you doing?" Stone demands when the tread-mill comes to a sudden halt.

Before he can turn it on again, I cover the display screen with my whole hand and ask, "Is this...is this about Cami going out on a date?"

"Hell, no. Already checked. Guy's a total egghead. It'll take me less than an hour to bury him if anything goes wrong."

I didn't even bother to reply to that one. "Then why are you down here, running in your business clothes?"

"I don't know, why are you here in North Carolina, living with some random aunt and a couple of kids you didn't know from Adam a year ago, when you could be in New York?"

"You're lashing out," I say, trying to stay calm, even as my skin prickles with the truth of his words. "Seriously, Stone, what's going on?"

"Blowing off steam."

"By steam, do you mean emotions?" I ask, tilting my head. "And by blowing off, do you mean running away from them?"

He gets off the treadmill, looks at me, then practically mauls me, pushing me into the wall with an almost violent kiss.

"Stone," I say, trying to pull back.

But he holds on to my waist, keeping me pinned between him and the wall. "I don't want to talk about it. Don't want to get gentle beasted by you. Don't dig deeper. Right now, all I want to do is fuck you against the wall." His words and breath are harsh against my lips. But his voice sounds desperate as he says. "I need...I need inside you. Can I get in there? Will you let me?"

I stare at him, all the questions piling up. Then I silently nod, wanting to help him more than I need to understand what's going on.

"Aw fuck, babe, thank you," he says, lifting me up to his waist, like I don't weigh anything, he carries me to the closest wall.

The panties I'm wearing under my Sunday dinner dress are just a barrier that disappear with a tug of his hand. Then he buries himself inside of me with a low groan. Driving deeper, then deeper still, filling me up with strokes that jerk my entire body as he claims me.

It's a crazy, but good position. He has to half hold, half counter-balance me to keep my hips right where he needs them on the wall. That means my clit gets plenty of stimulation as he pumps into me.

"Mmm, Stone, I'm coming," I tell him just a few minutes into it. Even though this is supposed to be about what he needs, not me.

But tell that to my body. My core quivers around his long staff, clenching it tight as the climax washes over me.

It doesn't take Stone long to follow me right over the cliff's edge.

"Need you...need you...need you..." he whispers urgently into my ear. His thrusts become faster, then sloppy. Then he groans long and hard before releasing with a full body shudder.

"Sorry..." he mumbles as he comes down. "Sometimes it's hard without pills. It's like I don't know how to process things."

Is this about his job, I wonder. The work he's been doing for the Ferraro family? This time without the numbing benefits of pills.

I worry, but I don't say anything, just press my forehead into his. "It's okay," I whisper, pressing soft kisses into his lips, his nose, his cheeks. Dragging him out of cotton, despite myself.

CHAPTER THIRTY

We sneak back upstairs, shower, change clothes, and come back down the stairs separately.

That totally works. My family notices my outfit change, but they all remain circumspect about it and don't bring it up.

Psyche! If you believed that, you're most likely not from a large Dominican family.

"Nice dress. Did your man pick that out for you?" my cousin Yara asks, elbowing me in the ribs. Then she glares at her soldier husband who is home on leave this weekend. "Why you never make me change outfits in the middle of the day no more, Lucas?"

"I'll give you three reasons," Lucas answers, pointing at each of their kids. They're all currently in a clear section of the living room with Garnet, arguing passionately over who should get to teach the baby how to walk.

"Mai, you're going to have to stop inviting us over on Sundays," Osner calls into the kitchen, after he vacates the recliner to let Stone sit down in his usual Sunday dinner spot. "Obviously our boy Stone's got other things he wants to be doing in the afternoon."

"Other things like what?" Juan, one of Osner's sons, asks. Then he looks around confused when most of her family bursts out laughing.

"He's trying to make sure you get another boy cousin to play here with soon," his father answers, cackling at his own joke.

"Okay, I'm going to go help Tia Mari in the kitchen," I inform the room, my whole face burning.

"You do that," Heaven advises. "Stay in here too long and Stone might decide he don't like that dress."

"I like your dress, *Tia* Naima!" Juan calls after me.

Gales of laughter follow my retreat into the kitchen.

Stone doesn't make me change again, but I can feel his hungry gaze on me all through dinner.

And when the rum and music comes out, instead of staying in his recliner to watch the conclusion of the Manhattan U. versus Virginia Tech game, he comes over to where I'm sitting on the floor with Garnet and Yara's kids.

"You wanna do this or what?" he asks, holding out his hand.

I stare at the hand, my eyes probably wide as saucers. "Are you serious?"

"Don't be stupid," he answers. His usual harsh rebuttal, but both his voice and expression are soft. Softer than I've ever seen them. I take his hand and let him pull me to my feet.

The next thing I know, I'm in his arms, swaying to the music, even though the current song has a fast beat meant for hip-shaking and twirling.

I don't protest. A... I'm pretty sure Stone doesn't merengue, and B...I kind of like being with him like this.

We never hug. Never touch even, unless it's a precursor to sex. Don't get me wrong, I've loved doing the sexy stuff with him these last few months. Technically that hard on was the best Christmas gift I've ever got.

But this is nice, too. Real nice. *As long as you remember it's only temporary, Almonte.*

We sway in a bubble while everyone spins around us, and eventually the music gives in, slowing down into a nineties' era Frank Reyes song.

"Hey, Stone?" I ask, feeling more comfortable with him than I have in...well, ever.

"Hmm?" His head is resting against the top of my forehead, and his voice rumbles low in my ear.

"What was up with you earlier? Why were you so intense? Did something happen after we walked Stallone?"

He tenses, and I wait, not sure if he'll answer.

But eventually he says, "Yeah, something happened."

Then he goes quiet again.

"Okay, what happened, Stone?" I demand, keeping my voice low but pulling back from his hold.

He doesn't answer.

And I brace myself. Wondering if this is the moment. The moment he decides he's done with me and better off with someone else.

But then he says, "The way you and me handled Cami, like a team, and all these talks we've be having, and you know, the sex. Today, I guess while we were out walking Stallone, I guess I realized, I was like, I dunno, maybe forty...fifty percent in love with you."

My heart doesn't just skip a beat. It stops. Dropping like a Looney Tunes anvil to my stomach.

"You're not answering," he says, after Frank Reyes plaintively sings a few more lines of Spanish.

No, I'm not. It feels like my brain has shut down, giving up on making words or full thoughts, much less on responding to Stone's lowkey announcement that he's halfway in love with me.

And after a while, he says, "Okay, me being sorta in love with you doesn't need doves and trumpets. We're already married. But I figured you would at least have a little something to say about—"

He cuts off when I kiss him. I don't know why. Maybe because I never in a million years expected to hear those words from his mouth. Maybe because I'm still not sure how else to respond.

Either way, a whole bunch of hoots and hollers rise up from my family, drowning out the prince of *bachata*.

"Watch out, Stone's going to make you change out of that dress!" Osner cheers somewhere in the distance.

And he's totally right.

"Okay, now I'm definitely at fifty percent," he informs me when we finish the kiss. "And I got a real good feelin' you're going to close in on fifty-five percent by the time the night is through. Think Mari can put Garnet down for the night?"

Stone's fifty-five percent in love with me. At least he thinks he is. I have no idea how to respond to that out loud. But when it comes to answering with my body...well.

I let Stone take me by the hand and lead me up the stairs.

CHAPTER THIRTY-ONE

STONE IS GONE WHEN I WAKE UP, AND GARNET'S ON the monitor protesting about not getting fed yet. *Maybe it was just the rum talking last night.* Relief floods through me at that thought.

If it was just the rum, I don't have to take his declaration seriously. Or think about how the part where someone says they love you comes right before they leave.

"We love you, but..." my parents had told me before announcing their decision to move back to Hispaniola.

"I just want to thank you for agreeing to raise this baby with me. Love you, bestie!" Amber had written just a few days before Luca crashed back into her life.

"I mean, I thought I loved you, but..." an uncharacteristically somber Rock had said while shuffling his feet.

Stone not really meaning what he said, means he'll stay longer, keep pretending we're a real family. I'm not sure when I went from reluctant bride to all in on this fairy tale, but somewhere between August and now I'm all in. And if there's one thing I'm sure of, it's that I don't want it to end.

When I come into the kitchen with Garnet, after breast-feeding her, I find him at the table, hunched over his phone. Not the iPhone, but the Samsung burner he uses for "Ferraro shit."

"Morning," I say to him, Cami, and Talia.

"Morning," the girls call back. But Stone just grunts.

Yeah, it was definitely the rum, I conclude, as I go to the side of the table where Garnet's highchair sits.

But Garnet has other ideas. "Un-uh!" She makes insistent baby sounds and reaches her chubby little arms toward Stone.

"She's upset because I missed our morning bottle meeting. Give her here," Stone says, putting down his phone.

Garnet's whole face lights up with gummy smile, when Stone stands up and takes her from me. Then she immediately grabs his tie and tries to put it in her mouth.

"How many times I gotta tell you, Prada ain't for munching?" Stone says, pulling it away before she can.

Garnet lets out a baby squeal and gives him another gummy smile. "Dada!"

Stone goes still as a statue and my stomach drops.

"Did she just say...?" I start to ask.

"Dada," Garnet says again before I can finish asking.

Then just in case, Stone's not getting it, she smiles at him and all but sings, "Dada! Dada! Dada!"

Cami and Talia cheer and coo. While at the stove Aunt Mari proclaims, "Oh, *angelita*, you love your daddy don't you?"

But Stone just stands there, his expression completely stunned. Then he says, "She's never going to meet him. He's gone. He's fucking gone."

"Who is he talking about?" Talia asks, her eyes going wide at the never-before-seen sight of Stone in clear distress.

"His brother," I answer, my heart constricting for Stone, who I suspect hasn't really let himself think about the twin brother he lost before this moment. "He died about a year and a half ago."

"Yeah, he died. He..." Stone rolls his neck. Right, left, as if trying to fight off a demon.

But he can't. The tears come squeezing out past the barrier of his eyelids. First dripping, then rolling as Stone's shoulders shake. "He's never going to meet her," he says, hugging Garnet to his chest.

It's like watching a mountain break down and cry. And we all seem to make the decision to rush to our most stalwart family member at the same time.

"It's okay, Stone," Cami says, patting his back. While Aunt Mari tuts in Spanish about how the Lord does everything for a reason, but that doesn't make the reason hurt any less.

I just cup his face and look into his eyes over Garnet's shoulder, while Talia pats his biceps and tells him, "Sometimes I cry, too. But usually when nobody's looking."

That makes all of us laugh. Including Stone.

And then it's over.

At least I think it's over.

After breakfast, he walks me to my car. "Have a good day, babe," he says, opening my driver's side door for me, and whoa, it doesn't even sound sarcastic.

He pulls me in for a soft kiss just before I'm about to get in the car. Then he says, "Now I'm at sixty percent."

I stare at him. Again, needing him not to mean that.

"But don't worry," he promises. "I'm not going to be a fuck nut about it."

CHAPTER THIRTY-TWO

STONE KEEPS HIS PROMISE NOT TO BE A FUCK NUT about his percentage point love proclamation over the next few weeks. And he doesn't bring up me not saying I love him back again. At least not explicitly. But somehow it's always there between us. Like an elephant in the otherwise tidy room of our relationship. One I can't look at directly, without shivering with fear.

He only heads out to New York every other weekend now, and he kisses me a little longer before he goes. Then he pecks Garnet on top of her head, and tells her to take care of me until, "Dada gets back."

The percentage points also seem to be ratcheting up. And I'm not sure how to stop that. I get points for everything. I reach 65% for giving good head, but he tacked on another five percent for filling out his DMV forms when they come up for renewal. "You're a 70% now, Nai. I fucking hate paperwork."

The points pile up for kisses and laundry and bringing him

coffee. One Wednesday before he's due to leave for New York, he even gives me five points for "this pussy."

"Fuck why do you feel so good?" he groans, right before he comes inside me.

It's May now. Nearly a year into our unexpected relationship. And somehow, I've found myself at 95% love. I know he's not really being serious, and I'm not even sure why I kept on adding up the points.

"You know this love thing is just pheromones, and you coming down from the pills," I tell him while we're both lying there in the dark afterwards. "When you're in New York this weekend, maybe you should consider experimenting a little."

A long beat of silence. "You want me to fuck around on you when I'm in New York?" he asks, his voice just as hard as it used to get back before he came off the pills.

"No, I don't...but yes, I kind of do. Our relationship is really unorthodox. And I think you should explore your options—your many, many options, before you make a decision you might regret. I mean, you're talking about having another baby."

"I'm talking about having more *babies*. Plural. And you're telling me to go bang some other chick."

"I mean...wear a condom of course."

"I cannot believe this shit..." Another long silence, then he asks, "You get that I'm a fucking psycho, right? If you cheated on me, I would kill that bitch. I don't care what side of the spectrum your shit falls on."

"Psycho is a strong word," I answer, keeping a reasonable tone despite his obvious attempt to bring me down to his level. "And you don't have to worry about me cheating. I've dated, at least a little bit, and believe me, I'm not looking for anything more complicated than this. But from what I'm understanding, you didn't date anyone seriously before me. I mean, as many drugs as you were on, were you even having sex?"

"The drugs didn't start giving me problems until my thirties. And I wasn't a monk. The Ferraro family used to own a bunch of strip clubs. I could go in any of them and get whatever I wanted."

Keeping my voice clinical, I answer, "Strippers aren't experience, and again you were heavily medicated. For all you know, you'd feel this way about any woman you fucked."

"You're my wife. The only woman I should be fucking. The only woman I want to fuck."

"That's a kind of problematic statement, since—"

"Jesus fucking Christ," he explodes in the dark. "I'm clean. I'm fuckin' killing this dada shit for Garnet. Now you're saying there's something else wrong with me because I don't want to fuck anybody but you?"

I wince, because yeah, he's summed my points up and it doesn't sound so logical when he puts them like that. "I'm just saying if you get the itch in New York, don't ignore it."

Another silence, this one even longer than the two that became before. So long I'm beginning to wonder if Stone has fallen asleep when he says, "Okay, expect a call this weekend when I'm in New York."

"So you're going to try it?" I ask, dual urges battling in my chest. I want to push him away, just far enough to realize this supposed love he's feeling could be applied to anyone now that he's off the pills. But I also have a crazy compulsion to lock my arms around his neck and never let him go.

Conflicted to my core, I wait in the dark for his answer.

But this time Stone doesn't reply.

CHAPTER THIRTY-THREE

STONE KEEPS HIS PROMISE ABOUT THE CALL, BUT IT isn't the one I'm expecting.

"Hello?" I say, when my phone erupts just as I'm walking to my car after getting off of work on Friday.

"Hi, is this Naima?" a friendly voice says. "Stone Ferraro's wife?"

"Yes..." I say carefully, my heart seizing. Did Stone decide to sleep with another woman, then have her call me after it was done?

"Hi, Naima, this is Dr. Nouri. I've been working with Stone, and he was hoping we might all meet on Monday when he's back in town."

Even as my heart starts beating again, I have to wonder out loud, "Meet? Meet about what?"

"Many patients find it helpful to have their spouse come in with them to an appointment."

"Oh, I know but Stone ..." I want to say "ain't most patients," but trail off. "Really, he wants me to meet with his therapist?"

"Yes, really," she answers. "Do you have 2pm on Monday available?"

"I can make it available," I answer. So we set it in the calendar and say our friendly goodbyes, even though I'm still so, so confused.

You want me to meet with your therapist? I text to Stone as soon as I get off.

No answer.

THE WEEKEND DOESN'T PASS BY FAST ENOUGH. STONE texts on Saturday to tell me he's not coming back on Sunday but Monday now. But he never answers my questions about Monday's appointment. Typical Stone, but still...

My stomach is a churning pit of anxiety as I sit at the breakfast table, feeding Garnet in a daze.

"Naima? Naima? Did you hear what I said?"

I look over at Cami, who's standing in the kitchen doorway with her Acer laptop in her hands.

"No, I didn't," I apologize. "Could you say it again?"

"I got a job!" she practically yells. "I woke up to the email this morning. One of Stone's friends has this kid named Barron. He's still in his teens, but he's been tapped to head up a new division of GoRobot. It's, like, biotech. Totally top-secret shit. And I got the job! I got the job!"

She sounds so happy. And I should be happy, too, but...
"GoRobot...isn't that in Portland?"

"Well, yes, but that's no big deal."

"A cross-country move is no big deal?" I repeat. "I mean, the other day, you were talking about staying here with us after you graduate, just so you could keep Talia in the same school district."

Cami's shoulders suddenly deflate. "Yeah, I was. But this opportunity seems so good."

"And you say the company's run by a teenager?" I ask.

"A really smart teenager," Cami answers, but sure she can hear how weak that answer sounds.

"I'm not trying to discourage you," I say, gentling my tone. "I'm just saying, don't put all your eggs in one basket. Keep on applying for jobs around here. Maybe you can find something that's a better match. Something in Charlotte where you have a support system."

My advice is solid, I know. It makes sense.

But all the light has disappeared from Cami's face, as she answers, "Yeah, yeah, you're right. I'll keep on looking."

The day doesn't go much better after that. It's an all paperwork Monday which makes it feel like the hours are ticking by particularly slow as I wait for the 2pm appointment.

I keep on checking my phone to see if Stone has called me.

He hasn't. Which only makes me worry more.

But eventually the clock strikes 1:30, and I call out my early goodbyes as I leave for the appointment. I know Stone's plane landed a little earlier this morning, and I'm hoping that maybe he'll be waiting when I hit the lobby of Dr. Nouri's office.

But all the seats in Dr. Nouri's outside lobby are empty, and Stone doesn't show up until the very last minute.

"Hey," I say when he enters the narrow waiting area. He looks like a bull in a suit. And he's glowering like I asked him to come here, not the other way around.

"Hey," he says, taking a seat beside me.

No kiss. No eye contact, aggressive, disassociated or otherwise.

"Is everything—" I start to ask, only to be interrupted by a woman, who looks to be in her forties opening the door.

"Hi, you must be Stone's wife, Naima. I'm Doctor Nouri." She wears her hair in a neat bob and her intelligent eyes crinkle behind designer glasses.

Friendly and capable, I think as we shake hands. I begin to feel a little more at ease as I follow her into her office.

Dr. Nouri doesn't bother with small talk, she gets right down to business. "Stone had some thoughts in his last therapy session. Thoughts he'd like to share with you."

So that's what this was all about. Stone had a breakthrough. My stomach untightens, and I feel even more at ease. His last therapy session was last Wednesday before I suggested he see other people in New York. So this session probably has something to do with his grief breakthrough with Garnet.

"So you have been talking to your therapist, not just sitting here in silence," I say, turning to face Stone.

"Course I have," Stone answers, as if I just accused him of not changing his underwear every day. "That's what you told me to do."

I crook my head, a little amused, because, "You don't always do what I ask you to do."

"Yeah, I do," he answers, his jaw ticking. "Other than going away and not dancing with you that one time, I've done every single thing you ever wanted me to do. And sometimes a few things you were only thinking about."

I open my mouth to argue, only to realize...I can't really think of a time when he didn't actually honor a request. Even the ones I never formally made. Like not self-medicating and spending more time with the baby.

"Thank you," I say, realizing as I say the two words how grateful I am for the work he's put in and the way he's apparently listened to me, even when he doesn't acknowledge it.

"You don't have to thank me," Stone says, shifting irritably in his seat. "You're always looking out for everybody, even when that shit's way above your pay grade. Least I can do is listen and follow through. Especially since we probably wouldn't be together, if you weren't trying to make sure even the people you weren't related to could live their best lives. That's one of the many reasons I'm one-hundred percent in love with you."

My cheeks warm. On one hand these words coming from Stone are a high compliment indeed. On the other, I'd like to edge away from the topic of his supposed love...and the felony-level cover up that led to our current marriage.

"Well, I'm glad you've started sharing with Dr. Nouri," I say to him. Then with a quick glance to her, I ask, "You were saying something about some thoughts Stone was having?"

"I'll let Stone start us off," Dr. Nouri answers with a serene smile.

Stone shifts irritably again, this time turning his huge body to face me. "Yeah, so I've been working real hard on this 'being normal' shit, like you told me to..."

"Actually, I didn't say..."

Stone huffs at the doctor, "See I'm not going to be able to tell her. She likes arguing with me too much."

"I don't like to..." I start to say.

"See?" Stone says jutting a hand at me before I can finish that statement. "She's too argumentative."

"I'm not argumentative! Most of the people I know would claim the exact opposite about me."

"I know, right?" Stone says with an annoyed shake of his head. "I thought once I put a ring on it, you'd calm down. Be that docile social worker Amber and Rock was always talking about. But the ring made it even worse."

I gape at him. Does he mean the ring he forced me to accept before agreeing to clean up Cami's crime scene? But of course, I can't say that aloud.

And before I can come up with a non-legally actionable

defense for myself, Dr. Nouri interjects with, "Perhaps try holding your thoughts until Stone is finished."

I clamp my lips, torn between my dutiful social worker baseline and my churlish need to defend myself against Stone's outrageous accusations. In the end, the social worker wins out.

"Sorry," I mumble. "Please tell me what's on your mind."

"So while I've been fulfilling your request for me to be normal..."

He pauses, obviously waiting for me to prove him right and take the bait. But I keep my tongue locked away behind clenched teeth, making myself be the good listener with Stone than I am with most other people.

"Dr. Nouri and my psychiatrist keep telling me I don't got to worry about taking pills anymore. I grew up believing I was a psycho who didn't know how to do nothing but fight and take out whatever Luca or his father pointed me at. But Dr. Nouri says maybe I was just an abused kid with some messed up scripts and you know, should maybe think about forgiving myself."

Oh, this confession is killing me! I want to say so bad that I agree about him forgiving himself, but instead I nod and take his hand, holding my tongue like I promised.

"So that's what I been doing. Working on my insides. Trying to wrap my head around Rock dying, especially after I lost my shit the first time Garnet called me 'dada'."

Oh, Stone... I think, but don't say. Still, I'm struck by the amazing work he's been doing. I can't wait to tell him that as soon as he's done with his revelation.

"I've been doing that," he said. "And it ain't easy, but you know I'm making progress. And last week I was telling Dr. Nouri all about it, how I was opening up, getting vulnerable and all that shit, not just pushing it all down. I was telling her how I liked the man I was becoming in this relationship with you..."

My heart is practically a melted puddle now, because I couldn't agree more with all his findings. God, I can't wait to encourage the heck out of this new mindset.

"The only thing holding me back now is the fact that I think you might be batshit crazy, and I didn't know how to tell you that. So Dr. Nouri was like, 'I agree. Invite her in. We'll session this shit out.'"

I pause, my hands going limp on top of Stone's fist. "Wait... what? You two brought me in here because you think there's something wrong...with *me*?" I ask, looking between Stone and Dr. Nouri.

"I would like to go on record as disagreeing with much of Stone's terminology, especially the words 'batshit crazy,'" Dr. Nouri says carefully. "And as I've told Stone many times I don't necessarily adhere to the notion of right and wrong when it comes to mental health."

"Yeah, yeah, yeah. Psycho is a strong word. We're all just trying to figure this emotion shit out," Stone says. "But the point is, you've got some head shit of your own to figure out.

This time I lift both hands from Stone's fist. "Okay, *what?*"

A grimace passes over Dr. Nouri's previously serene face. "This is why I advised Stone to have this conversation with both of us and not attempt it on his own. Here is what I think Stone might be trying to say. In the beginning, when your marriage was one of convenience, he knew that you wanted him to leave. It felt like a fact of your relationship."

"Because it was," I answer. "It's not unreasonable to not want to enter into a marriage of convenience—which by the way I didn't really get a say in."

"Yes, we've discussed why his actions most likely made you feel controlled...but has this marriage inconvenienced you in any other way? Kept you from something or someone else?"

"Is this about Amber?" I ask Stone. "I thought we dealt with that. I'm not—"

"No, it ain't about Amber," he answers, cutting me off. "Almost wish it was, then this shit you've got going on wouldn't feel so complicated."

"I'm not even sure what you're referring to, what you think I've done wrong here," I answer.

Stone huffs, then looks over to Dr. Nouri, "I'm going to let you explain it, because I don't think either of you are going to like 'my language' if you let me do the job."

Dr. Nouri must agree with him. "I think Stone has a fear that he needs to address with you," she says, once again serving as his emotion translator. "He feels that the issues in your relationship no longer stem from you wanting him to leave, but instead, *expecting* him to leave."

I crook my head, because, "I don't...I don't understand what you're trying to say?"

"Stone desires to transform your marriage into a loving relationship. Do you have that same desire?"

Here's that question again. *What do you want, Naima? What do you want?*

My heart speeds up, and suddenly I can't answer. I can't even breathe. It feels like I'm on the verge of a panic attack.

"Okay, how about this?" Stone asks when I don't answer. "If I said tomorrow you could have a divorce, no harm, no foul, would you take me up on that?"

My heart skids to a stop, a terrible ache taking bloom. "So you want a divorce?" I ask.

"No, I don't want a fucking divorce. I'm Catholic Italian Mob. You got better chances of breaking out of Guantanamo Bay, than getting me to agree to that shit. But say, I had a stroke or something, and was like, 'yeah, be free, little bird'."

"Then I'd be suspicious, because that doesn't really sound like you." I shake my head, irrationally irritable at the question I can't answer. "Why do you even care what I want anyway? It's never mattered to you before."

"Because I'm in love with you!" Stone roars. "And that's what falling in love with somebody does to a man. Makes him fucking care."

"Stone," Dr. Nouri says, her voice a soft warning.

Stone takes a deep breath through his nostrils and visibly calms himself down, but his voice sounds like it's straining to stay level as he says, "Right now you're sending some real mixed signals. Riding my dick all night, then waking up the next morning and telling me to stick it in some other snatch, instead of saying 'I love you, too,' like a normal wife."

The word normal hits me hard. No, I'm not normal. That's why Rock dumped me, and why Stone eventually will, too.

"I wasn't trying to send you mixed signals," I explain to him. "I was just saying you'd moved awfully fast from being able to have sex again to love."

"We been together for almost a year now. Been banging since December. You're acting like it's been two weeks. And you still haven't answered one of my goddamned questions. It's real simple? Do you want to be in this marriage? Yes or no?"

"Yes, but..."

"Great, me fucking, too," Stone says. "So then, why are you trying to get me to leave you?"

"I'm not trying to get you to leave me," I insist, feeling helpless and attacked. "That's just what people do, eventually. I'm only preparing you and myself for what comes next."

Dr. Nouri leans forward. "Is that what you believe, Naima? That everybody leaves? That all relationships end with one person leaving the other."

"No, I don't think all relationships end that way," I answer, thinking of Luca and Amber, who will probably be together forever now that they've found each other again. Also, my parents whose long-term relationship is so secure, they've made a game out of cheating accusations.

But... "That's how my relationships end. All of them." Something jagged and raw twists through me and a crushing heaviness presses against my heart. "My parents left two years ago—I mean they had their reasons. Good reasons, but I didn't have any other family in New York, and they left me behind. Then my best friend Amber decided to make another go of it with her ex-husband instead of raising her baby with me like she'd promised. And then Rock dumped me..."

I trail off.

But Dr. Nouri picks up my lost thread. "That's a lot of people unexpectedly leaving during a relatively short time period," she observes, her tone thoughtful. "Maybe you felt lonely during that time. A little abandoned. Is that right?"

"Yes, abandoned...I'd invested hardcore in those relationships and ended up with nothing," I answer, my heart constricting. "They all left, with, like, no hesitation. That's what hurt me the most. But you know, I'm not lonely now. I mean, I've got my baby."

"A person who's incapable of walking away from you, at least for several years," Dr. Nouri points out. "But how are you dealing with the people in your life who can walk away? People like your Aunt Mari, and the two girls you've invited to live with you."

"Fine..." I start to insist. But then I remember the conversation with Cami from this morning. How unnecessarily angry I'd felt when she announced that she gotten that dream job in Portland.

Also, how many times had I refused to go to church or any other family event with Aunt Mari? Even though I'd technically moved down here to be closer to her and the rest of my dad's side of the family? "I guess I can be a little withholding. I'm not trying to be."

"I think a lot of people who'd experienced loss on the level you have would be a little hesitant in what is still a relatively new relationship," Dr. Nouri says sympathetically.

I nod. It's the right answer. The professional answer. Perfectly balanced to make me understand my reaction to Stone's profession of love, without feeling ashamed.

"I'm sorry," I find myself whispering to Stone. "I'm sorry I'm like this. Sorry I can't believe your 'I love you' and say it back. I know I've got issues. I wish I didn't. I wish I could act like a normal wife."

"Fuck normal," Stone answers, his face hitching into an ironic smile. "A normal wife never would've married me. Never would've done what you did for Cami and Talia. A normal wife sure as shit wouldn't have stood up to me about the pills. You hold down the fort. You're always there when I want to talk. Plus, you're going to give me a son any day now. So believe me, if I've got to choose between you and normal, it's you every day. I shouldn't have to fight for a love you ain't willing to give. But I'm doing it. And I'll keep on doing it. I don't care how fucked in the head that makes me. I'll keep fighting for you as long as it takes."

Did I really think nothing had truly changed after Stone stopped taking those pills?

Stone's words melt my heart.

But then his face scrunches, all the softness disappearing. "And by the way, you might as well get the thought of me leaving you out your head. I could fuck a thousand broads, and the only one I'd really want to be fucking is you."

He reaches for me, enveloping one of my hands in both of his and bringing them to his mouth. "Love me or don't love me back, I'm staying put either way."

Okay, we just talked about my parents moving to another country, my best friend casually abandoning all the plans we'd made together, my ex-boyfriend dumping me right before he died.

So why is this the moment that breaks me? When Stone kisses my hand, his eyes blazing, like he couldn't be madder at me—or love me more—the flood gates burst open.

"Thank you," I whisper to him, tears streaming out of my eyes. Suddenly I'm so grateful that this rude boar of a man charged into my life and refused to leave. "Thank you for saying that. For being you."

And in the next moment I decide out loud and inside my heart, "I'm going to try to believe, to learn how to trust. For you and Garnet. I'm going to try, too."

CHAPTER THIRTY-FOUR

Before Stone, relationships had always felt like something that happened to me. A boy at church passing me a folded offering envelope note with "I like you," scrawled across the back in pencil. A co-worker I never even considered like that, asking me out to coffee. A man who looked identical to the man who'd just dragged me by gunpoint out of my home inviting me to dinner.

Relationships have always been an opportunity dangled, grasped for, then snatched away.

The session with Stone's therapist reframes everything, though.

Stone's not passing me notes, or asking me out, or inviting me to dinner. He's telling me straight up that he's fallen in love with me. One hundred percent and now he wants me to totally fall in love with him, too.

Will I? Can I?

My mind grinds away at both of those questions over the

weeks that follow. Wage a full out battle between ominous warnings from relationships past and old Naima, the woman who used to be capable of believing in love.

"Our relationship anniversary's coming up next month."

I pause in the middle of buttoning up my work slacks, which are getting a little tight, thanks to all the good Dominican food I've been shoveling. I almost say, "No, we got married in August," but then I realize he's counting from the first time he showed up at my door.

Does he really consider that the start of our relationship? And has it seriously already been a year? The Stone invasion and life takeover still feels like it happened just yesterday somehow.

Not Nice Naima keeps on warning me not to fall, but Old Naima sighs. *You've been together for nearly a year, but it still feels like we just met. Isn't that what happy couples always say? This must be. This must be—*

Stone interrupts before Old Naima can drop the L-bomb. "I already talked to Cami. She says she'll keep an ear out after Aunt Mari puts Garnet down if you want to go out or something?"

I freeze a little at the offer. Stone and I spend plenty of quality time together. Breakfast, dinner, every other weekend, plus lots of walking the dog around the block. And don't even get me started on the magic that happens in the late night hours after everyone else has gone to bed. It's become a problem, truth be told. I had to add a third late afternoon cup of coffee into my rotation this month just to stay awake.

But we've never been out on a date, just the two of us. Which is weird, when I think about it. My relationship with Rock went just the opposite way. Lots of chaste, fun dates at first, until I had to be returned to Luca's condo prison.

I'd thought not having a weird curfew hanging over our heads would bring us closer together, when Luca let me go. But as it turned out, our relationship couldn't hold up under the pressure of day-to-day intimacy without a bunch of fancy restaurants, movies, and dance clubs to pad out our time together.

Would Stone's and my relationship suffer in the opposite way once we introduced dates into it? Could our strange dynamic withstand a full dinner conversation that wasn't broken up with chatter from the patchwork tribe we'd managed to acquire over the course of the year since he showed up on my doorstep?

Old fears start to rise up, threatening to engulf me—but then I remember Dr. Nouri's office. The promise Stone made while kissing my hand. The promise I made about trying.

"Okay," I answer after taking a deep, brave breath. "Sure, why not?"

The phone, Stone keeps charging on top of his dresser starts vibrating and lights up.

"Sure, why not?" Stone throws me a surly look as he picks up the phone. "Real romantic, babe."

He answers his phone, before I can tell him what a big step this feels like for me. "Yeah, whaddya want?" he asks into the phone.

But then the surly look disappears as he says, "Yeah, this is Stanley Ferraro."

Stanley Ferraro Jr....Stone's real name, I remember from the marriage certificate and DMV paperwork I filled out for him. I finish buttoning my pants, but stay right where I am instead of heading downstairs for breakfast.

The conversation doesn't last long. It's basically a series of "yeahs" until Stone ends it with, "Yeah, I'll let everybody know. You don't have to call my ma. Yeah, let me tell her."

Then he hangs up, walks over to the settee, and sits down.

Something's wrong, I sense immediately. Something he doesn't necessarily want to talk about.

But I walk over and sit down next to him anyway. Just letting him know I'm there, as I wait for him to talk.

"My pop's dead. Heart attack," he says eventually.

The words "I'm sorry" don't feel right, given their history, so I ask, "How are you feeling?"

"Like I want to take four pills. Right now. Before I can feel a fucking thing," he replies, his answer instant and frank. "So I don't *have to* feel a fucking thing."

He sits so large and rigid beside me. But when I tug on his arm, he immediately caves. His large body curls around me as I slip my arms around his waist.

"This emotion shit is for the birds," he grouses, holding on to me tight.

"What do you need from me now?" I ask, rubbing his back.

"I want you to come with me to the funeral. But you know, Luca's going to be there. He'll probably bring the wife and the kids. And even if he didn't, you know somebody in the family would break and go squealing to Amber."

"I don't care." My words are both a decision and a suddenly realized truth. "I'll come back to New York with you. Anything you need."

"The baby, too," he says. "And Cami and Talia. They need to see a monster buried. Closure and all that shit."

"If they agree to it, then they'll come, too," I answer. I want to comfort him, to provide him something better than pills, but I don't know if the girls are ready for that.

To my relief, Cami and Talia agree to come up to the funeral at the breakfast table, without even pausing for a few seconds to decide.

"I always wanted to go to New York. See that Statue of Liberty and Times Square," Cami says, reminding me that technically, she was one of those tourists real New Yorkers like me hated so much.

"We're staying in New York, but the funeral will be in New Jersey," I answer. "We'll have to see if we have time to go sightseeing."

"We can go wherever you want," Stone says to Cami, totally contradicting me. Then he asks, "What?" when I shake my head at him.

"You are way more indulgent than I thought you'd be when we first met."

"You think that's indulgent, wait till you see what I'm getting her for her college graduation."

Showing how far she's move past the overly prideful girl she was when she and I first met, Cami asks, "What are you getting me?" Her voice unabashedly excited.

Stone just smirks.

"C'mon Stone, tell us. I wanna know... c'mon," Talia whines over her breakfast plate, proving that even a traumatized kid will eventually return to a baseline setting of whining about anything and everything.

But Stone remains impervious to their pleas, at the breakfast table or on the multi-hour first class plane trip we undertake the following weekend.

And the girls abruptly break off with all the questions about Cami's graduation gift when the car service drops us off in front of a glittering Manhattan skyscraper.

Talia gasps. "This is where you *live*?"

"Technically, the building belongs to the Ferraro Family," Stone answers. "But yeah, I snagged one of the top floor apartments."

Cami just shakes her head. "If I lived here, I'd never come back to Charlotte."

"Yeah, but here don't have all you guys," Stone answers.

He squeezes my hand and murmurs in my ear, "Now I'm at a hundred and ten percent."

Weirdly indulgent, I think as we all enter Stone's luxury apartment building together. *Also, weirdly sweet.*

It's been nearly a year of breakfast and dinners, not to mention all the holiday celebrations and Sunday dinners at our house. But strangely, I never feel as much like a family, as I do when we all walk into the building where Stone's other life takes place. Together.

CHAPTER THIRTY-FIVE

ALL OF THOSE WARM FAMILIAL FEELINGS DISAPPEAR when we walk into the New Jersey funeral home for the wake the next day.

A ton of people have gathered, wearing sharp black suits and designer dresses. Most of the men have black or gray hair, and most of the women are either blonde or the darkest brunette. They speak with thick Jersey accents "like ya heard about." And they all seem to freeze when we step through the door.

"Did you not tell anyone about us?" I ask in a hushed voice, drawing Garnet a little closer at the abrupt silence that follows our entrance.

"I gave Luca a heads up."

"Luca, that's all?"

Before I can point out that he probably should have pre-warned the rest of his large Italian family that we were coming to the funeral with his dead brother's baby in tow, Stone's mother descends on us.

She's one of the older women who's opted for blonde side of the not gray spectrum. She's thin, but her face has that plump dewy cast without a hint of wrinkles, only Botox can provide to a woman her age.

"What's this?" she demands, coming to stand toe to toe with Stone, even though he has a good foot on her.

"Peg, calm down," a taller and even thinner woman comes over to stand behind her. She has long, silky black hair, and bright blue eyes. Luca's mother, I realize, looking at the "best friends" in a new light as she tries to pull Stone's mom away. "Don't want to start anything. It's a wake. C'mon now."

But Stone's mom doesn't budge. "You brought your *moolie*?" she hisses at Stone. "To your own father's wake?"

Okay, I'm not sure what a *moolie* is, but I get the feeling it isn't good.

"Not my *moolie*, Ma. We're married just the same as Luca and Amber," Stone answers, proving that even off anti-depressants, he's the kind of guy who pulls out lighter fluid, instead of quietly trying to putting a small fire out.

"Maybe we could move this to..." I start to suggest.

"You got married?" another relative screeches in the background. "Without telling your mother?"

"And who's the two other kids?" another stage whispers so loud, she might as well be shouting. "They both got Italian eyes, but one of them looks like she's mixed."

"Maybe they had her first and it took the *moolie* this long to get him to agree to marry her," another relative suggest. Way too loudly.

"Then why's the other one white?" the original stage whisperer asks.

"Okay, maybe we shouldn't have come," Cami says, her voice nervous.

Talia's now trying to hide from all the blatant stares behind her sister.

"Can we not be that stereotypical Italian family for maybe one whole second," Luca calls out, appearing like an angel in a bespoke black suit and getting between us and the rest of the crowd.

Proving why he was able to take over the family at such a young age, Luca calms everyone down.

He directs Stone's mother and him to the viewing room to see the body. Then he hands Cami and her sister over to one of his personal bodyguards, telling him to "make these kids a plate and introduce them to Daniella and Luca Jr."

I look in the direction of Luca's adopted daughter and the son I was originally slated to raise with Amber. Luca Jr. is almost two now and a perfect match to his beautiful parents' set. His huge eyes and curls put me in mind of a Botticelli angel. However, unlike those darling cherubs, he's already shed all his baby fat, as if his genes decided something as pedestrian as kid chub wasn't befitting of a boy who was destined to grow up to be movie star gorgeous.

To my surprise, looking at him doesn't hurt like it used to. As I watch him play on a Nintendo Switch with his adopted sister, I no longer see the baby I didn't get to co-raise. Now he's just Amber and Luca's weirdly good-looking kid.

"Thanks," I say to Luca when he's done shutting everyone up and issuing orders. For more reasons than one.

Luca doesn't say you're welcome, though. "Kidnapping you is the gift that just keeps on giving, isn't it?" he asks with an annoyed sneer. "Now I have to figure out how to tell everybody that this is actually my dead cousin's kid without causing another scene."

He glares at the both of us for a few moments. But then his face drops into a silly look, as he tickles Garnet's belly and says, "Yes, you are, aren't you? You're a little friggin' soap opera come to life!"

He reaches out to pull her from my arms, "I'll take her while you go talk to Amber. She's waiting for you in the bathroom."

"Oh, I'm not sure if she'll go to someone she doesn't—"

But I'm cut off by Garnet's happy squeal as she practically jumps into Luca's arms.

Ugh...even babies aren't immune to Luca's ridiculously good looks.

Feeling completely out of my element, I cross through a sea of staring Italians to finally face the friend I've been avoiding for nearly two years.

CHAPTER THIRTY-SIX

Amber's standing at the sinks when I come in, and her head turns in my direction at the sound of my entrance.

"Hey, Amber, it's Naima," I say. Still too trained in dealing with the blind not to announce myself right away.

Amber doesn't answer. And I know it has nothing to do with the fact that she's blind. Amber is basically Daredevil in an always zipperless dress.

She can hear me, smell me, and fight me, easily.

In fact, she looks like she wants to fight me when she finally answers, "I know who you are, even if you seem to have forgotten who am I in the twenty months since you left New York."

"I'm sorry," I say pre-emptively, even though I know that won't stop Amber from lambasting me.

And I'm right about that.

"You didn't return any of my calls or texts, not even one.

And I had to find out from Luca that you had a baby *by Rock* and then, *married* Stone? What the hell, Almonte. I thought you hated him!"

"I did hate him," I concede. "But now I don't anymore."

"Why? Because he was there, available? The latest wrong guy to wander into your life?" Amber demands in that vicious lawyer way of hers. I've heard her use the tone so often with others. But only once before with me. When she predicted Rock's and my relationship would fall apart.

"That's...that's not fair," I answer, trying to find the right words to defend myself and my decisions. God, fighting with Amber is like facing down an even more vicious and particularly articulate version of Not Nice Naima.

"What's *not fair* is my supposed best friend, dropping out of all contact for almost two years!" Amber instantly shoots back. Of course, she has all her words ready to go, locked and loaded. "Me questioning the validity of a relationship that began with Stone *kidnapping you from your home* is *entirely fair*."

She shakes her head in my general direction. "And I see after ditching me, you decided to surround yourself with people who don't question your obviously broken decision maker. Luca told me you and Stone took in two more of your case files."

Her words hit me like slaps. "You don't know anything about this. Anything about us."

"So what? You didn't case file him?" Amber asks, closing in for the kill. "Didn't see a broken toy and pull another 'oh no, look, he's so wounded! I must fall in inappropriate love with him, stat!'? Because according to Luca, the last time he saw you and Stone in a room together, you were kneeing him in the crotch for calling you a lesbian."

"People change, Amber," I answer between clenched teeth. "He's changed."

"Nobody changes that much," Amber answers with a dismissive roll of her neck. "If they did, I wouldn't be here with you having the same damn conversation about Stone that I had with you about Rock."

"Stone isn't anything like Rock."

"Oh yes, I know he isn't anything like Rock," Amber answers, pointing both her index fingers in the air. "Rock was an almost sane choice under the circumstances. I have no idea what would possess you to..."

Okay, Amber's smart and one of the most capable people I know. When it comes to most things, Amber's usually right. But she's not right about this. And suddenly I can't take her *lawyerier* than thou attitude anymore.

"Shut up!" I scream at her. "Shut up. You have no idea who Stone really is, the lengths he's gone to, the way he's up-ended his life..."

It feels like I'm realizing my next words at the same time I'm saying them. "Stone is a good man. Better than Rock even. At least he's authentic. At least he loves me flaws and all. He one hundred percent loves me. He told me that, and he continues to tell me that every day, even though I'm so messed up, so scared to make myself vulnerable and get left, that I still haven't figured out how to believe him. Or to say it back. But you know what, Amber?"

I roll my neck even more fiercely than she did when she was trying to dismiss me. "I'll say it to you. I'll say it proud right here and now. Stone isn't a case file, and this isn't Stockholm. I love him. I one hundred percent love him. And I'm sorry for not telling you about us earlier, but I'm not going to stand here and let you drag his name through the mud."

By the time I'm done yelling, the "know it all lawyer" look has faded from Amber's face.

"Oh, Nai..." she says, her voice going soft as a flower. "Do you really? Do you really love him?"

I study her sharply, but the judgmental expression has disappeared along with her disapproving tone. All I see is my best friend. Amazed at the words that just came out of my mouth.

"Yeah, yeah, I do," I answer, a new lump forming in my throat. Then I admit to my best friend. "And it scares the hell out of me."

"I get it." Amber does that graceful thing where she makes it seem like an exploratory swipe of her arm is actually an intended move all along, and pulls me into a hug. "Believe me, I get it more than most."

I can hear her and Luca's own epic romance in her wry tone.

"I still don't get it," a gruff voice says behind us. "But I'll take it."

Amber and I draw apart to see Stone, filling up the restroom's doorway. "Came in to tell you two broads to quiet down. This wake's already got enough drama without you two getting in a fighting match."

"Sorry," I mumble.

But Amber resets right back to Super Lawyer and asks, "You really love my best friend, Stone? This isn't just a bunch of fucked up psychology wrapped in a marriage license?"

"Well it ain't *not* psychology," he answers, shrugging his head to the left. "But it is love. One hundred and twenty percent now. At least for me."

He turns from Amber and looks down at me, his eyes asking questions that don't make it all the way to his mouth. Did he hear me right? Do I really love him, too?

"It's love for me, too," I answer his unspoken questions, my voice soft but not tentative. Not tentative at all. "One hundred percent. I'm all in."

And would you look at that? The sky doesn't come crashing down. The funeral home doesn't collapse on all of our heads.

Stone just lets the door swing close behind him and pulls me into his arms. "Thank fuck. But you know I'm going to wanna hear you tell me that again. A lot more times. And at least once, while I'm fucking you good."

My cheeks warm. "Okay," I agree quickly to get him off the subject.

But apparently Stone doesn't care about Amber's nearby presence, he continues to stare down at me, his eyes burning with hunger. Hunger that is all for me.

Wow...I've been getting ignored in rooms with Amber for the majority of my life. Even Rock unconsciously stared at her, like she was a painting when we are all in the same space. But Stone acts as if Amber's presence is barely on his radar, as he says, "Promise? I will drag your ass in for weekly marriage counseling with Dr. Nouri if you try to take it back. I swear to God."

"I promise," I answer with a laugh, suddenly also not caring so much about Amber being in the room.

"Good," he says, looking deep into my eyes. "Amber, I suggest you give us the room unless you wanna hear what's about to happen next."

Stone's already kissing me by the time he locks the door behind her. And the next day at the funeral, all the terrible stage whisperers have something new to gossip about.

Not just that Stone married the mother of his dead twin's baby, but also that they heard we "*did it*" at his father's wake.

All the gossip is totally true. Just like my love for the man who survived the cruel father we put in the ground that day.

And somehow that makes me feel like Teflon as all the gossip and stares bounce right off me. Stone's crass and bullish and pretty much nothing on the list of qualities I wanted in a husband.

But he's everything I need.

CHAPTER THIRTY-SEVEN

Despite us kicking his wife out of the bathroom and giving the entire Ferraro clan something to gossip about, Luca invites us back to his house after the funeral.

They've moved out of the Tribeca penthouse Luca jailed us in when he was trying to convince his ex-wife to give their relationship a third chance. Now they live in a huge compound in Alpine, New Jersey that makes our house in North Carolina look like a tiny shack.

But the comparisons stop there. I'm nothing but happy for Amber as her sweet daughter proudly shows off their open plan first floor to Talia and Cami, explaining how the entire estate was designed for her mom. Each wall is differently textured to make touch navigation easier for Amber, and the floors are heavily dynamic, with small bumps at the boundaries of every living section.

What a dream house for Amber. Suddenly I'm not just resigned, but glad she chose Luca.

I'm also glad our families get along. Amber and I end up talking on the couch, like the old days, while the kids play with Cami, and Luca and Stone talk business over whiskeys and beer.

"I don't have to ask if you're really happy, I can plainly see," I tell my best friend.

"Yeah, I am," she agrees, with a Cheshire cat smile, like she's gotten away with something. "Did I ever think this was how I'd end up using my law degree? No. But now I can't imagine my life any differently."

"I know how you feel," I tell her. "Two years ago, I never would have guessed I could be happy with Stone. I thought I hated him, in fact. But now, all I want is to stay in this fairytale with him forever."

I laugh at myself, but stop when a weird expression comes over her face. "What?" I ask.

"Nothing," she answers. "It's just, I don't think we've ever had a conversation like this. About your happiness. About what you want. Oh, wait, we did. And it turned into a huge argument, because the one time you fought back against one of my plans, I acted like you'd gone crazy."

"We don't have to talk about this," I say, shaking my head.

"No, I think we do. I've had a lot of time to think about where our friendship went wrong over the last two years. And if I'm being honest, it wasn't just you deciding to up and leave. It was me letting you being a good friend to me, but never the other way around."

"That's not true. You helped my parents with their landlord suit," I point out.

"Like a decade ago!" Amber counters with a laugh. "And I helped your parents. Not you. You were always there for me, no matter what, but when you needed me, I wasn't there. In fact..."

Tears suddenly pool in Amber's usually hard eyes. "I told you to go away. I was such a selfish idiot. No wonder you stopped talking to me after Rock died."

"No, you weren't a selfish idiot. You were moving on with your life. And that forced me to come out of the limbo I was living in and get on with my life, too. I was pretty bitter about it back then. But girl, trust me. You going back to Luca was the best thing that ever happened to me. Please don't cry."

Amber sniffs and wipes at her tears. "You know, I didn't see it at first, but no wonder Stone decided to become a *caporegime* down South. He obviously knows a good woman when he unemotionally observes her."

"Capo-what now?" I ask.

"Capo for short. It's like a rank they use for the heads of offshoot branches of a mafia operation," Amber explains, but then she frowns. "Stone didn't tell you this? He told Luca he wanted to stay down south and run his own operation last August. Luca gave him a year to get it up and running, and the plan is for Stone to move down there full time in August. Anyway, it'll be a lot less exciting but also a lot less dangerous than enforcer work."

"No...he didn't tell me," I answer as my stomach drops with the realization that Stone always intended to live full time with me and Garnet, even when he was dragging me into our courthouse wedding. "He doesn't like talking about that kind of stuff with me."

"Oh, a lot of them don't," Amber says with an understanding nod. "If your wife isn't also your mob lawyer, there's really no reason not to leave work at work when you come home in this line of business."

She changes the subject, but warm, loving feelings continue to rush over me as she continues to talk.

Stone always believed in the long term future of our relationship. From the very beginning, before and after he stopped abusing pills.

My heart flooding with feelings, I look over my shoulder at the man who will officially be the Ferraro's North Carolina-based capo after August. I am so grateful and so awed.

Because he believes in us. And now I do, too.

As if sensing my eyes, Stone suddenly looks up. But instead of smiling at me from afar, like any other guy would, he leaves his conversation with Luca without a word of explanation.

By the time he makes it across the room, I've stood up, like a marionette being lifted on strings.

"Hey, Naima," he says, stopping in front of me.

"Hey," I answer, suddenly feeling self-conscious.

"You alright?"

"I'm fine," I answer. I look down at my feet, then back up at him. "I just love being here with you and the girls. I just love...us. One hundred percent."

He looks at me for a long, warm moment. "One twenty percent," he says.

Then he kisses me when I giggle. In front of Amber. In front of Luca. In front of the whole world.

CHAPTER THIRTY-EIGHT

THINGS HUM ALONG HAPPILY AFTER WE RETURN TO North Carolina. I start texting every day with Amber again. Like the last two years of estrangement was merely a bad dream and totally over now.

And Stone continues to play the part of an amazing husband and exemplary father, both surrogate and adopted. He helps Cami make a plan for moving and living in Portland for her new job. Then he surprises me and Aunt Mari with the announcement that he's chartered a plane to take us and whoever else we wanted to the Dominican Republic for Christmas.

Life is perfect. Our relationship is perfect. I've never been happier.

Which is why I try to ignore it when he comes back from a trip to New York the weekend before our anniversary dinner suddenly not feeling up for anything.

"I'm tired," he says, instead of kissing me, when he climbs into bed. "I can wife you, but I'm not up for much else."

"That's okay," I answer. "I can wait until a night when you're not tired."

"Thanks, babe," he says with a tired smile.

He falls asleep instantly, but I spend a long time lying there in the dark, repeating what he said to me in Dr. Nouri's office. And trying not to worry.

However, that not tired night never comes. And though Stone's back in town, it feels like I never see him. He starts coming home, so late I'm already asleep, but waking up so early, I don't see him until we're sitting across from each other at our crowded breakfast table. Which is not the place to ask about where he was all night and what he was doing there.

I love Stone and I believe in us, but the old fears start nibbling at the back of my brain, threatening my newfound trust that a relationship involving me could actually work out.

But then something crazy happens the morning of our anniversary. I find myself in the agency's bathroom, staring at a small plastic stick.

It has a baby head on it.

I'm pregnant, again.

This time with Stone's baby.

I can't believe it. For like fifteen minutes I haven't been able to believe it. I've just sit there open-mouthed, gaping at the stick, like I stared at my wedding ring, not believing it.

I might have sat there for another fifteen disbelieving minutes if not for the sudden buzz from the Fitbit smartwatch Stone got me for Christmas, alerting me that I've got a text from Amber. ***"Have any plans tonight? Need to talk!"***

I grab my personal phone out of the purse I'd just stuffed a couple of new toddler diapers into this weekend, because Garnet's gotten so big.

She won't even be two when the next baby arrives though, I think as I type back, ***"Sorry. Relationship anniversary dinner with Stone. Raincheck for tomorrow? Is it important?"***

"Yes, just finished that J.R. Ward book you recommended to me on Audible. Want to talk. Way more important than your anniversary."

I laugh. And for a moment I'm tempted to share the big news. But I guess Stone and me really have leveled up our relationship. I used to tell Amber everything first, but now I can't imagine not sharing it with Stone before anyone else. And maybe this will clear up some of the weird distance I've felt between us over the past week.

"I'll beg for your forgiveness tomorrow, girl. Now start the second one. It's even better. Mary and Rhage are my favorite couple."

A FEW MORE TEXTS WITH AMBER AND A DOMINICAN blowout from Aunt Mari later, I arrive at the restaurant in my going out dress. Much like my work clothes it fits a little tighter these days, but now I know why. And I can't wait to tell Stone.

He's already sitting at a table when I get there with two glasses of wine. And even though, I won't be able to enjoy the drinks he ordered, I beam at him as I cross the room.

He doesn't stand up when I approach the table like Rock used to, or even say hi. But who cares? "Hey you!" I greet him enthusiastically as I carefully set the purse with the pregnancy test on one of the empty seats, then grab and pull out my own chair.

"You're late. I said seven."

"Oh..." I look at my Casio watch. He's right it's like, 7:15. "Sorry. I didn't mean to keep you waiting."

"Well, you did. Better figure out what you want to order before the waiter comes back," he says, picking up his own menu.

I'm starving, but I don't pick up the menu, which is waiting a lot more patiently than Stone on top of my place setting.

Instead I study my husband, trying to figure out the reason for his surlier than usual mood. I'm aware Stone can be a general about time, but there's something off about him as he scans the menu with an irritated look...

"Did something happen today?" I ask him.

"Yeah, I showed up here on time and you didn't," he answers.

"Something other than that?" I ask, trying to keep both my voice and my emotions level.

Stone doesn't answer.

And that makes me frown even harder, as a new gut-wrenching suspicion makes it to the top of my hypothetical list. "Stone, look at me."

Without any hesitation, Stone lowers the menu and looks at me. "What?"

Just like I suspected, his eyes aren't blazing with fire. They're cold. Almost dead.

"Are you on something tonight?" I ask, my heart chilling over.

Stone doesn't answer. But that's answer enough.

Anxiety clutches at my throat and something heavier presses against my heart. "Stone," I say. "Why?"

I need to know what happened. What major event would make him turn back to his pill bottle when everything was going so well. I reach across the table for his hand.

But before I can get to it, he picks back up the menu. Like choosing an appetizer is way more important than telling me why he's decided to go back on mood-altering drugs. Ones I'm fairly sure his "Stone is learning to trust himself" therapist didn't prescribe.

"Stone," I say, grabbing on to the top of his menu. "We need to talk about this—"

"Jesus fucking Christ. No we don't! We don't have to talk about this! I bought you a house. Nice car. That'd be enough for most women. But not you. Every fucking thing, you got to run it into the ground. Nothing's ever enough for you."

I stare at him, aghast. Not just because he's yelling so loud that half the restaurant seems to be looking at us now, but also because, "That's not true."

"Why? Because you being a nagging bitch doesn't fit into the 'hey, look at me, I'm a nice social worker' story you're always trying to push?"

Did I say just half the restaurant before? Nearly everyone's looking at us now. And a waiter who seemed to be headed in our direction to take our order, abruptly cuts left, now avoiding our table at all cost.

Humiliation crawls through me, but I keep on trying to get through to him, to drag him out of that cotton. "Stone, I'm just trying to figure out why you would—"

"See, you can never let shit go," he interrupts, his words coming out like arrows through his clenched teeth. "Get it through your head, I don't want to talk about it."

"Don't want to talk about it," I repeat. "But I thought that's what we did these days. Talked, communicated...with one hundred percent love."

I search his eyes, desperate to find any hint of the man who so passionately argued our case in his therapist's office. "Remember our big breakthrough?"

For a moment, Stone falters. But then his face resets to hard. "Fuck Dr. Nouri. Fuck talking all the stupid time, just to raise a kid who ain't even mine. Rock's dead. Not me."

It's like every moment of doubt, every single fear I've ever had about our relationship has suddenly combined like Voltron to bring this nightmare to life.

"Stone..." I whisper, my heart begging for him not to be serious. For him to wake me up, and kiss me and say, "Happy anniversary," like he did this morning.

"You know what? I'm so sick of this," he says instead of Happy Anniversary. And instead of waking me up, he throws down his napkin. "I'm done with you, Naima. Call yourself a ride home. I can't do this pretend shit with you anymore."

With that, he gets up from the table. And I realize he's actually planning to leave me here in the restaurant before we've even had a chance to order.

"Are you serious?" I ask, standing up myself to grab his arm. "What happened to a hundred percent?"

He tenses, his bicep expanding under my hand. "Look, I thought I could do this. Raise a kid that wasn't even mine. Put up with you. But I was deluding myself. We both were. I think we always knew this wasn't going to work out."

"Wasn't going to work out?" My heart skitters as his doomsday prediction, so close to the one I used to carry, even after we started having sex. But then remembering how many times we uttered I love you in New York, I remind him, "Stone, I'm your wife. The mother of your children. You can't just call this off—"

I'm wrong about that. Stone proves how easily he can just call it off in the next moment, when he yanks his arm away and continues toward the door. Like he can't get away from me fast enough.

I watch him go, reeling with a conflicting urge to both scream and throw up. In the end, I settle for standing there frozen. Still not believing what just happened, long after Stone disappears out the restaurant's front door.

We haven't paid for the drinks Stone ordered. That's the only reason I don't run after him. Though Stone is apparently A-OK with both causing a scene, and stomping out of restaurant without paying, I'm not. Unfortunately, I only have a single $20 in my wallet, and this seems like the kind of place that charges at least two digits for a glass of wine.

Too Nice Naima, I think as I sit back down to wait to give someone my credit card...and try not to cry.

CHAPTER THIRTY-NINE

DESPITE THE ARGUMENT, AND THE APP I HAVE TO fumble through for a ride home, I'm sure this is some kind of misunderstanding.

Stone might have left the restaurant, but he didn't really leave me. I just know it.

Except I'm wrong.

Aunt Mari and Cami meet me at the door, their faces the same kind of stricken.

"He just came barging in, saying he couldn't do this anymore," Cami tells me.

"Yelling at the top of his lungs," Aunt Mari adds. "He woke me and the baby! It took me a good minute to calm her down. By the time I was done, he was slamming out the door with a bag full of his stuff."

"Luckily Talia didn't hear," Cami says casting a mournful look towards the room they share. "But I don't understand. Did something happen between you two?"

"Yeah, what did you say to him?" Aunt Mari asks, assuming this is somehow my fault.

But it isn't. At least I don't think it is...

Rock's sudden dumping of me chimes like death knell in the back of my head.

"I'm sorry," I say to them, over the bell's ominous chime. "He just...he just left." My voice gives out, and "left," comes out of my mouth as little more than a choke.

Then I rush up the stairs without saying anything else. What else can I say? Stone was here, and now he's gone.

I was so excited about telling him that I was pregnant tonight, but we never even made it past the first course.

The room is half empty when I walk in. No more suits in the closet. No more overnight bag sitting on the suitcase rack. He didn't bother to close any of the drawers he yanked open while packing his bags, so now I can see clearly how empty he left them.

He's gone...Oh God, he's really gone. And I'm still not sure why.

I wake up in my going out dress the next morning, to the sound of rain pounding against the windows. North Carolina's first spring rain. They always make spring rain sound so airy and cute. But the world outside the bedroom looks miserable. And the darkest gray.

Like my mood put in a special order with Mother Nature.

In the distance I hear the baby calling out, "Dada! Dada!"

screaming it, because we're off routine. Usually Stone gets her up in the morning. By now, he's usually sexed me, gotten in a work out, and grabbed a bottle of breastmilk for her from downstairs.

I need to get up. Go to her.

But I don't. I just lie there wondering how...why... I let myself get played like this again. Gave yet another person my all, only to get dumped.

Too Nice Naima...you stupid, stupid idiot.

"Dada! Dada!" Garnet cries out.

Okay, okay, Almonte. You're not some young girl, living in a rom com. You've got a baby and a job and you've got to get up.

I haul myself out of bed, both my body and heart aching. It feels like I'm dead...but walking around anyway.

That walking dead feeling never quite goes away as I drag myself through my work day.

Amber texts to confirm our J.R. Ward book club talk, and I text back that I'm busy at work.

The "I told you so" part of me says I should tell her she was right in her first assessment of Stone's and my relationship, then ask her for recommendations for divorce lawyers who are just as vicious as her, but licensed in North Carolina.

But the Naima I was trying to be is just too sad to do anything more than get through the day.

Which is why my heart slams into the front of my chest

when I come home to find a dark Cadillac, sitting in front of our house. Oh, God, he's back!

Not even bothering to grab my purse from the passenger seat, I rush into the house.

Only to find two men in dark suits, nodding to Aunt Mari politely as she pours them coffee.

"Thank you, ma'am," one of them says. He's young, tall and built, while the older guy sitting across him is short and wiry.

"We surely appreciate it," he says, eyeing Aunt Mari with another kind of appreciation.

She eyes him right back. "You're welcome. And call me Mari, please."

"What's going on?" I demand, too confused to be polite.

The older guard stops making flirty eyes with Aunt Mari to answer, "We just wanted to knock on the door to introduce ourselves, seeing us how we'll be watching the house from our car until further notice. Mari was kind enough to invite us in for some coffee."

"Watching the house?" I repeat. "You mean, like guards?"

"Yeah, exactly like that," he answers. "So if any of you are going anywhere, just come out and tap on the window. One of us will go with you. You should let Camille know that, too?"

"I sure will," Aunt Mari promises him, setting a carton of half-and-half on the table. "And that will come in so handy when I'm getting the groceries."

"Aunt Mari!" I say.

"What?" she asks. "You try carrying in enough groceries to feed a family of six. Eight now that Nick and Joey will be joining us."

"Oh, you don't have to feed us, ma'am," the younger one says.

"Handsome men are not allowed to call me ma'am. *Mari*, I insist," she tells him, like this is all some kind of joke.

Before he can respond, I demand to know, "Why are you here? We never needed guards before."

"Ah..." the two men exchange quick glances. "Extra security measures while Stone's out of town."

"He's out of town?" I ask, alarmed because he'd made a big deal out of the fact that he wouldn't have to return to New York until July on the plane ride back.

"Yeah, he had some business," the older one answers, his expression a bit wary.

"Do you know when he'll be back?" I swallow down all sorts of pride to ask, "If he'll be coming back here?"

"Stone doesn't share his personal calendar with us," he says with an apologetic look. "Maybe you should ask him. You could send him a text or something."

I try that as soon as they leave, but receive no answer. And when I pick up my phone to check my messages the next morning there's a "Not Delivered" and a circled exclamation mark next to my question.

"It's not delivering," I say, holding the phone up to Nick and

Joey, when I come out of the house for work. I'm still not sure which one is which. "Do you have another number for him?"

Another exchanged look. Then instead of answering, the older one says, "We'll have to get back to you about that."

Something breaks inside me and I ask harshly, "So he doesn't want to be with me anymore, but he sent you guys to protect me?"

The older one just looks at me blankly, like I'm talking in Greek.

"Don't follow me," I tell them before stomping away. I know it's petty, and it's not their fault that Stone did what everyone does to me.

But I'm not going to lie. It hurts. It hurts so much.

CHAPTER FORTY

ALL MY TEXTS TO STONE FAIL TO SEND, AND I GET A "Not in Service" message when I try to call. Nick and Joey honor my request not to be followed. But a few days into my supposed freedom, I notice a dark car with tinted windows in my rearview. And I sight the same car, sitting across the street from the agency when I come out at the end of the day.

I know it's one of Stone's men in my gut, and I try to cross the street to ask him the same questions Nick and Joey refused to answer. But he speeds away as soon as I step off the curb.

I hate this. Hate Stone for claiming to love me, then doing what I knew he would from the start. When my parents left, I threw myself into work. When Amber killed the plan, I went back to my real life job again, grateful to wade through all the backed up case files. When Rock dumped me and died soon after, I transferred all of my attention to finding a new job in a new state, and beginning a new phase of my life with my unborn baby.

But this time, none of my old coping mechanisms make a dent in my sadness. Not throwing myself into my job. Not trying to focus on Garnet. In fact, it feels like the harder I work to accept his leaving, the more I ache for him to come back.

Why did he do this? I keep asking myself. *Why did he go back on the pills and ruin everything?*

Somehow I drag myself through the rest of the week, but when the weekend comes around, I just give out.

I thought getting dumped by Rock was bad, but this is on a whole other level. Without a job to go to, I can't find a reason to get out of bed. No more tears left to cry. No more give left to give. I'm too hollowed out to do anything but stare at the monitor.

"Dada! Dada!" Garnet cries out, making it even worse. Even after several days, she refuses to get with the new feeding program. Or forget the man who used to deliver her morning bottle.

Eventually Aunt Mari takes over. "Ssh, *mija! Titi* is here, and I've got your bottle," she says in Spanish on the other side of the monitor. "It's okay. Everything is okay. Your *mai* and *pai* are having some trouble and that is making her a little sad."

Did I say I had no more tears left to cry? Not true. Not true at all. I find that out when I begin weeping at Aunt Mari's words.

It feels both like the whole world has stopped...and that time is rushing by too fast for me to catch up.

If I was living out a romcom, I might have spent the whole

day in bed. Eating ice cream and crying over a man that did me wrong. But I'm lactose intolerant and Dominican aunties are the worst.

Aunt Mari makes sure the toddler she still calls "the baby" is happy and fed. But she leaves me in my room to starve. And she must have put Cami and Talia under strict commands not to visit me, too. The rain stops and the sun sets without one person coming to my door.

But when I finally come downstairs late in the evening to root around for something to eat and drink, guess who's sitting there? Aunt Mari, big as day, at the kitchen table.

Cami's there, too, eating straight from a bag of Doritos while obeying Aunt Mari's hard and fast rule that food only be eaten at the table.

"Oh, *mija*, what happened to the blowout I gave you? You look like you just got done whoring at the docks!" she tells me upon seeing me, with the affectionate tone only a Dominican auntie can pull off.

"What are you two still doing up?" I ask, not bothering to act happy to see them.

Usually on a Saturday night, Cami would be out with her boyfriend and Aunt Mari would be snoring under a sleeping mask, thanks to St. Lunesta.

"Well, we noticed you were kinda sad..." Cami begins carefully over her chip bag.

"So we decided to wait down here until you came down for something to eat, then pounce and do an intervention," Aunt Mari finishes in a much harsher tone.

Then proving she really doesn't know the difference between an intervention and an interrogation, she demands, "What happened? What did you say to your man to make him go and stay away so long?"

"Maybe it wasn't her fault." Cami waves a bright orange chip as she comes to my defense. "He's the one who packed up all his stuff and wouldn't even tell any of us why!"

Aunt Mari dips her head, her eyes going as intent as a telenovela heroine finally figuring out that her identical twin sister is really a duplicitous schemer, who's trying to steal her man. "He's probably decided to go live with whatever *cuero* he was keeping back in New York."

"What's a *cuero*?" Cami asks.

At the same time I demand to know, "Why do you think he has a mistress?" Great, this is exactly what I needed. Another possible scenario to obsess over.

"A *cuero* is a slut, Camille," Aunt Mari answers Cami in an educational tone. "In this case, the kind of woman that fools around with a married man, knowing good and well he has a wife at home. And as for why I think that..."

She turns back to look at me, her eyes judgmental and all-knowing. "Of course, he was going somewhere else to get his needs met on those days he was away in New York. That's what men do! That's why you have to put more effort into your appearance, *mija*. Straighten your hair and keep it that way. Wear more makeup. Make yourself beautiful, like I keep on telling you!"

Cami, who's wearing her hair in two messy afro puffs squints at Aunt Mari as she points out, "Straight hair and makeup don't make you beautiful or keep somebody from leaving you."

"It helps!" Aunt Mari insists, her voice pitching high with outrage. "I mean, look at her!"

Cami glances over at me, and backs down with a cringe.

Yeah, I imagine the slept in blowout and wrinkled pajamas look isn't one of my best.

"I'm sorry. I'm sorry I left you two to deal with Garnet today," I tell them, feeling like an f-up in every way.

"It wasn't any problem," Cami assures me.

At the same time Aunt Mari says, "You *should* be sorry! Why are you all day in the house moping, when you should be on the first plane to New York to get your man? Whoever that other woman is, I bet she isn't Dominican. That means you can beat her ass!"

"Tia Mari!" Cami and I gasp at the same time, our mouths dropping open wide.

"What? I am just saying if it was me, I would be at the Vietnamese salon with my cousins, getting my nails done up nice and sharp..." Aunt Mari answers, sweet voiced until she finishes with, "so I could scratch that *cuero's* eyes out!"

Cami leans back in her seat, her expression totally impressed. "Forget Nicky and Joey. If anyone ever tries to cross me, I'm coming to you."

"You better," Aunt Mari says, pointing at her. But then her razor sharp gaze swings right back to me. "And as for you, *mija*..."

"As for me, nothing!" I cut her off, swiping a hand across my body. "That's not how life works. I can't just beat up the reasons Stone left me. Even if one of them is walking around on two legs..."

At the thought of the hypothetical woman Stone might have replaced me with, my anger fades, leaving a sad bitterness behind. I bet she's perfect. Perfect and normal and easy. Just like Rock wanted.

"I'm sad...really sad," I tell Aunt Mari and Cami. "But there's nothing I can do. He's obviously going through something. Something I can't fix. Something he's no longer interested in fixing."

"Nothing you can do?" Aunt Mari repeats. She waves a hand at Cami. "Do you think if this one had said the same thing about getting back her sister, she'd be sitting here right now? Eating junk food she didn't pay for, even though she barely picked at the *pollo guisado* I made for dinner?"

Cami freezes, then puts down the bag with a guilty look, before trying to defend me to Aunt Mari.

"You have to understand. Naima's not like us," she says, casting me a sympathetic look. "She doesn't know how to fight for stuff. Plus, she has a kid to think about. She can't just get on a plane and tell Stone he has to come back. That's just not who she is. It's not in her nature."

Cami is exactly right, but her words shrivel something inside of me. No, I'm not the type to gather all my cousins to fight over a man. I tend to play a more sympathetic role with the people I love, encouraging and nurturing them, then finding it within myself to understand when they leave.

And Stone's left me. Despite the promises he made to me in his therapist's office, he left. There's nothing I can do about it. Only an old school thinker like Aunt Mari would blame a mother for making do the best she can with the cards she's been dealt instead of getting on a plane, like some kind of desperado.

But something about Cami's pitying assessment of my character doesn't sit well with me. "Do you really think I'm that weak?" I ask her. "Like, I'm completely incapable of defending myself or the people I love?"

Cami quickly looks away, too polite to answer my question. But Aunt Mari says, "Well, we're not sitting in your apartment right now, are we? And from what I can see, Stone's been calling the shots in your relationship this whole time. He doesn't care what you want, and I guess you don't either. Because you've already given up."

With an aggrieved, huff, Aunt Mari snags the bag of Doritos off the table. "You're right, Cami girl. She just don't have it in her to fight for her man."

All my defenses go up at her words. "I shouldn't...I shouldn't have to fight for somebody who doesn't want to be in a relationship with me—"

A sudden memory stops me cold in that moment.

I shouldn't have to fight for a love you ain't willing to give. But I'm doing it. And I'll keep on doing it. I don't care how fucked in the head that makes me. I'll keep fighting for you as long as it takes.

Stone....he'd said that to me. The exact right words to get me to believe in him. To believe in us.

Hot tears spring to my eyes. I can be a bitter woman. Sometimes it feels like I'm all sugar on the outside with a sour nugget. But in that moment, disgust replaces my bitterness. And the disgust isn't directed at Stone—I'm disgusted with myself.

He fought for me for months and months. And when he dragged me into Dr. Nouri's office, he was nowhere close to backing down.

But when he pushed me away, like I did him all those months, did I fight? No....

I know. I know in my gut and my heart that there's something wrong with Stone. A reason he's back on his pill crutch. But instead of fighting to figure out what made him fall off the wagon, I went back to work. And instead of dragging him out of the cotton, I wasted a whole day of my weekend holed up in my room, feeling sorry for myself.

But that all ends now.

"Give me that! I need something for the road," I say, snatching the bag of Doritos out of Aunt Mari's hands.

"No, don't eat *that* when there's some perfectly good dinner available!" Aunt Mari snatches the bag back from me, as if I'm a child who's accidentally opted for rat poison.

But then she stops and asks, "Hold on, where are you going?"

"To get my man back!" I declare. "If he doesn't want to be with me, I don't care. I'm his wife and he's my husband, and it's going to take more than an embarrassing restaurant fight to get rid of me!"

CHAPTER FORTY-ONE

"Are you serious?" Cami asks. "Are you really flying to New York right now?"

"Yes, she is," Aunt Mari answers for me, her voice practically singing with approval. She hops out of her seat. "But hold on, let me warm you up a plate. You can eat it on the way to the airport!"

Okay, I can tell as hard as Aunt Mari was being with me, it probably killed her to leave me in my room all day without once offering of food. But as I wait in the living room for her to bring a bowl out, it feels like I have a revving engine inside of me.

"What's taking so long?" I call back into the kitchen after what seems like an eon has passed.

"Just need about ten more minutes. It's still heating up on the stove!" Aunt Mari calls back.

What, seriously? "Can't you just heat it up in the microwave?"

"Those microwave heat rays are full of cancer. I give you that, you'll be dead less than a year after you get your man back."

"I am really, really sure that's not true," I tell her.

"Radiation!" Aunt Mari yells, like she's a medical scientist, stating facts, not an old lady set in her ways.

I'm about to tell her that's alright, I'll just pick something up at the airport, when a knock sounds on the door. "Pizza delivery!" a squeaky voice calls from the direction of the front door. I immediately recognize it as Gino the third, the grandson of the original Gino.

We've gotten to know this particular pizza delivery guy well in the months since Cami and Talia moved in. I'm fairly sure he has a crush on Cami, though he's barely just graduated high school, and still has a lot of squeaking in his voice, unlike the academic baritone of the T.A. she's been dating since March.

Mari sticks her head out of the kitchen. "You ordered a pizza?" she asks Cami, in the same tone of voice, prosecutors use to interrogate suspects accused of heinous crimes on the stand.

"No!" Cami insists, even though I can see Gino the third through the peephole, big as day.

"Uh...the guys sitting outside said it was okay to come straight up to the door," he says, smiling at me nervously, on the other side of the magnified glass.

"Maybe it was Talia," Cami says, wringing her hands. "I thought she was asleep, but she was playing on my phone before bed, she might have triggered later delivery on the app..."

"What are you two trying to say about my *pollo guisado*?" Aunt Mari demands, spreading her arms.

No worries I decide as I open the door on their argument. This unexpected pizza order is a God send. Now I'll have something to take with me to the...

The word "airport" dies inside my mind when I see that it's not just Gino standing on our porch.

There's also a man, dressed all in black. And he has a gun with a silencer attached, pointed straight at our high school delivery boy.

"I'm sorry!" he squeaks, his eyes terrified. "He said he'd kill me if I didn't do everything he says."

Cami accused me of having no natural instinct for defending myself or the people I love. But in an instant, I find out she was wrong.

"Run!" I scream at Aunt Mari and Cami, throwing my entire body into closing the door in the killer's face.

I'm not quick enough though. The assassin tosses Gino aside and jams his foot into the door. "Let me in, bitch. Or I'm really going to make your death painful."

"Run!" I yell over my shoulder at Aunt Mari and Cami. "Call 9—"

I break off when the man forcibly shoves the door open, sending me stumbling back.

Cami screams, "Pass me a knife!" somewhere in the background.

"No, no, run... save yourselves!" I yell back at them, even as I scoot backwards away from the gunman on my hands and feet.

With a cold look that puts me in mind of Stone at the kitchen table, the man raises his gun.

He's going to shoot me, I know in that instance. No words of explanation. Just a bullet straight through my forehead. Cold and efficient. Exactly like Stone.

I squeeze my eyes shut, and soon comes the muffled but lethal whoosh I've heard so often in movies. But this isn't a movie. This is my life. My life and my unborn baby's, suddenly cut short.

Except...except... I'm still breathing, I realize after a few seconds.

Blinking, I open my eyes. Just in time to see the gun man slump forward, his forehead seeping blood.

His drop reveals my unexpected savior: an expressionless Stone.

He blinks at the man's fallen body. Then with the same demeanor of an insurance agent, making a quick risk calculation, he lowers his gun and shoots my would-be assassin several more times. We all watch the body dance under the bullets impact until Stone runs out of slugs.

Only then does he look up at me and ask, "You alright?"

CHAPTER FORTY-TWO

I AM NOT ALRIGHT. NOT ALRIGHT AT ALL. YET somehow I find myself an hour later, sitting at a table with Gino Jr. Jr. as Stone explains to him what did and didn't happen here while peeling hundreds off a large stack of bills.

"Sorry for the inconvenience..." He peels off a hundred.

"I'm sure this messed with your delivery schedule." He peels off another hundred.

"Tell your grandpa it was my fault." He adds a third hundred.

"Also, make sure he knows how much I appreciate doing business with him." Then he puts one more hundred on the pile.

"And if you or him got any questions about any of this..."

This time instead of peeling off a hundred, he pushes the entire stack toward the delivery boy.

Gino's only in high school. I'm not sure if he'll understand. I mean, Aunt Mari had to put a towel down before he sat at the table, because somewhere along the way, he'd peed his pants.

But the peach fuzz on his upper lip quivers, once…twice. Then he reaches out. "Thank you for choosing Gino's, Mr. Ferraro," he says, stuffing the loose hundreds and the stack in one of his rain jacket pockets.

"That kid is about to buy all the weed this summer," says Cami as we watch him rush out past the spot where the dead body used to be before Nicky and Joey showed up just a few minutes after Stone.

They'd been full of apologies. Apparently the assassin had used a stooge, a man who'd come up to the house and waved a gun, then run off when Nicky and Joey got out of the car, forcing a foot chase. They'd had no idea that the real assassin was just waiting for them to leave before making his move on the house.

But now everyone's gone, including the dead body. Leaving just Stone, Cami, Aunt Mari and me to talk.

"Welcome back, Stone…" Aunt Mari says setting the bowl of *pollo guisado* she'd heated up for me down in front of him. "Now why exactly did you go away?"

What follows is a long story, told in Stone's usual staccato verse. Basically dealing with the Lunettis had been a lot more complicated than Stone had let on.

Apparently Cami's father had embezzled some of the money he'd been washing for the local mob to pay off a balloon mortgage on the McMansion he couldn't afford and other debts. A couple million dollars had been lost.

Stone had been in negotiations with the Lunetti family for months, but hadn't been getting very far. The eighty-year old head of the family wouldn't just settle for a buyout. He was insisting on taking Cami's and Talia's lives, for the sake of his family's reputation.

"And while the Lunetti family ain't as big or as powerful as the Ferraros, they ain't exactly small either," Stone tells us. "So it wasn't like I could just shoot my way into making them see things my way."

Things were getting top heated. And that was part of the reason he'd asked Cami and Talia to come with him to his father's funeral, he confessed. But when he got back from New York, things went from heated to worst.

The head of the Lunetti clan had died while they were away. "And guess what this bitch decided to make his death bed wish? Revenge on the girls for what their rat bastard father did. And revenge on me for moving into their territory. Unfortunately the son was just as bad as the father. According to my intel, he started talking about the coming war at the funeral. At that point negotiations were over. The only way we were solving that shit was with blood. Lots and lots of Lunetti blood."

I jolt, suddenly understanding. "That's why you started up with the pills again. Because you knew you'd have to kill and you didn't think you could do it without them."

He gives me a sheepish shrug. "Yeah, pretty much. And I faked breaking up with you because the Lunettis ain't exactly honorable. Last war they engaged in, the other boss lost his wife and kids. I had hoped by splitting up in public like that, they'd be less likely to come after you while I tried to sort out this mess."

Stone throws me an apologetic look. "But I'm back to managing my emotions on my own if you're worried about that. I like my head better off those fuckers."

Instead of acknowledging his return to sobriety, I ask, "And how about going to New York? That's where Nicky and Joey said you were."

Another sheepish look. "Yeah, that was just for show, too. I stayed in town. More trying to throw the Lunettis off our scent. Plus, when I'm using the enforcer side of my skill set, I find it's better to operate like a ghost. It worked, kind of. I took out the new Lunetti boss and my crew ended most of his loyal soldiers, too. But when I got a hold of the dead son's computer we found out he'd put in a kill order on the girls with an outside party. That's when I decided to double down on watching the house."

"So if you hadn't been watching, too...if you hadn't shown up, those guys would have murdered Talia and me," Cami summarizes, her eyes wide. "Just because we were the daughters of somebody I despised—oh God, this is all my fault. I'm so sorry I put you all in danger! If I hadn't killed him..."

"It ain't your fault," Stone insists. "And the only reason we were in danger was because that Lunetti family has some fucked up ideas about ethics. The world's better off without them if you ask me. And now I'm capo of the whole territory. No competition."

Cami blinks back tears. "Thank you," she whispers. "Thank you for saving me again and again."

"No problem," Stone answers, his tone all no big deal. "Hope you can forgive me for confusing you a little bit to get the job done."

"No forgiveness necessary," Aunt Mari assures him.

Cami nods in fervent agreement. "I'll never be able to thank you enough."

"I knew you didn't really mean it when you said you were leaving anyway," Aunt Mari says, like Stone is some rapscallion who'd come home later than he promised from school.

They both gaze at their hero and protector with pure adoration in their eyes.

I stare at him, too. But when I open my mouth, I don't thank him, I say, "I want a divorce."

The whole table pauses, as if my telling Stone our relationship is over was hands down the most surprising thing that's happened this evening.

"Naima!" Aunt Mari starts to exclaim.

"You said you'd never leave me, and then that's exactly what you did," I say, cutting my aunt off mid-chastisement. I train my eyes on Stone, cutting her and Cami out. "You yelled at me in a crowded restaurant. Then you left me there like I was last week's trash."

"I had to make it look believable," Stone says, as if he's explaining to me why water is wet. "You think I wanted to give Italians a worse reputation for bringing the drama in restaurants? I mean, we're already all over the reality shows."

"I don't' care! I don't care what you wanted!" I shout back. "You knew Cami, Talia, and pretty much everyone in this house was in danger and instead of telling me about it, *you left me*. You took my biggest fear and you decided, fuck it, Naima's feelings don't matter, I'm going to run this mind game on her anyway!"

I over-enunciate each word that comes out of my mouth next. "*I want a divorce.*"

The room goes deathly silent, until Cami whispers, "Is this what kids with real parents feel like when their mom and dad say they're getting divorced? Now I know why they act so traumatized about it."

"We're not getting a divorce." Stone replies to Cami with his eyes stay locked on mine.

"Oh, yes we are," I answer my voice just as hard as his with promise.

"Stone, *mijo*, I think she's just hangry. You know she has had nothing to eat all day," Aunt Mari tells him, like I'm a willful child. "Here, *mija*, I'll heat you up another bowl of *pollo guisado*."

"You can't leave me," he says, his tone thick with menace.

"Oh, watch me," I answer, rolling my neck. "Amber and I are besties again and she loves helping people get divorced from controlling husbands who don't care about anybody's feeling but their own. I will call my lawyer, and I will get my own place, that I choose by myself. And you and your two groupies can visit me on the court mandated days."

"You can't do that." His face, so calm when he was telling us all about how he and his soldiers pretty much mass murdered the Lunetti family, turns thunderous.

But I'm not scared. For once in my life, I'm not scared to speak my truth. "You asked me what I wanted. I want a husband who talks to me. And tells me the truth, no matter what. I want a husband who would never break my heart the way you did at that restaurant. One who would never go a whole week, letting me believe he was done with me. What I want from you is a divorce. That's all I want from you."

Stone shakes his head, his eyes bright with emotion. "Well, that's the one thing I can't give you."

"You can!" I insist, slamming a hand on the table.

"No, I fucking can't, because it would destroy me," Stone roars, standing up from the table. "I'm talking a hundred percent backslide into fucking oblivion because that's the only way I'd be able to deal with you being gone. This thing between us. It was binding from the start. I tried to deny it, to you and myself, but you think I didn't feel it from the moment we kissed? I *felt* you Naima. Even cottoned up beyond all reason on blue label pills, I felt you in my fucking soul." Stone pounds on his chest, his eyes blazing now.

"And months later, I couldn't bring myself not to come down here and check on you. I said it was for Rock, but I knew you were mine from the moment I saw you were pregnant. I thought it'd be cut and dry after that. I'd make you come back to me to New York. Set you up in the lap of luxury and keep you close, even though I knew I couldn't be the same kind of man for you that most guys could. But I couldn't figure out how to get you to cooperate. And then the next thing I knew, I was living in this house with you. Happy to spend my nights with you and the Island of Misfits Toys family you put together, instead of making deals in titty bars."

Stone shakes his head. "Luca thought I was out of my goddamn mind when I told him I wanted to branch out into the South. I didn't know how to explain it to him. Didn't know how to explain it to myself. It took coming off the pills and months of fucking therapy for me to get it."

His eyes burn into mine as he says. "I love you. I'm so fucking in love with you. And no, sometimes I don't always make the right decisions. Looking back at it, I can see now how you might not appreciate me blowing up all your triggers to keep you and our family safe. I was willing to do anything to keep you safe. To keep our family safe. Even break your heart. But know this, from now on I will be that husband. I will tell you when work goes from bad to lethal. I will tiptoe around your triggers, like I'm in a minefield. I will be *everything* you want."

He spreads his arms like a martyr. "Because I'm out of my mind in love with you, babe. So, please don't leave me. It will *fucking destroy me.*"

We all stand there stunned. I'm pretty sure these are the most words any of us have ever heard come out of Stone's mouth. And definitely the most passionate.

Both Cami and Aunt Mari turn to see how I'll respond.

I don't respond. I don't say anything for a long, long time as his words echo through me.

But then I release a shaky breath, look deep into his eyes, and say, "Okay, in that case, I was just kidding about all that getting a divorce stuff. Now I've decided you're never getting rid of me."

It takes a moment before Stone fully comprehends what I'm saying. That he's forgiven for everything, just like that. But when he does, his devastated expression is replaced with the sun of his smile.

"See how she treats me?" he says to Aunt Mari and Cami, even as he rushes around the table and pulls me into his arms. "Always making me work for every inch of her heart."

"You know, she was headed out the door to get you back right before you showed up and saved all of our lives," Aunt Mari tells Stone, tattling like only a woman without a feminist bone in her body could. "If you ask me, she needs to be nicer to you. That mouth of hers isn't no way to keep a man."

"Oh, she don't ever have to worry about me going nowhere," Stone promises Aunt Mari while smiling down at me. "And even if it looks like I am, I'm always coming right back. I promise you that."

"You better always come right back," I say, my own smile teary with emotion. "Or else I'm going to threaten to leave you again, just so I can get another heartfelt speech."

That threat makes the smile disappear clean off Stone's face. "You better memorize what all I said, because I swear on my father's grave I'm never saying shit like that to you again. From now on I'm going to be so fucking unromantic. Watch, at our fifty-year vow renewal ceremony, they'll ask me about you, and I'll be like, 'She's alright.'"

He might have gone on, ranting about how unromantic he planned to be from this point forward, but I cut him off when I pull him down into a kiss.

Because we both know good and well neither of us are going anywhere after that speech. In fact as I kiss Stone, I begin to suspect for the first time ever that I'm in something for life.

"Oh, and by the way," I say, pulling back after we've sealed our once-again one hundred percent love with a kiss. "I'm pregnant."

EPILOGUE

We end up escorting the two kids I care for way above my paygrade to Portland in the BMW hybrid Stone bought Cami for her graduation a few weeks later. We move them and Stallone into a dog friendly condo Stone bought in Cami's name as a "first job gift," then visit the girls every month like doting grandparents, until my expanding belly puts me in the no fly zone.

"Don't worry," Cami tells me on our last visit as we hug good-bye. "We'll see you at Thanksgiving. This little bird might have left North Carolina, but I'll always come flying back to you."

Then she tells me not to cry. And I blame the hormones for making me too sentimental. But I get on the plane without a doubt in my mind, Cami's and my unspoken mother-daughter bond is made of industrial elastic. It will stretch, but never break.

Luckily Stone really hated his dead dad. He breaks his

"father's grave" promise to become positively unromantic several times in the months to come.

We're at four hundred percent love these days. I got one-hundred points after my pregnancy announcement, and the number still ticks up by five points, every time I give him head. He's also taken on a rather unfortunate habit of introducing me as "the fucking love of his life," at doctor appointments, at my work functions, and at Mass, which we begin dutifully attending once a month to keep Aunt Mari happy.

My Dominican family now welcomes him like a king at all our functions. Goodbye to only seeing them on holidays and Sunday dinners at our home. Shortly after Stone gifted Yara's oldest daughter with a laptop for her *quinceañera*, Heaven and her maybe daughter, Alaysha, got a nail salon gang level of cousins together to inform us we were expected to attend all family functions from now on. Exceptions will no longer be allowed.

"See this is why you don't stunt at *quinceañeras*," I hissed at Stone after they left. "Now they're going to invite us to *everything*."

Stone, who I suspect, misses his big Italian Catholic family back up in New York just laughed and gave me so much wifeing that night, I began to wonder why I was so upset in the first place.

Yes, life is good. It's so, so good.

Which is why it's startling to be awoken by a middle-of-the-night phone call shortly before Thanksgiving.

"It's me," Stone says, sitting up in bed. Next, I hear the wooden slide of his nightstand drawer being opened.

I turn on the bedside light as he snatches up his phone. Not the iPhone I call him on, but the Samsung burner he uses for business. "What?" he answers with a surly growl.

However, his face drops when he hears the voice on the other side of the line. "Rashid, calm down, I can't understand you. Talk slower..."

I don't have to ask if everything's all right. I already know that it isn't.

This isn't the phone people call when they need to talk to Stone. This is the one they call when they need him to do something dangerous. Or really, really bad.

I'm sitting all the way up in bed by the time Stone hangs up.

"Rashid? Isn't that the friend who hasn't returned any of your calls or texts since he lost his wife and daughter?" I ask, remembering the tragic story with a pang.

"Yeah, the freeze out's over," Stone informs me, his face grim. He gets out of bed, and starts pulling on pants. "He's got a new woman now, and she's in danger. So he needs my help."

Who is this mystery woman? Find out in
RASHID: Her Ruthless Boss,
the third and final installment of the Broken and Ruthless series.

Thank you so much for reading, STONE, the second book in the Broken and Ruthless series. I think we all know a Naima.

Someone who gives and gives, eventually becoming so insecure, she loses hope of ever finding true love for herself.

I'm so glad Nai finally received the love she deserved, even if it did come in one large, complicated package. And while I realize it's no one's job to fix another person, I do believe in the power of being fixed by the generous gift of love. These two healed each other, and I couldn't be more thrilled that this mishmash family found their way to a happy ending.

I'd also like to give a huge shout out to all the big, noisy extended families out there. I'm blessed to hail from such a family, and even when it feels like an introvert's curse, I know my ridiculously large fam is one of my best blessings.

*If you loved Naima and Stone's love story and their crazy patchwork family, **please do them the further favor of leaving a review on Amazon**.*

Curious about that outrageously hot best man? Keep swiping for an excerpt of KEANE: Her Ruthless Ex

*Wondering about Luca and Amber?
Get thee to Amazon to read their epic romance.*

*So much love,
Theodora Taylor*

KEANE PREVIEW

Spring Break, Eleven Years Ago

"Yo, look at Graham. He found a 3-pointer!" one of Keane's teammates yelled over Fergie caterwauling from the Daytona Beach bar's sound system about her better than yours glamorous life.

The last person Keane expected to find when he looked up to see who Graham had netted for their Spring Break Bang-Off was Lena Kumar. But there she stood, dressed in a yellow bikini. One that confirmed beyond a shadow of a doubt every lewd thought he'd had in high school about what she'd been hiding under that uniform. Big hips, big tits, she'd finally let them out, and they were on full display.

Unfortunately, her big eyes were currently peeping up at Graham Diener, a mediocre second-string wing—though Keane had overheard him telling a girl he was a starter earlier that night. And Lena didn't know the only reason Graham was talking to her was because she was fat and brown, which meant instead of the usual one point per girl, he'd start the Bang-Off with 3 points if he closed the deal.

Fuck if Keane would let that happen. He hadn't laid an eye on Lena in four years, but a new possessiveness rushed through him when he saw her flirting with that piece of shit.

"No cock blocking, bro!"

Keane didn't realize he'd started advancing in Graham's and Lena's direction until a hand grabbed his shoulder and pulled him back.

It was Tim, the team captain and a fellow Bostonian. He'd been the one to put together the week-long Bang-Off rules, and he though he wasn't descended from a Founding Father, he was rich enough to fund the $5000 pot.

5K Keane had been sure he would win until he saw Graham trying to run his lame game on Lena.

"I know her," Keane said. "I don't want Graham flirting with her."

"Know her. Like she's an ex-girlfriend?" Tim sent a skeptical look in Lena's direction. Probably because she didn't fit the normal profile of a hockey player girlfriend. Which tended to lean more Carrie Underwood than brown and fluffy.

"No, I went to high school with her..." Keane admitted, his eyes still on Lena. Another girl had joined the conversation. She was shorter than Lena but also fluffy...and falling down drunk. Lena looked concerned as she settled her friend on a stool. But drunk girls didn't qualify for play in the Bang-Off, so Graham was ignoring her and still trying to close the deal with Lena.

Keane had never seen the drunk girl before, but he found himself feeling grateful to her for cock-blocking Graham in his stead, since Tim probably wouldn't accept "knowing her from high school" as an excuse to go over there.

As if to confirm his point, Tim declared, "The cock-blocking rule still applies. She's not drunk and she's a three-pointer, so that means Graham's free to play."

Of course, Keane's other teammates nodded along, like referees making an interference call. For a competition that was supposed to be fun and games, they were taking this shit way serious.

Yeah, good thing the drunk friend showed up...

But then another second-stringer said, "Fuck, what's he doing now?"

Keane looked back over his shoulder to see Lena was no longer with her drunk friend at the bar, but hitting Graham with her purse, shit spilling out of it, as he dragged her towards the beach bathroom.

The fuck?

It would have taken a stronger guy than Tim to hold him back at that point. Keane ripped his shoulder out of the captain's grip and rushed over to them, like Graham was trying to light a lamp for the opposing team.

"Stop. Let her go, dumbass," he said, getting in front of Graham.

Graham and Lena stared up at him. Lena looked like a ghost had appeared out of nowhere, but Graham just looked pissed.

"No fair, Keane, I saw her first!"

Keane nearly lost it when instead of letting her go, Graham curled his hand even tighter around Lena's wrist. "End of your life coming down in five..."

"Bro, c'mon," Graham whined. "Fights off the ice are an automatic three-game suspension."

"Four..."

"You're going to risk your draft chances on this shit?"

Truth be told, Keane could barely hear him. All he could see was that little fuck's hand still touching Lena. "Three..."

"Fuck, Keane, c'mon. Cut me a break, it's just pussy—"

"Two..."

Like the coward Keane had already guessed him to be, Graham dropped her wrist before he could get to one. "I fucking hate you, bro. But whatever. Plenty of pussy in the sea. Bet I can find another brown one, too."

Graham probably thought that was some kind of comeback, but Keane had already forgotten about him by the time he disappeared back into the crowd of spring breakers.

His eyes were glued to one thing and one thing only. "You all right, Lena?"

She stilled. Like a forest critter that had just been spotted by something that wanted to eat it.

Looking at her in that bikini, Keane couldn't say she was wrong about that.

"I'm...I'm fine...um thanks?" she finally managed to say,

appearing wary as hell to be talking to him after all this time.

"You're welcome," he answered, smirking at her questioning tone. She probably didn't ever expect to be thanking him for anything after what went down their senior year.

But then he thought about what could have happened with Graham, if he hadn't shown up. "You sure you're okay? Real serious. I will beat that fuckhead into the ground if he has hurt you."

She looked back at him with blank shock, and Keane could almost hear her smart girl mind trying to reconcile him of all people offering to defend her as she said, "I'm fine."

Yeah, she was fine, he realized, continuing to stare down at her. Still. He'd never seen her hair out of the studious braid she kept it in back in high school. It was pretty down. Like a black cloud of curls framing her cute face. He didn't let his eyes roam lower than that this time.

The swim trunks he'd worn to the bar wouldn't provide much camouflage if he sprung a boner. And that was exactly what would happen if he let himself look at her body in a bikini again, without Graham here to distract him from all of that "yeah, you know you want this, Keane." Still.

"What's a goodie like you doing in Daytona anyway?" he asked, channeling all his irritation at not being able to ogle her the way he wanted to into the question.

She pulled a face. And Keane wonder if she was asking herself the same question after her run-in with Graham.

"Trying to blow off some steam before finals. It was my friend's idea to come here—"

She cut off, glancing over her shoulder. "Sorry, I've got to go. It was..." She shook her head as if searching but failing to come up with a word to describe their unexpected reunion. "I've got to go."

"Wait, hold on—"

She disappeared into the beach crowd, before he could come up with something to convince her not to leave. To stay and keep talking to him.

He thought about running after her. It felt like he had so much he needed to say. But when he tried to find the words, he couldn't think of any.

What could he say anyway? "Sorry for ruining what should have been the funniest part of your senior year by accusing you of being a psycho. But hey, ran interference for you with Graham, soooo...wanna fuck?"

Keane couldn't say he'd met other girls like Lena at UBoss, but he'd scoped them out from afar. Always headed in some specific direction, never wandering around campus. They didn't flirt. Never showed up at his frat house's parties. Always had the right answer in class, because they actually studied that shit before the test. Somehow, Keane doubted she would jump at his offer of makeup sex.

A strange disappointment swept over him as he headed back in the direction of his boys.

Graham had already come back to the three tall tables they'd claimed for themselves. To tattle as it turned out. He was waving around what looked like one of those moleskin journals and complaining loudly to Tim about getting cock-blocked.

"What? You didn't close the deal either?" Graham shouted over the Ludacris club thumper that had started playing when Keane got back to the tables.

"She was a friend from high school. That's the only reason he interfered," Tim answered, coming to Keane's defense. Keane gave him a "good looking out" chin up. Sure, Tim had told him not to interfere, but when worse came to worse, starters stuck together.

"That shouldn't count—hey, what are you doing?" he shouted, when Keane snatched the moleskin journal out of his hands.

Keane didn't answer, just let Graham's whiny-ass voice fade into the background as he checked to see if his suspicion about Graham not being the kind of guy capable of reflective thought panned out. It did.

This journal belongs to Salena Kumar. If found, please call...

There it was. The number he'd never been able to get in high school, written out in the neat handwriting Keane still remembered right on the front page.

And just like that, his heart started pounding again, with "More Than a Feeling" blasting in his head.

As it turned out, he didn't post any points on the Spring Break Bang Off that night. Instead, he ended up texting Lena: *This is Keane. Shouldn't have run off like fuckin Cinderella. Got your journal. You want it back, come meet me tomorrow. Lucky's on Seabreeze. Noon.*

The journal turned out to be a diary. And Keane spent the hour before their noon meeting reading it, even though he was supposed to be doing inventory at that time. That was the deal he'd struck with the retired "uncle" who owned the bar, but never wanted to be bothered with any of the technical aspects of running a legitimate business. In exchange for his boring service, Keane could stay for free in the room above the bar and enjoy all the drinks he wanted to pour himself.

Keane needed the deal. He had stopped party dealing after a close call during freshman year. He'd been collared by a campus security officer and if not for his taking the offer of one of Keane's front row Friends and Family tickets for the rest of his time at UBoss, he might have gotten kicked off the team.

Rule #2 still applied, so he'd said goodbye to the lucrative activity that almost got between him and the NHL and hello to college life on the barter system. Usually it didn't matter. He lived in a frat where food always seemed to magically appear. However, the annual hockey team spring break trip had been a little trickier. The rest of the team paid top prices to stay at the Daytona Beach Benton Grand, but he was too poor to afford a 3-hundy a night room for a whole week.

So, he'd made up a story about his uncle making him stay at the bar to work. Family, right? Plus, it's a fact of life that rich kids like nothing more on this earth than free shots, so everyone was happy with the arrangement. He shouldn't be doing anything to jeopardize it.

But Lena's diary was just too good to put down. In fact, a few pages in, he poured himself a bowl of peanuts and sat behind the bar to finish reading what had been written as a series of letters to her dead mother.

Apparently, Lena had gone on to Mount Holyoke, an all-girls school in Western Mass, and had spent her senior year in an actual real relationship with Band Nerd's older brother. Some fuckhead named Rohan. But get this, Rohan had insisted on waiting until marriage to have sex. Several months into what sounded like a boring as fuck relationship, he'd asked her to come back to Boston for the weekend before Spring Break. She'd thought he was going to propose, and Keane noted she wrote a whole page about how happy her dad would be when she told him, and exactly zero words about whether she really wanted to marry dick she hadn't test rode yet.

But as it turned out, that ass tool had called her down to Boston to break up with her. And he didn't even come up with a good lie. He told her straight out his mom was too racist to accept a half-black Indian girl for her oldest son—especially now that she wasn't speaking to the youngest one for coming out as gay. What in the entire fuck?

Lena was all angry and broken up about it for a couple of pages. And there was a lot of Dear Mama, *how am I going to tell Dad Rohan dumped me?* But if you asked Keane, she'd dodged a bullet. What kind of little bitch dumps a girl because his mommy doesn't approve?

Keane flipped to the Sunday night entry from two days ago to see if she'd come to her senses.

Dear Mama, I've decided to be more like you. Instead of crying over Rohan, I'm going to try living on the wild side.

With that in mind, here's my SHAKE IT OFF Spring Break Bucket List.

Keane scrolled his eyes down to what he'd figured would be the usual good girl break-up list. You know, get your nails done, have a spa day, eat a fuck ton of Ben and Jerry's like you seen them other girls do in the movies. But no...

   1. ditch my V-Card

Keane nearly choked on his bar nuts, definitely not the opener of a good girl break-up list. He then quickly scanned the rest of the list.

2. look into therapist programs

3. learn to Dance

4. kiss somebody in public

5. have sex not in a bed

6. do something wild

7. wear a bikini

8. smoke Weed

9. say yes to everything that scares me

10.

He briefly wondered why she left number ten blank, but then playfully filled it in for her. He probably would have read the entire diary a second time, if not for the alert from his uncle's over the top security system—hey, you can take the mobster out of Southie....

She was here.

Little Miss Shake-It-Off was at the door. Ripe for the taking. By him.

And, okay, admittedly, if you're looking to hook up with a girl you fucked over back in high school, holding her college journal hostage probably ain't the best look. But it was all Keane had, and hey, it worked. She was here.

Keane went to the front door but waited for her to knock, so he wouldn't look too pressed. However, when the knock never came, he was forced to open the door himself.

He found her standing there in a pretty yellow shift dress and flip flops, her good girl hands wrapped primly around her beach purse.

Fuck, she was cute. "You just gonna stand there all day?" he demanded, trying to cover up all the "More Than a Feeling" popping off inside his head.

She reacted with a startled look. Guess, she'd gotten unused to straight talk after four years at her all-girls school.

"Hi...hi again? I'm here for my diary?"

"Yeah, I got it inside. Come on."

Keane jerked his head, but she just stood there, looking like a frightened animal too scared to be alone with him. Normally he wouldn't mind intimidating a girl. Especially this one. But he got a feeling this had less to do with him than what happened last night.

And he hated that she'd been scared. Even for a second.

"I'm an ornery bastard, but I'm not Graham. I'd never force you to do anything you didn't want."

Keane expected her to accept his words. Maybe even thank him again for getting Graham to leave her alone. Instead she thinned her lips and gave him a skeptical look, "Yet here I am after getting no answer to my texts asking you to drop it off at my hotel's front desk."

He snorted. "Yeah, I'm not in the hotel delivery business, princess. You want this diary or not? I got shit to do."

Again, not the best tact when you're looking to be the number one on a good girl's Shake It Off list. But again, it worked.

A few seconds later, she was standing inside his temporary lair.

Asshole or get assholed, he reminded himself as he watched her pick up the journal he'd left lying on the bar. Out loud he said, "Would've given it back to you last night, but you rushed off before I could let you know you dropped it."

"Thank you," she mumbled. Keane watched her look everywhere but at him. "And sorry for rushing off."

"That's okay. You're here now," he answered, still watching her closely. There was a skittishness to her, like she could take off at any second. He brought out a bottle of tequila, the official base of Girly Spring Break. "You want something?"

She raised her eyebrows. "It's only noon."

"Yeah, only noon in Daytona," he pointed out. "Bet ya half

the town's already tied a couple on. How's your friend doing by the way? She was pretty out of it last night."

"You saw her?"

"Yeah, clocked you as soon as I saw you at the bar. Blast from the past. But I guess you didn't see me."

"No, I didn't..." She still wouldn't look at him. And it was taking all the patience Keane didn't have not to grab her chin and make her look him in the eye.

"She okay?" he asked instead. "You didn't have to take her to get her stomach pumped or nothing like that? That alcohol poisoning is a fucker."

"No, she's fine. I kept her hydrated and now she and her other friends are out for lunch. Probably tying one on just like you said."

Lena gave him a tentative smile, but she was still wary of him. He could tell. And it made him wish he'd punch Graham's teeth in last night, even if it violated his second cardinal rule.

"I talked to Graham. Made sure he understood I'd report him to the college board my fuckin' self and beat him within an inch of his life if he ever tried that shit again. Got there as fast as I could, but I'm sorry I didn't jump in sooner. Seriously, let me get you a drink on me."

She shook her head. "Seriously, it wasn't your fault."

Keane clenched his hand around the bottle of tequila not knowing what to do here. Truth be told, getting girls to fuck him had only gotten easier in college. They showed up at hockey frat house parties like clockwork every weekend, and usually, "You want something to drink? Let me get you something," was all the game he'd needed.

Up until now.

But Lena didn't day drink, even on her Shake it Off spring break, and Keane didn't know how to deal with that. Or how to talk to her. Fuck, why was this good girl making him feel like such an insecure pussy?

"Do you work here or something?" she asked, looking around the dark bar.

"Or something," he answered. "Bar belongs to my uncle. He pays for my ticket down here, and lets me stay in the room upstairs, just so long as I do all the boring ass set up work before the bar opens and the spring inventory. He hates that shit."

"Wow, a zero spend spring break. I'm impressed."

"Yeah, you probably are impressed, ya nerd. But trust me, I'm not coming nowhere near bar work after the draft in June."

"So, you think you might play professionally?"

"Know I will," he answered, his cardinal rules humming inside his head.

"Well...good for you."

Yeah, good for him. He could do a 360 spin to slap shot a puck into the goal, but he couldn't figure out how to talk to this girl without a whole lot of awkwardness. Fuck, he wished she would just take the drink.

"I should get going," she said instead, stuffing the journal into her beach bag. "If I rush, I can still make it to brunch."

"Yeah, brunch is the most important meal of the day," he joked. Even as his brain-screamed, *Fuck she's leaving. She's just going to walk out the door and I'll probably never see her again.*

She hesitated, then said, "Thank you. I really appreciate it."

"Yeah, alright," he said, brain scrambling to think of something to keep her there. "But before you go, we should talk about it."

"Talk about what?"

"High school. I was a dick to you."

A lot of girls would have played it off, but Lena...her face read like CliffsNotes. He could see all the hurt she was still carrying around from that day in her eyes, as she gave him a stiff nod of acknowledgement.

There was probably a right thing to say in a situation like this. Sorry or some shit like that. But Keane had never been good at that sensitive shit.

And in that moment, it seemed like the most natural thing in the world to follow up with was, "Here's how I'm going to make it up to you. That Shake It Off list of yours—I'm going to help you get 'er done. Starting with number one."

Her eyes widened and her shoulders stiffened. "You...you read my diary?" she sputtered.

Keane scrunched up his face. "Course I did." *I mean what was she expecting?*

Apparently better. Instead of answering, she threw him a bitter look, then turned and walked away.

"Wait, Lena, hold on. Just hear me out," he said, running to stop her.

She stopped but only because he got in front of her, blocking her way.

"I know I was a rat bastard to you in high school," he rushed out before she started thinking he was like Graham. "I was going through some shit."

Understatement. But Keane wasn't the type to go into the finer details of the shitshow his home life had been those two years. Pretending like he was King of the School at Boston Glenn while having to go back to that shithole he called home on weekends to keep his dad from wailing on his little brother. "I liked you, though. I liked you a lot. From the day you got between me and Band Nerd's lunch money."

"Band Nerd," she repeated, her eyes blazing. "Vihaan had a name. He was a scholarship kid just like me. And you."

"Yeah, I know he had a name, but..."

Keane wasn't one of those saps on TV. He never saw himself pouring his heart out to a girl. There was never any reason. However, the look on Lena's face was giving him a bad feeling that if he really wanted to be her number one, then he was going to have to get real with her.

So, he used a tactic he'd never tried before. The truth. "I was jealous, so I didn't bother to use it. Didn't stop being jealous till he showed up to prom with another dude. But I'm sorry. I'm sorry for how I acted."

Silence. She stared at him; her big eyes wider than he'd ever seen them. Even that day in the hallway. "Is this a trick?" she finally asked, her voice tight.

"What? No!"

She shook her head at him. "Because if it's a trick, it's a really horrible thing to do. You are so privileged. So, so privileged, because of your talent and your looks. You could seriously have any other girl in Daytona right now. Why pick on me? Play these mind games?"

"Exactly! Why would I pick on you? Trick you?" he answered, spreading his arms defensively. "Girls come easy to me. Why would I put myself through this shit if I didn't want you?"

And no, he didn't do details or vulnerability or any of that pussy shit. But in this case his voice dipped low as he told her straight out, "Six years I been wanting you. Ever since the first time we met."

More silence. And now she was really looking at him, her eyes searching his face like he was a puzzle she had to figure out. "You really want to have sex with me? Help me ditch my V-card?"

Was she fucking kidding? He dipped his head down so that he could look her straight in the eye as he answered, "Yeah... yeah, I do."

"But why?" she asked. Like he'd offered to crash her car, not be her first time.

"I already told ya," he answered, his own mind as clear as hers was confused.

They were standing so close now. Even a millimeter closer, and she'd feel just how much he wanted to be her first against her belly.

"One kiss," he whispered. "One kiss will prove I'm dead serious. I know I'm the high school idiot and you're the smart girl who knows better, but can I kiss you?"

Second shock of the evening...she nodded. She actually nodded yes.

Ho-ly Shit. Six years of wet dreams. Four of regrets. Both his dick and his heart started pounding like war drums.

No way was Keane going to give her the chance to have second thoughts. He fucking devoured her, covering her sweet lips with his and kissing her like he'd been dreaming about since day one of meeting her.

It was probably too much. In the back of his mind he worried about overwhelming her. But no...she kissed him back. Just as hungrily. Like she'd been waiting six long years for this exact moment, too.

They kissed like that and for a while all Keane's rules fell away. Who cared about getting assholed or the NHL or anything fucking else? This...was all he wanted. He'd do anything for this.

But she pulled away. "Keane, wait! Stop!"

Keane blinked, something dangerous inside of him commanding him to go on, but no...it was Lena. He didn't want to hurt her, never wanted to do anything to make her look at him the way she had that morning in the hallway, when instead of asking her out, he'd dicked her over in front of the whole school.

With a shuddering breath, he made himself release her and take a full step back.

But instead of running off, she asked, "Is Keane your first name or your last?"

"My last," Keane answered, probably looking as confused as she did when he told her he'd been liking her for six years.

She nodded. "What's your first name?"

Keane inwardly jerked at the question. He never told people his first name. If they wanted to know it, they had to look it up, then wait to get punched if they ever dared to call him that to his face.

But for Lena he answered. For Lena, he confessed, "Desmond."

If he was expecting her to be a lady about it, he was sorely disappointed. She snorted. "Desmond. That's kind of nerdy."

"Yeah, why do you think I go by Keane?"

Still grinning, she asked, "May I call you Desmond?"

"Fuck no. Why would you even ask me that?"

Her expression suddenly sobered. "Because if I'm going to have sex with you, I kind of want to be on a first name basis."

He stilled, now the one unable to believe the words coming out of her mouth. "You serious?"

"Yeah...yeah I think I am." She peeped up at him, her big

brown eyes shy, even as she said, "My first time. I want it to be with you."

How had he never noticed just how fucking disgusting his room above the bar was before he opened the door a few minutes after getting the yes from Lena? Back at UBoss, Puck Girls came by their rooms daily to tidy up, like a maid service—but one that was totally willing to spread their legs if you asked nice.

But apparently without that particular service, he was a fucking slob. He realized that as soon as he stepped through the door with Lena. Dirty clothes laid everywhere but in the laundry basket his uncle had given him, and thanks to everything being closed, it smelled worse than a locker room.

"Sorry," he mumbled, picking up the clothes and throwing them in the laundry basket as fast as he could. "Wasn't expecting company."

"You didn't know I'd say yes?" she asked as she watched him throw the laundry basket in the closet and close the door on it. Her tone was all "you're fucking with me."

But he wasn't. "I didn't let myself get my hopes up. Just knew I had to ask you—fuck it still smells in here. Want to go back to your hotel?"

"I'm on a fold out couch in the living room," she answered with an apologetic look. "No privacy."

"I'll get us a room then." It didn't even take Keane a second to decide to reallocate his spring break pay on a hotel. "Give me a minute to ask my uncle if I can take an advance on my pay out of the till."

But she closed the space between them and took him by the wrist, before he could get his phone out of his pocket. "Don't. This is fine. Really."

Keane shook his head, insisting, "You deserve better for your first time." Nobody had ever accused him of being a romantic. More like down to fuck anywhere. But Lena wasn't like the others. He wanted it to be nice for her.

But then she hit him with a pleading look. "Keane, I don't need hotel sheets and rose petals," she said, her voice soft. "I just...I just want to be bad for once."

Fuck, did she know, have even one clue what her words did to him? It felt like his dick was ready to punch through his pants. "You want to be bad? With me?" he asked, challenging her. Not to be a dick, but because he was still having a hard time believing this dream was coming true.

"Can you help me do that?" she asked in return. "Be bad? With you?"

His cock ached, with an intensity that could not be denied or put off by a search for better accommodations.

Next time...

Next time, he'd borrow that money from his uncle and next time they did this, it would be in a queen-sized bed at the Daytona Beach Benton Grand. He'd give her the kind sweet, soft-light sex she deserved with the band, Boston, hitting that baseline in the background while he hit it from up top.

But this time...

They fell back into the kiss, devouring each other. And why did he think she was shy?

He found out how wrong he was about that when he felt her hands tugging on his shirt.

He didn't hesitate to rip it off his body in between kisses. He wanted her hands on him, felt crazed with the need to be inside her. Especially when she tore away from him for too many seconds to take off her shift dress and bikini top.

Yet, when she tried to fall back into the kiss, he found himself stopping her. "Hold on. Let me look at you, bad girl."

He curved a hand around her neck to keep her there and maintain some skin-to-skin while he took her in. "You filled out since I saw you last."

Her eyes shifted up and away like she was wishing to be anywhere but here, under his gaze. "Yeah, some people go for the freshman twenty, but I decided to double down."

Did she ever. Her tits were even bigger than he'd imagined. Heavy and ripe. Begging for his hands. "You got nice everything. Can I touch?"

He could see the wheels in her mind turning, and he tightened his hand around her neck, wondering if she would turn scared woodland creature again and bolt.

But in the end, she nodded. Making him feel like he'd won another championship trophy.

He pulled her forward for another kiss with one hand while finding a breast with other. Best of both worlds and that made it easy to go slow. To pull her down to the bed and kiss her for a long and leisurely time, while they lay on their sides.

Eventually she started pushing her breast into his hand along with kissing him back. He let his hand drop from her fantastic tit and pushed it below her bikini bottom to check.

She was a little damp, but it wasn't enough. "Get wet for me, bad girl." He pushed two fingers into her while his thumb started rubbing circles over her clit as he told her the God's honest truth, "I want you ready to fuck as soon as I sit you on my dick."

He'd never talked this much in bed with a girl before. There was never any reason. He was a catch and most of the girls he hooked up with went out of their way to make it as easy as possible for him. He got the feeling Lena would need things spelled out for her though.

And from the way she gasped, surprised like, when she began to enjoy it, she'd didn't have any experience with the below the waist stuff. Jesus Christ, had that Rohan fuck not even bothered to do this for her?

Keane found himself both irritated that she wasted her senior year on that assclown and prideful that he was giving her something she'd never had before.

But when she started moaning, he stopped just short of letting her come on his hand. Selfishly he wanted her first time coming to be with him inside her. "You ready for me?" he asked, pulling his fingers out of her pussy.

Her hips kept moving even after he pulled away, begging for his hand back. The sight of her writhing hips hit him hard, made him take a moment to think about hockey drills so he wouldn't blow his wad right then and there.

He was surprised he was able to sit up and get his jeans off in that state. When he pushed them down along with his underwear, his cock sprung out. More than ready. Already dripping pre-cum in fact.

His eyes flew up to his good girl turned bad, hoping the sight of his raging hard-on didn't scare her.

Her expression had glazed over. But not with fear...

He nearly lost his mind when she closed one hand around his dick, then brought her mouth down to lick off the pearl of pre-cum at the tip.

Fuuuuckk! His stomach kicked, his body momentarily losing sight of his main mission, it wanted to come so bad. And then she had the nerve to press her tongue into his slit.

"Fuck no!" Cupping both his hands around her neck, he tugged her up and off the bomb she was creating between his legs. "What the hell were you thinking? Your lips wrapped around my dick...that isn't something I can withstand. We would've had to wait a couple more hours before crossing number one off your list."

"Sorry," she murmured. But the look on her face didn't look sorry at all.

She was playing with him, and if he didn't watch out, he was going to lose control. Flip her over, push her face into the bed, and fuck her the way he wanted to, forget that sweet shit.

But no...it was her first time. He had to get it right.

Determined not to let himself preemie creamy, he grabbed a condom, sat sideways on the bed, and slid it on over his dick.

"C'mon," he said, beckoning her forward when she looked questioningly at the new position.

Telling her to get on top worked. She morphed from saucy minx back into the good girl whose asswipe ex had taught her absolutely nothing about how to be a woman to a man.

"We're going to do this slow, okay?" he assured her. "You start feeling some kind of way, you tell me to stop. I'm not looking to hurt you."

She nodded, but continued eyeing his lap and erect cock like it was a pop quiz she hadn't been prepared to take.

He took pity on her after she awkwardly climbed on. "Watch me. Watch me, take your virginity, Lena."

With those words, he parted her pussy lips with one hand. He was so hard he didn't even have to guide himself in. All he had to do was pulled her hips forward with his other hand and watch as her wet slit sank down over the tip of his erection. "Watch me. Watch me take your virginity, Lena."

The sight of her pussy slowly consuming his entire cock was nearly enough to make him come. And he hissed when she started to adjust and readjust herself after sinking down all the way to the base.

"Am I hurting you," she asked with a truly adorable worried look in her huge brown eyes.

"No, you're not hurting me," he answered in a mocking tone, silently thanking her for helping him out with her silly question. For at least a moment or two, his basic Masshole need to tease her outweighed his baser instinct to come in her tight pussy. "Not in the way you think anyways. I'll be alright. You do what you need to do to get comfortable. Just let me know when you are alright to move."

Somehow he made it sound NBD. *No big deal, baby, keep on grinding your hips all over my dick. I'm not struggling at all.*

But his patience was soon rewarded when she went from trying to get comfortable on his big dick, to circling her hips with a natural rhythm.

"Ah, baby, yeah..." he threw his head back, struggling to hold on as she rode him. "You're fucking killing me. Yeah just like that."

The feeling of Lena Kumar riding his dick...it was un-fuck-ing-believable.

"Yeah, fuck. Fuck this dick," he told her, his voice getting rougher and rougher the closer she got. "It's yours. All yours."

Her moans came faster, and then she cried out, her pussy clamping down on his dick.

"You came. You came, right?" he asked, hoping to God.

"Yes," she answered, looking just as shocked as him that it happened so quickly.

"Thank, fuck."

There was no holding back after that. He flipped her on to her back and plunged back into her, his body roaring as he finally let the dog off the chain.

He pounded into her, too far gone to be nice about it. And this girl, this girl. What the fuck, instead of lying there waiting for him to get done, she wrapped her arms and legs around him. Joined him right on that edge. She came again, and this time her clamp down undid him. He spilled into the condom with a coarse yell, his body going rigid, paralyzed by the sensation of finally realizing this dream.

No, better than the dream...he thought as he pulled out and collapsed on the bare mattress beside her.

"Why are you laughing," she asked beside him, her voice breathless.

He told her the truth. "That was even better than I imagined."

"You imagined us...together like that?"

Yeah, he must have been an Academy Award level actor in high school. She sounded like she had no idea of the dirty thoughts he had harbored about her until that hallway confrontation guilted him into cutting that shit out.

But they weren't in high school anymore. And now he told it to her straight. "Fuck yeah, I did. A lot. Whacked off to it, too. But the real thing was way fuckin' better."

And...cue the awkward silence. He knew he sounded a little rough—what a prep school English teacher once referred to as unnecessarily crude, but in the game of Asshole or Get Assholed, the guy with the biggest "don't give a fuck" accent always wins. Plus, he knew the way he talked held a lot of appeal with girls looking to fuck on the wild side. Which was fine by him, as long as they knew he was a short-term rental, not available for lease.

But in the moments after his rough confession, he almost regretted not losing his South Boston accent, like a few players he knew had after playing on elite teams too long. He wanted to be better for her. Better than the guy she'd known back in high school.

He was trying to come up with a f-bomb free sentence, when she started to get out of the bed.

"Where you going?"

She looked down at him, her brown eyes back to confused and wary. It made him long to take her again. To see them glazed over with lust instead of "what did I just do?"

"I thought you had to work today. And I should get going. Back to the hotel."

No, he had to keep her here. Letting her leave would be a disaster. She'd get back with her girls and talk herself out of the Next Time he was already hardcore planning.

This was the problem with fucking a virgin. She didn't have enough experience to know that real life sex wasn't anything like what had just happened in this bed. Didn't matter how hot he was—most girls didn't come twice on his dick in one session. And he for shit sure didn't lose his mind like that when it came time to get his. Or start thinking about the next time before he'd come down from the first.

"Fuck work. Let's take a nap. I was out late last night."

She tugged back, her expression hesitant. "But, my best friend, Dawn, is probably wondering where I am, and you should—"

"Let me have this, baby, okay? You don't know how long I waited."

This time he didn't act. Didn't try to prove to the academy that his heart wasn't pounding a Boston song for this girl.

And thank fuck...it worked. She settled back into the bed with him, and maybe her nerdiness was rubbing off on him. For he found himself taking a big whiff of her hair as she lay her head down on his chest. It smelled like coconuts and flowers. Like a vacation no man in his right mind wouldn't want to take.

"That Rohan dickweed is a fucking joke. If you were my girl, no way would I have let my parents have a say."

She froze in his arms.

Alright, guess it was still too soon to talk about all the stuff he'd read in her diary.

"Relax. We don't have to talk about the personal shit if you don't want. But when we wake up, we should have a conversation about taking care of the rest of that Shake it Off list of yours."

She didn't leave. In fact, she did exactly what he wanted and fell asleep in his arms.

But the rest of that wish didn't come true.

When he woke up, it was to the sound of insistent knocking in a room darkened by the afternoon sun.

Shit. He'd totally lost track of time. That was probably his uncle wondering why the bar was not set up for the night service.

It wasn't his uncle. Later and for many weeks afterward, he'd wish it had been his uncle.

But it was Graham, and his eyes widened as soon as he's saw the girl in Keane's bed. "I knew it!" he whined. "She was *my* three-pointer, *mine!*"

Oh my gosh, you have GOT to see how this story ends!!!
Please click here to finish reading
KEANE: HER RUTHLESS EX.

ALSO BY THEODORA TAYLOR

BROKEN AND RUTHLESS

KEANE: Her Ruthless Ex

STONE: Her Ruthless Enforcer

RASHID: Her Ruthless Boss

RUTHLESS TYCOONS

HOLT: Her Ruthless Billionaire

ZAHIR: Her Ruthless Sheikh

LUCA: Her Ruthless Don

HOT AUDIOBOOKS WITH HEART

The Owner of His Heart

Her Russian Billionaire

His Pretend Baby

His Everlasting Love

Her Viking Wolf

THE RUTHLESS NAKAMURAS

Her Perfect Gift

His Revenge Baby

12 Months of Kristal

(newsletter exclusive)

RUTHLESS RUSSIANS

Her Russian Billionaire

Her Russian Surrender

Her Russian Beast

Her Russian Brute

THE VERY BAD FAIRGOODS

His for Keeps

His Forbidden Bride

His to Own

HOT CONTEMPORARIES WITH HEART

The Owner of His Heart

The Wild One

His for the Summer

His Pretend Baby

His One and Only

ALIEN OVERLORDS SERIES (as Taylor Vaughn)

His to Claim

His to Steal

His to Keep

Theirs to Mate

THEIR ALPHA KINGS

Her Viking Wolf

Wolf and Punishment

(The Alaska Princesses Trilogy, Book 1)

Wolf and Prejudice

(The Alaska Princesses Trilogy, Book 2)

Wolf and Soul

(The Alaska Princesses Trilogy, Book 3)

Her Viking Wolves

THE DRAGON KINGS

Her Dragon Everlasting

Her Dragon King

THE BROTHERS NIGHTWOLF

NAGO: Her Forever Wolf

KNUD: Her Big Bad Wolf

RAFES: Her Fated Wolf

THE SCOTTISH WOLVES

Her Scottish Wolf

Her Scottish King

Her Scottish Warrior

HOT HARLEQUINS WITH HEART

Vegas Baby

Love's Gamble

HOT SUPERNATURAL WITH HEART

His Everlasting Love

12 Day of Krista

(only available during the holidays)

ABOUT THE AUTHOR

Theodora Taylor writes hot books with heart. When not reading, writing, or reviewing, she enjoys spending time with her amazing family, going on date nights with her wonderful husband, and attending parties thrown by others. She now lives in Los Angles, California, and she LOVES to hear from readers. So....

Friend Theodora on Facebook
https://www.facebook.com/theodorawrites

Follow Me on Instagram
https://www.instagram.com/taylor.theodora/

Sign for up for Theodora's Newsletter
http://theodorataylor.com/sign-up/